# *Capital Bound Series, Book 1: The Lion's Roar*

**By Michael Rogers**

Writers Exchange E-Publishing

http://www.writers-exchange.com

# CHAPTER ONE

Terran stood on the cracked sidewalk and scanned the deserted street. To his left was the Lessers' territory. The buildings weren't in the best shape; some were worn, and the original color on the concrete had faded, but they were tall and sturdy. The buildings in the Outskirts territory to his right weren't so lucky. Made of red brick, they were short and squat, with hundreds of cracks running along their sides. The windows of most of the buildings were broken, allowing him to see the vacant interiors covered in mold. *It looks just like home.*

Terran glanced toward the sun that was dipping below the horizon, then down at his watch. Barely three o'clock and it was almost dark. Steeling himself against the wind, he crossed the street toward the alley. Without the buildings acting as a buffer, the full force of the chill wind hit him. Terran hunched over, trying to conserve as much heat as possible. Potholes and black ice threatened his unsteady steps, but he trudged on towards his goal.

Reaching the alleyway, Terran stood tall again and took a better look at what the alley had to offer.

Four dumpsters lined the side of the Lessers' building, followed by several trash cans and two large plastic bags. On the Outskirt's side, trash was piled in rotting heaps that stretched the full length of the building. *I wonder what smells worse, me or the trash. Not much difference between us anyways.* He forced the dark thoughts away. He had a job to do--to find food. Otherwise, his family went hungry again.

He opened the first dumpster. Empty. He flipped up the lid to the second dumpster. Empty. *What is going on? Trash isn't picked up till Tuesdays.* He flipped open the next two in quick succession. The third dumpster was empty, but the fourth was about half full. He hopped in without hesitation and began sorting through it.

From somewhere in the building a bell let out three sharp rings. As if on cue, the Tenets rolled through his mind. *Sisera creates life and thus creates Man. Sisera sustains life and thus sustains Man. Sisera is Man's deepest desire.* With the Tenets came the familiar memories of life before his family had been thrown to the Outskirts. His days had been filled with dozy evenings in reclining chairs by the fireplace, schoolwork from the Academy, warm food every night. His childhood had been more than happy; it had been perfect. Until his father, and all the money they had saved, disappeared.

Terran planted a hand on the rim of the dumpster and tried to hop out. His foot caught and he tumbled onto the alleyway, landing on his back. He got up quickly from the ground and began kicking the dumpster. When he couldn't take the pain in his foot anymore, he slammed the lid shut. Reverberations continued to echo through the alleyway as Terran caught his breath. *That was probably a bad move.*

A rat scurried behind him. Its high pitched squeals just adding to the rage inside of him. He took in a large breath, then exhaled. *Remember why you're here.* He closed his eyes, calling to mind his sisters and mother. They all shared the same features, fair skin-like all Siserian women, rich blue eyes, and straight black hair. The only physical difference between them was age. Even with all their similarities, their personalities couldn't have been more different. After they had been carted to the edge of the city and left to die, Kelly had remained positive. She was the glue that kept him together.

Terran rested his head on the lip of the dumpster, staring at the ground. One of the patches on his right shoe had torn--either from the fall or his tantrum. Anna would have to fix it. He cringed at the thought of asking her. The opposite of Kelly, Anna was sharp and critical. If he brought home some good food, it would lessen the scolding.

Terran moved on to the trash cans, dumping them onto the alleyway. There was plenty of food in them, but even after seven years of looking through garbage, he still had a hard time knowing what was safe to eat. Almost every week or so someone got sick, which made the cramped rooms at the boarding house that much more unbearable.

It was better than sleeping outside though, so Terran kept that complaint to himself. If Linz heard one of them complaining about the lodgings, who knew what she would do. With a snort, he wiped his hands on his jeans and moved on to the trash bags.

He squatted next to the first one and tore it open. The stench forced him to fall backwards and his body fought between trying to cough and choke at the same time. He rolled to his side and threw up on the alleyway. After his body had finished emptying itself, he wiped the tears from his eyes and walked a few steps away from the small puddle of vomit. Every so often Terran would find a bag like the one he had opened--the leftovers of a gang fight or some other victim left in the street.

His frustration returned and he walked over to a small pile of refuse. With a small wind-up, he kicked the trash as hard as he could. Putrid smells threatened to overtake him again as garbage flew in all directions. The rat, caught unawares in the pile, slammed into the wall. It fell to the ground, ran a few feet, and then collapsed. Terran smiled. *Not every day we get some meat.* Walking over, he stuffed the rat in the hidden inner pocket of his long jacket. No need for everyone to know he had one.

He looked through what remained of the pile the rat had been in. It had to have been eating something good if it had been still long enough to be kicked. After another moment of scavenging he found his prize--a molded loaf of bread. He tore it into pieces and began stuffing his outer pockets, careful not to make them bulge.

"Get out of my alley, you piece of trash."

Terran turned to see who had shouted just in time to dodge a bottle. It crashed into the wall besides him, peppering him with shards of glass. The young man who had thrown the bottle retreated out of the window on the second floor for a moment before returning with another. Terran turned to run down the alleyway as another bottle crashed by his feet.

"Get a job!" another voice yelled.

A quick glance towards the building showed all the windows leading to the road were open. This was not going to be a good afternoon. He ran to the street as bottles and insults rained down around him.

"Look through your own trash."

"Get out of our territory!"

"Why don't you do us a favor and die."

As he reached the corner of the building, Terran turned to retort to the teens. A bottle crashed into the wall by his head. He felt the shards of glass dig into his skin as it exploded inches from his face. He ducked back around the wall and ran down the street. The kids wouldn't chase him--they wouldn't dare go into Outskirts territory; too many gangs. Terran continued running, despite the wind that tried to suck the life out of him. He glanced around him at the run-down buildings, keeping track of the signs painted on their sides. Blood dripped into his eyes and he wiped it away, cringing as the glass shards sank a little deeper into his skin.

The streets were deserted, which coupled with the growing shadows, made it easier for scavengers to get ambushed. *Nothing I can do about that now.*

Terran rounded another corner and almost hollered in joy. A neutral building stood amongst its neighbors, basking under the dim light of a streetlamp. In a hurry, Terran burst into the building, unsurprised to find it empty. *Everyone else is already home.* It was the only reason he had been so quick to barge in. A small puddle of water sat in the center of the room. Terran made his way over and gingerly began washing the blood off his face and hands. It took time for him to find all the glass, but eventually he could touch his face without cringing, which was a good sign. Anna could help him get the rest out when he got home.

He walked back to window and scanned the street for any signs of a trap. Neutral buildings were supposed to be safe, but as soon as you stepped out, you were a goner. Grabbing a pane of glass, he examined his face. Cuts peppered his skin, but none looked too deep. There was plenty of blood still on his face, although now it was smeared. On his dark skin it was hard to tell the difference between dirt and dried blood, so he wasn't too alarmed at the amount he saw. His blues eyes looked almost ethereal amidst all the red. He lifted the shaggy mess of brown hair around his ears, looking for any more cuts or hidden shards of glass, but apparently, his face had taken the bulk of the damage.

Terran jumped as the sound of breaking glass outside the front of the building surprised him. He ran to the back of the building and burst out the door. He had learned the hard way that you don't investigate, you run. The street was empty and Terran took the advantage to sprint as hard as he could. One of the benefits of constantly running from gangs in the Outskirts and overseers in the Lessers' territory was that he was good at it. *It's about the only thing I am good at anymore. Astrophysics don't matter to people without food.*

He heard the door to the neutral building slam open behind him as he turned the next street corner. He didn't have much time to get back to the boarding house, but he would make it. As the streets became more familiar, he ran harder. He took another tight corner and suddenly the street was full of people; men and women headed to their shelters. Finally, he was safe.

He joined a small group of people with their heads down, walking in the general direction of Linz's boarding house. There were no sounds except for shuffling feet and his pounding heart. He glanced around him at the people he was travelling with, and saw that each one wore the same blank expression. They were victims, defeated by the system. Terran spit on the ground. He would find a way out of this place. He just needed the chance.

## CHAPTER TWO

It was pitch black in the city as Terran reached the last street to the boarding house. The shelter stood out among the ones surrounding it, since it was the only one not covered in graffiti and had all the windows intact. Linz was particular about her image and made sure the tenants cleaned up any and all messes that were created as part of their rent.

He crossed the cracked asphalt to reach the small concreted porch leading into the building. The door opened before he reached it, and a harsh light blinded him. Taking a quick step back, Terran felt his foot slip on the damp cement, and he tumbled onto the sidewalk. He felt something warm and wet in his pocket and Terran knew he had fallen on the rat.

"Well, that was unexpected," a calm and lighthearted voice said.

"Is that all you're going to say?" Terran asked while struggling to pick himself up. He slipped in the rat's fluids that covered his side.

"Well, I do apologize," the calm voice said.

The man stood to the side of the door frame, no longer silhouetted by the light behind him, revealing a thick beard, blue jacket, and a faded pair of blue slacks.

"You squished my dinner," Terran dug into his pocket and flung the broken rat at the stranger's feet. "How am I supposed to eat this now?"

"Cooking it might be a start," the man said "Or you could just eat something else."

"You have some nerve you pomp..." Terran cut his insult short as the figure of a woman stepped into the doorway. The back lighting made it hard to see any details of the woman other than her slight build.

"Rictor, what do you think you're doing?" she sounded tired.

"Just having a bit of fun Naomi," Rictor said. "He and I were talking about dinner plans."

"That's not why we are here," Naomi replied without the slightest hint of amusement.

"Well, we should. Neither of us has eaten all day and I am famished."

Terran stood confused for a moment and stared at the pair. *What in the world is going on?*

"Rictor, get the ship ready," Naomi pleaded.

Smiling, Rictor turned back toward Terran and bounded down the steps. Putting his arm around Terran's shoulders Rictor gave Terran a half embrace.

"Just listen to the whole story, ok?" Rictor asked.

Finally recovering his composure, Terran pushed away from Rictor's arm.

"What is wrong with you? And listen to what? Who in the name of Sisera are you?" he shouted.

"We are not associated with that name I assure you," Rictor said. Without another word he turned and walked down the road a distance, then ducked into an alley next to the shelter.

Terran watched him go for a moment before turning back to the woman. She was sitting on the steps of the porch with her arms crossed on her knees.

No longer back lit, Terran was able to observe her. She was wearing the same uniform as Rictor, but hers seemed newer and the blue stood out brighter against her dark skin. Her hair was pulled back into a tight bun that sharpened her already angular features. Catching his gaze, Naomi patted the space next to her. Terran walked over to the steps and sat on the far end leaving space between them.

"Well, now we can get to what's really important," Naomi said with pep in her voice.

"And that is?" Terran asked. He shifted uncomfortably in the light. He wasn't used to sitting in plain view of the world around him. Seven years of avoiding notice urged him to either run inside or out into the night.

"Do you like Sisera?" Naomi asked, interrupting his thoughts. "Do you feel provided for by it? Do you feel obliged to it? Do you feel as if it is as important to you as the very air you breathe?"

Terran paused unsure of how to answer. While there was no official punishment for not following the Tenets, dismissing them could make life more difficult.

"I already know your answer, Terran," Naomi said in a soothing tone. "I know you want more out of your life, I know you want more for your family, and I know for a fact you hate what this planet has done to you."

Terran stopped himself from responding and tried to figure out what Naomi wanted with him. Silence settled over them, broken by the soft scraping of trash on the streets. He shivered, wishing he still lived in the insulated dome of the inner city.

"What do you want with me?" he asked in a low voice. He tensed his muscles, ready to spring at a moment's notice. He might only eat every other day, but he could still put up a fight.

"I want you to be free," Naomi said in that same soothing voice. "I want to take you off Sisera and show you something bigger than you could ever imagine." Her voice picked up in speed as excitement crept into it. "I want to show you the stars, the moon, and the planets; but most of all I want to show you the Capital."

At the mention of the Capital, Terran sighed and relaxed his muscles. Naomi and Rictor were a part of the Capital Bound. A group of people who claimed to travel between the stars on their way toward paradise. A group of them usually came around the shelter every few months or so, preaching how a ship would come from the stars and rescue them. It was all garbage. No one could travel to other planets, the technology just didn't exist. He looked over at Naomi again. She was so different from anyone else he had ever seen. No one on Sisera had skin that dark. It could have been a mutation, of course, but he wanted her to be different. He wanted what she said to be true. He was so tired of living off scraps, of skirting around the Outskirts begging for handouts, and living in fear of the prowling gangs. *Am I desperate enough to leave?*

Terran took a deep breath and tried to quiet his emotions. No matter what he wanted, he had other people to look out for. He wouldn't leave behind his family. If he said yes and left them alone he knew what could happen to them. There were a lot of prostitutes that worked their way into the Lessers' territory. That was assuming a gang didn't just nab them from the street for their own use.

"Have you talked with my family?" Terran asked. "Three women, two with short hair, one with long. They live in apartment 322."

"I do recall talking to a group of women matching that description. Two of them were teenagers? The youngest is a bit snarky?"

"That's them," Terran said, "Did they decide to go?"

"Of course they did. Who would give up the chance at paradise?"

She took his hand and they stood up together. "Come with me, Terran. Let me show you a better life than the one you're living."

Terran stared at the street. If Kelly and Anna were going, it wasn't like he could stay. He would be lost without them.

"I'll go." he said, casting a last look at the third floor window where his apartment was. Even if it was all a hoax, he needed to protect his family.

"Good choice. We must hurry then or else we are going to be late," she said. "If we are late, we get left behind. I do not particularly like Sisera, as nice as the people are, so we are going to have to run to catch up with Rictor."

Tugging at his hand, Naomi pulled him south down the street to the outer boundary of the city. Terran was caught off guard by the sudden movement and almost tripped on the cuffs of his pants. With another strong pull, Naomi helped him regain his balance and they began making their way down the streets. They didn't talk as they ran, giving Terran time to sort through everything Naomi had told him. One thing was for sure, there were a lot of questions he needed answers to.

The closer to the outer city they ran, the worse the buildings around them became. Instead of just missing windows and having cracks along their sides, the buildings had huge holes in them. Some of them were nothing more than heaps of brick, having fallen long ago to the elements. The wind picked up intensity, making Terran wish they could take a break in one of the rundown buildings for a few minutes to warm themselves.

At last, the edge of the city came into view. The road led into a desert pockmarked with shallow craters. The craters were haphazardly spaced and filled the entire expanse to the mountains in the distance. As they passed the final buildings and stepped into the expanse, the full force of the wind smashed against Terran, knocking him off balance and pelting him with sand. He fell to one knee and looked up to yell for Naomi. Instead, he found that he was lost for words.

A massive ship lay sprawled over two large metal rails that extended far into the distance. He was used to seeing the rails. They were a part of the natural landscape and were one of the few mysteries that science couldn't answer. Made of an unnatural metal, the rails were unable to be scratched, resistant to weathering, and made a continuous humming sound. The ship itself lay on top of the rails shining in the last rays of the meager sun. It was a long and thin vessel, beautifully curved and glowing like a spear tip just taken from a forge. Its two wings extended along its body and came to an end at the back of the ship. On its hull a golden emblem of a lion stood out against the crimson exterior. A large hatchway was open on the back and Terran saw a few people making their way inside. Naomi stopped running and turned toward him. With the ship behind her, she seemed to have a glowing aura. She motioned for him to stand, he forced himself to obey. Grimacing, Terran trudged toward his last hope.

Terran kept his head down, and didn't even notice they had reached the ship until his foot hit the loading dock. An arm fell across his shoulders guiding inside. The loading dock hissed behind him and he turned to see it closing with a loud click. He was blind in the darkness until lights flickered on across the ceiling. He was in a rectangular room. A small, four-wheeled vehicle was parked on one side and plastic containers were strapped to the floor behind it. A thick net was attached to the floor on the other side of the room. Terran assumed the collection of bags and suitcases must have belonged to others trying to escape from Sisera.

"Well, let's get you situated," Naomi said. Her breathing came out in shallow breaths, and Terran somehow felt better that the running and cold had affected her as well. "I suppose you will want to sit next to your family?"

"Yes, please," Terran said wanting nothing more.

They left the cargo hold and entered a wide corridor. The wall to his left had two large bulges in it that extend far into the corridor, making the hallway seem small. Sitting in front of each bulge was a comfortable looking chair.

"I need you to sit here for a second if you would," Naomi said, gesturing to the seat.

Terran sat down and his seat automatically reclined until he was staring at the ceiling. Shocked by the sudden change in orientation he could only watch as wide belts slithered from the sides of the seat itself and fastened him in. After his body was locked into place, a smaller belt went over his forehead and latched his head down with a bone chilling click.

*They were lying the whole time.* He jerked his head left and right, seeing nothing but empty seats around him. His heart raced, sweat began pouring down his brow. *They're just going to harvest my organs or something.* He opened his mouth to start screaming when he felt a small prick in his neck and his mouth locked. Frantic, he leaned as far out of the chair as possible, trying to see if he could locate Anna or Kelly. *Maybe they were back at the boarding house, but no. That woman, she had described them to him. That means they're already gone.* He fought against the restraints as tears rolled down his eyes, but with every passing second his strength faded.

Then, the world went black.

# CHAPTER THREE

Naomi stepped back from the chair and put the syringe into the disposal. He was dirty, mangy, and covered in fleas. He had been kicked to the curb and abandoned by the people he looked up to. Amidst all of that he chose to stay with his family and provide for them. *And I just killed him.* Her heart pounded in her chest as she stepped away from the chair. *It had to be done. Remember, this was for Nathaniel. It was a life for a life.* Naomi tried to quiet her nerves as she pushed a small button to the right of the chair and it slid into the wall of the ship. A moment later a small noise from the console let her know the chair was locked firmly in place.

Usually, the chairs were for people who became hysterical or violent, but in this case, they were the perfect tool for the job. *It had to be done.* She took a deep breath and continued down the corridor. Leaving the holding area, she began walking through the passenger cabins. Faking a smile, she took plenty of stops and chatted with the nervous passengers. She knew the questions they would ask; she had asked them all herself.

"Yes, you are really leaving the planet,"

"No, you won't need oxygen masks for the flight."

"We will explain how the jump ships work aboard our main vessel,"

"No, we don't know when we will reach the Capital,"

*No one ever asks if we will ever reach it, they always ask when.* Naomi's thoughts turned bitter as she smiled at everyone seated in their tidy blue chairs. So many families were seated together, sharing smiles and laughter. They were excited for the new adventures that awaited them. Reaching the last cabin Naomi checked the seating chart. A full one hundred and sixty-two people were onboard the Gungir.

"Excuse me, miss," A young girl's voice pierced her thoughts.

Turning, Naomi saw Terran's sisters seated near the front with an empty seat between them.

"How can I help you?" she asked with a grin that didn't reach her eyes.

"Have you seen Terran? Commander Rictor said you would talk with him about coming aboard." The younger girl spoke with desperation and tears were in her eyes. "I know he would come. Please could you tell him to sit next to us before the ship leaves?" Naomi's smile faded as she looked at the girl. *Better practice the lie now.*

"When we got onto the ship, your brother started going into hysterics and had to be restrained. When we reach the main ship, you will undoubtedly see him, but for now he needs his rest."

Both sisters seemed shocked by the news; the younger sank down into her seat and began to sob. The older however, kept her eyes on Naomi.

"Is he in trouble?" the girl asked.

"No," Naomi replied. The difference between the two girls was striking. Although they looked remarkably similar to one another, the manner that they carried themselves was quite different.

"Buck up, Kelly," the older said. "Terran just freaked out a bit and needs some time to cool off. You know how he jumps to conclusions." The younger girl regained some of her composure, and the sob turned into a soft whimper.

"I just have a bad feeling is all," Kelly said looking at her feet. "I know that he's in trouble."

"Well, don't worry about that," Naomi said forcing warmth into her voice. "It's expected that some people can get overwhelmed by the ship. We have special seats just for them. He isn't in any trouble at all," Naomi kept the forced smile and gently squeezed the girl's hand. "Don't fret, everything is OK." The young girl looked up from her feet and directly into Naomi's eyes.

"Promise?"

"Promise."

The girl breathed a deep breath and tried to sit up straighter. "How much longer until we start flying?"

"Not too much time at all. Now, I need to go to the bridge to make sure everything is OK. Are you going to be all right?"

"Yes ma'am." The girl flashed a smile as Naomi turned back to the bridge.

As she reached the door, she paused and took a breath. She had just lied to two young girls who would be devastated by what she had done. Now she just had to convince Rictor and the Captain. Taking a few more breaths to steady her nerves, she entered the bridge.

The bridge was a single deck, smaller than one would think for a ship this size, and was filled with busy officers at their stations. At the front of the ship a blank screen was attached to the frame of the ship. Although the screen could be used to show their surroundings, most of the time it was off. Naomi preferred windows. They didn't really need to see anyway, since the computers on board were connected with the Lion's Roar and would do all the travel calculations themselves. However, more than one guest had grown unnerved by the continuous wall of metal that surrounded them. Most of the crew were seated either at their stations or in one of the chairs that lined the walls. Rictor stood in the center of the bridge with his back to Naomi.

"How are our happy guests?" he chirped not looking back at her.

"They seem to be doing well," she replied.

"You handled yourself well out there. Not bad for your first time planetside."

"To be honest, I feel I could have done better."

"Oh," Rictor asked, finally turning around. "What stopped you?"

"You did," she replied. "Your approach to people is so far out I'm surprised you haven't been beaten or worse, killed."

The other officers on the bridge stopped moving. Silence permeated the room as Rictor turned around to face her. His usual smile replaced by stoicism.

"Naomi, go sit down."

"Yes, Commander," she said through gritted teeth. She could feel him watching her as she walked to the small seats that lined the walls.

"Besides," Rictor said, his voice growing lighter returning, "I have been beaten. I don't recommend it."

Naomi held her tongue and sat down. She and Rictor had been up well before dawn preparing for this last push into the Outskirts and she wanted sleep more than an argument.

When they had first arrived on Sisera a year previous, they had focused on the inner city of Debe. After a small team had been established, they had journeyed into the Lessers' territory right outside of the dome of Inner Debe. They had been more receptive, but many had the stubborn pride that plagued the working class. After two months of talking with the Lessers, she and Rictor had moved into the Outskirts. She had not had the easiest life before joining the Bound, but it was nothing compared to what she had seen over the last few months. She shivered as she remembered one of the last buildings they had entered. It had been filled with bodies--The result of some dispute between rival gangs. Men, women, and children, all murdered for a piece of land that no one wanted.

The people had come in droves to them. Some wanted food, others just the medicine, but there were plenty who had wanted to leave. It confused her how many people had chosen to stay on Sisera. Even if they never reached the Capitol, life on the Lion's Roar would be so much better than what they had. She had talked with hundreds of people, and most had been more than polite. However, there was a difference between listening and taking something to heart.

She chuckled at the bitter irony of her last statement. Opening up her tablet, she sent a quick encoded message to Dagor. "It is done." Closing her eyes, she rested her head on the cushion of the seat. Now, finally, she could be reunited with Nathaniel.

"Hey, you sleeping already? I asked you a question." Naomi opened her eyes and stared at Rictor.

"What?" she growled.

"I asked you how Terran handled seeing his sisters." His eyes shone with sincere concern.

"He didn't see them. He was growing hysterical when we entered the ship. I had to administer Brixatol to quiet him down, and then I had him restrained in a sleeper."

The lie was well prepared and her voice didn't waver. She had been through too much in her life to let emotions show unless she wanted them to.

"You did what?" Rictor asked breaking from his usual jovial rhythm. "Why did you use something so strong?"

"Well, probably because he was hysterical and becoming violent," Naomi said. "You saw him at the boarding house. He was covered in blood, probably from a fight over that rat, and he stank of alcohol. I did what I had to do. Besides, there is nothing we can do about it now, we will have to take care of it aboard the Lion's Roar."

Rictor locked eyes with her, and for the briefest moment she saw a hint of suspicion behind his concern for Terran. She would have to be careful around him for quite a while. *At least it's my last job for Dagor.* She had done her job and could focus on the things she really cared about. *I wonder how much Nathaniel has changed. Will he still smile at me the way he used to? Will he forgive me for leaving?* She closed her eyes again and sighed.

*Why does Dagor even care about someone like Terran anyway?* She cut off the thought before it could wander. It didn't matter, she had to remain focused. This was about her and Nathaniel. No one else mattered. If she could see him for even a moment, it would be worth it.

As the rest of the crew found their seats, Rictor sat at the main console and gave a final command. The ship lurched forwards at breakneck speed and Naomi felt the G's pressing her into her seat. With another sudden lurch the ship changed direction and she knew they were headed toward the main ship. Glenn would most likely have a lot to say to her. Naomi knew her only choice was to stick with the story she had created. *Once they see it was just a safety precaution gone wrong I will be free.* As her heart sped up in apprehension she tried to tell herself it was just the ship flying and not the gnawing sensation of guilt trying to worm its way into her mind.

# CHAPTER FOUR

Naomi kept a careful eye on the Captain as she retold the story of the events leading up to the administration of the brixatol. She watched as his face changed from one of passivity to cold steel. Now aboard the Lion's Roar, she couldn't help but feel like a child seated before a headmaster. Seated in the small wooden chair in his office, she awaited his reply.

His office was generously furnished with a carved desk of some dark wood which matched the filled bookshelves that lined the walls. The back wall was a solid window that showed the streaking lights of New-Space as they danced around the ship. Taking away from what would otherwise be a beautiful room, there was the Captain himself.

Captain Denner was a giant among men. Fully six-and a-half feet tall, he towered over everything in the office. His uniform, although precise and neat, seemed barely able to restrain the muscle underneath. He would be handsome if not for the scars completely covering his face. It was almost mesmerizing in a horrific way to trace them, trying to find where one started and ended. Yet, through all the scars, in perfect condition, sat two bright and intelligent eyes. You could see who the Captain really was by looking into them--now emotionless and hard, for once they seemed to match the rest of his body.

Sitting across from him, her resolve began to crack under his gaze. Not much, but just enough for her shoulders to slump and her guilt to build.

"What do you have to say for yourself?" he asked in a voice that could have come from a statue instead of a man.

"I am deeply sorry, sir," Naomi said, avoiding his eyes and bowing her head slightly.

"I want to believe you, Naomi..."

"Then do it," she pleaded, cutting him off.

"Well, I can't. Because I know you are lying," his reply hit like a bullet.

"About what, sir?" she asked keeping her head bowed.

"I don't know yet."

There was a loud creak as the Captain got up from his chair. Naomi looked up to see him walking over to a painting. The massive frame of his chair seeming oversized without the Captain to give it perspective.

"What are you going to do to me?" she asked, adding a small tremble to her voice.

"You will be confined to your room until an investigation has been completed. If you are found guilty of negligence or sabotage, you will be left at our next stop."

"What if our next stop is the Capital?" The sarcastic comment escaped her mouth before she could stop it, and she cursed herself inwardly.

The Captain turned slowly to face her. He moved with an easy grace that defied his size. He seemed too surreal to be a man. *Who were you before the Capital got ahold of you?*

"Then, the Emperor himself will judge you for your actions." The Captain's tone shut down any more remarks she could have said, and she knew the meeting was over.

"By your leave, sir," Naomi said bowing her head again and getting up from the chair. The Captain did not respond as she walked awkwardly across the small office practically crumbling beneath the weight of his gaze. As the door closed behind her she let out a long sigh of relief and became aware that her heart was thudding like a jack hammer. She didn't drink often, but meetings with the Captain often left people a little shaken, to say the least. *Too bad there isn't any aboard.* She started walking down the hallway.

"That went well," a silky voice whispered into her ear.

Naomi shuddered, but started walking toward the elevator at the end of the hallway. There were no other rooms in the hallway, just the Captain's office, but people were still lingering about.

"Hello, Dagor," she mumbled in reply. "Now is not the best time."

"We just had a huge victory," his voice was positively bursting with joy. Naomi always imagined Dagor as an imp. A small man with a smooth tongue. She had no way to prove it, but she was almost certain it was true.

"Well, we can talk as soon as I get to my room instead of while I am walking in a hallway," she grumbled, trying not to draw attention to herself. It didn't work, of course. Everyone knew by now what had happened to Terran. Another group of people walked by and began whispering once she had passed-- she began to think maybe getting off at the next stop would be a good idea.

"Very well then, but don't forget about your little reward for this wonderful deed."

Naomi's heart skipped a beat at the thought of talking to her son again. "I want to talk to him once I get to the room."

"Of course," Dagor's voice whispered.

With that he was gone, and Naomi felt the distinct need to shower. She hated talking with him. He seemed to be able to magnify every bad feeling she was experiencing and bring it to the forefront of her mind just by talking. He could have been asking her about her day, and she would have felt like a cold slime had been dripped down her back.

*It will all be worth it to see Nathaniel again.* She couldn't forget the prize. It had been four years since she had seen his face or heard his voice. He would be sixteen now. He had taken after her, and she had loved seeing his dimples when he smiled. Her heart began to ache at the thought of her son. *He will understand, they have surely told him what happened and why he was left behind. He would understand that it wasn't her fault.* She repeated these thoughts to herself as she finally entered her room.

It was a simple room. A bed sat in the corner, neat and orderly. There was a couch and some lounging chairs surrounding a small table in a small depression in the center, but it was bare of decorations. *First things first, I need to take a shower.* After she had washed away Dagor's voice and the worries of the day, she dressed and readied herself for her son.

Sitting on the couch, she picked her up her tablet and input the code to open the underlying operating system on it. She no longer used the ship's OS as it could be traced too easily. Noticing an email notification, Naomi mindlessly clicked on it.

*Probably just some meeting or other useless notification.* Naomi hated the meetings that accompanied the newcomers' training. Surely, they wouldn't ask her to speak to them again after what had happened. The email was not from a committee, however, but from Rictor. The subject said it was a brief from the planetside operations, but it was addressed solely to Naomi. Opening it, she read through the first few lines of pointless information, then stopped in her tracks. One line stood out to her from the rest.

<u>Just to be clear, Terran is expected to make a full recovery from his accident.</u>

Naomi couldn't help but stare at the words. Surely it was a lie. She had given him the precise amount that Dagor had told her. Terran should be dead. She read the sentence again, then again. Tears began filling her eyes. As she expected, another email notification appeared on her screen. With trembling fingers, she reached out and touched the symbol. A quick email from Dagor appeared with five words. <u>Terran Alive means No Deal.</u>

Naomi set the tablet down and lay on the couch with her head on the pillow and began to cry. In a few moments, the email erased itself and the tablet shut off. The lights dimmed with a simple command between sobs, and in the darkness of her room Naomi cried herself to sleep.

# CHAPTER FIVE

"Wake up, sleepy head," a sweet voice whispered.

Terran's eyes snapped open, and he sat up ready to fight off the attack. A wave of nausea struck him, and he fell onto his back putting his palms to his eyes to fight against the light. Terran moaned and tried to gather his bearings. Something was different, the chair wasn't the firm material from before, but soft and bouncy. It reminded him of the plush couches his family had owned when they had lived in Inner Debe.

"What are you doing Kelly?" Terran asked. There was an awkward silence as Terran realized who he was talking to. Once again, he sat straight up in the chair, this time fighting through the nausea and the brightness of the room. Kelly was sitting at the foot of the soft and narrow couch he had been resting on. Her eyes were bright and she was smiling at him, her hair washed and falling in soft waves below her shoulders. She was no longer in the mismatched clothes they had been wearing in the slums. Instead, she was in a blue tank top with a grey jacket and matching slacks. The lion insignia he had seen on the hull of the burning ship was on her jacket's shoulder. *No, it wasn't burning, just glowing.* That seemed odd to him the more he thought about it. Looking beyond his sister he surveyed his surroundings.

They were in someone's office, several bookshelves lined the walls of the small room and a wooden desk sitting in front of a large window gave hint to its use. Terran's eyes almost skimmed over the window before his brain registered what he was seeing. Out of it, the whole of space spread out before him. He stood and walked unsteadily to the window until his forehead was resting on its thick glass, all else forgotten.

"You're lucky," Kelly teased. "I didn't even fall asleep like a little baby through the hard part of leaving planetside. I was up the whole time."

"I didn't fall asleep," Terran said absent mindedly, still looking at the beautiful scene before him. Shining stars, more than he could count, sparkled at him across a backdrop that tried to smother them in darkness. He could see the sides of the ship; they were dark grey and fell away from him in a gentle curve. *The crimson must have been a trick of the light.*

"If you didn't fall asleep, then why did you just wake up?" Kelly asked, playfully nudging his arm.

"I didn't say I wasn't asleep, just that I didn't fall asleep," Terran said, a little annoyed at his sister. "I was..." Quickly, Terran began to run his hands along his body. Looking down at himself, he noticed that his clothes had been changed as well and matched the style that Kelly was wearing.

"They probably took care of all your fleas, bro," Kelly said laughing. "They made all of us take showers when we boarded. Get this, the water was hot the whole time. They told us to take as long as we wanted."

"I was looking for stitch marks," Terran said with a frown. "Why the heck did they put me to sleep like some type of animal?" he snapped. "I thought they were going to harvest my organs or something."

As soon as Terran finished, Kelly began laughing so hard that she fell over double, tears beginning to stream down her face.

"How in the world is that so funny? Terran asked, "Maybe for you it would seem strange, but I was strapped down and drugged. What else was I supposed to think?"

Finally, regaining her composure, Kelly didn't reply. Standing up, she walked over to him and hugged him as tightly as she could. Terran's anger disappeared instantly as he wrapped his arms around her in a fierce bear hug.

"I am so glad you're here." She said. "It's nice having the family back together again."

"Mom and Anna came too?" Terran asked hopefully.

"Of course, silly," Kelly said as she headed back to the couch. "Why would anyone pass up the chance at paradise?"

A smile began creeping to his lips as he walked across the room to plop on the couch by his sister. Staring out the window, he noticed two small streaks of light racing toward the ship. *I wonder if those are comets.* As they tore into the ship, however, he knew they were not. More beams of light came tearing through the black sky, piercing the vessel. Terran could see the hull boiling around the perimeter of each hole punched in the ship.

"No" he screamed as a beam of light began heading towards the window.

He jumped on top of Kelly as the beam of light crashed into their room. The force of the blast threw him into the wall and he crumpled to the floor. He watched as Kelly flew away from him, out of the small room. He reached out to her, somehow hoping he could draw her back in to him.

He didn't know what exploded behind him, but he felt the explosion fling him out of the window. He rocketed past his sister, no longer moving, and began spinning wildly in the air. Then, fire exploded within him, and he screamed as the flames spread throughout his body. Whimpering, he curled into a ball, hugging his knees. With a final shudder his body gave out and a numbness spread all over. He glanced up and everything was gone. Instead, he was surrounded by darkness. Featureless and soundless, this darkness had a cold feel to it. It seemed immeasurably large, and yet it seemed to be rushing inward into him, as if to devour his very body and soul from the inside out. Suddenly, his body convulsed as lightning shot through it and the darkness burst away from him. The pain from the lightning was very real, and once again, Terran screamed.

"Someone shut him up," an unfamiliar voice yelled through a wall of static.

Terran opened his eyes again to a blurred world full of dull lights and slow noises. There seemed to be a disconnect between his eyes and ears. He would see something move, then hear it moving a second after. *I wonder what those fuzzy things are? They seem so nice.* He tried to reach out and touch one of the strange and twisted pieces of fuzz, but he was unable to move his arm.

"How much longer does he have?" said another voice. This one had a rough edge to it and seemed very concerned about something.

"You can't have my organs," Terran failed to say, slurring every word. One of the featureless fuzzes leaned toward him, and he began to fall away again. He watched the scene around him drift away until it was just a speck of light in the distance. His own personal star. Then, even that light was too far away to be seen. He drifted down for a million miles until he finally landed upon his old couch from Inner Debe. The darkness around him was a comfort this time, filled with the sweet warmth of rest.

# CHAPTER SIX

Terran awoke to the harsh smell of antiseptic. A sudden beep caused him to jerk away from the sound--which he immediately regretted as a sharp pain shot up from his hand. An IV had been stuck in him, and following the tube led back to the small, beeping machine beside him. *I'm in a hospital?* He turned to his left and jumped when he saw a large man in the chair next to him reading a rather small book. The book looked more like a pamphlet in his scarred hands. The man looked toward Terran and smiled. Scars almost completely covered his face, forming crags and valleys against the wrinkles that were already there. His gray hair was trimmed neatly, but his scalp bore several large scars that disrupted the orderly haircut. He stood, and Terran fought a sense of vertigo as he forced himself to look up at the man's face. *This has to be the orderly sent to keep me in line, or to finish the job that Naomi started.* That didn't make sense. If this man had wanted him dead, he would have killed him in his sleep. *What is he here for then?*

"Wha..." a fit of coughing stopped Terran from finishing his word.

The man tossed the book he had been reading onto the chair and stared at Terran. Unable to get away from the giant's gaze, Terran sat in silence and looked down at his hands.

"Hello, Terran," the man said, finally breaking his silence. "My name is Glenn Denner, and I am the Captain of the Lion's Roar. Do you know where you are?"

"I'm in a hospital," Terran whispered. He swallowed a few times to make talking less painful. "Where the hospital is, I don't know."

"You had a very bad reaction to a sedative you received when you were onboard the Gungir. Do you remember boarding the ship?" Glenn asked, pulling the chair next to the bed and sitting back down.

"Why was I given a sedative?" Terran rasped, wishing he didn't have to talk anymore. Every time he talked it felt like a piece of sandpaper was scraping inside his mouth.

Glenn handed Terran a clear glass of what appeared to be water and sat down. Terran sniffed the liquid, then drank just enough to wet his mouth. He fought the urge to gulp the rest of the water for a few more seconds before downing the cup, spilling water down his chest. A contented sigh escaped from him as he set the cup down. Water had never tasted so good. *Of course, the water I'm used to was never this clear anyway.*

Glenn gave Terran a few more moments before continuing, "You were given a sedative because a Voice had an over inflated sense of urgency. We have talked it over, and she has been reprimanded. How are you feeling?" Terran tried to look into the Captain's eyes, but turned away.

"Truthfully?" he asked.

"Truthfully." Glenn replied.

"I'm already tired of this Capital nonsense. If your 'Voices' or whatever can't handle something as simple as boarding someone on a..." Terran paused mid rant. What did he call that ship? The Gungir is what the Captain had called it.

"It is called a jumping vessel," Glenn said, noting Terran's confused expression. "It makes the jump from the ship to planetside and back again. Luckily, the jumps don't take any large amount of time, and Rictor made sure that everything was right on schedule. We were able to get you into the O.R. quickly and pump some life back into you." After a brief silence, he added, "You were gone for a little bit there."

Terran shuddered, thinking back to the darkness that had almost smothered him.

"How long have I been out?" he asked.

"Two days," said Glenn. "Everyone else has been assigned their duties and cleaned up. After another day or two you will be assigned your duties, and we can get you briefed on the details of what exactly we do and what is expected of you. Unfortunately, even if you are tired of this 'Capital business', you can't leave until we reach the next assigned planet. It will take us three months to get there. If you do decide you don't want to be a part of our mission, you can stay in the room we have prepared for you."

Terran struggled to keep his emotions in check. *I'm really gone? No more Sisera to haunt me?* "Sir," he said, unsure of protocol on a space ship, "I have a lot of questions about all this."

"I understand," Glenn said as he got up from his chair. "However, we will have to continue this talk at a later time. I made a promise to some...persistent girls that when you woke up, I would let them know. There will be plenty of time for Q&A before we reach Torga." Glenn left the door open as he left. The bed's position made it impossible to see out of the room, but Terran was able to see the blue carpet that stopped in the doorway. He wondered who his visitors would be. His sisters? His mother? All of them? Maybe it was just Naomi, coming to explain why she had almost killed him.

The last possibility caused a knot in his stomach and he hoped it wouldn't be her.

Minutes passed, and Terran began inspecting his room to pass the time. It was small and white with two uncomfortable looking chairs sitting neatly in front of his bed. There was a small side table to his left and a number of bright monitors to his right showing his vitals. As he began to read the monitors, he heard footsteps pounding down the hallway. He looked to the doorway just as two breathless girls entered the room. They both wore grey sweatpants and a blue shirt with the lion emblem emblazoned on the chest. Panting and leaning on one another, they looked at him and smiled. Even with shaved heads it was easy to see the resemblance.

"You have no idea how happy I am to see you two. Where's mother? What happened to your hair?"

The two girls straightened, their breathing softer now though obviously still winded. Kelly held up a finger to silence Terran, and the girls took another moment to catch their breath. Anna spoke first, "Mother stayed behind to wait in case dad ever came home. She has been waiting this long and didn't see any reason to stop. Before you get mad, know that it was her choice and nothing we could have said would have changed her mind. I guess we can figure out where you get your stubborn side."

Kelly started in before Terran could respond, "You are the reason we lost our hair. We both had positively massive amounts of lice and bugs and unmentionables in it. At first, they tried to save it, but by the time they had cut out the split ends, combed out the bugs, and tried to wash it, it had practically all been cut or fallen out. Besides, you have no reason to laugh."

Terran reached up and rubbed his head. Rough stubble covered it. "How do I look?" he asked with a grin.

"Horrid!" Kelly replied at once. "Of course, losing your hair didn't change much." His sisters rushed the bed and they wrapped their arms around him.

"I had the most terrible dream," Terran whispered. "I thought I had lost both of you."

"Well, unfortunately for you we are still here to pester you," Anna said giving him a faint smile. "We can't stay long, we have duties to attend to, and you need your rest."

"Very well," Terran said, already feeling worn out. "I love you, don't forget that."

They pulled away slowly. Kelly wiped her eyes, and they both backed away from the bed "This is going to be a grand adventure, Terran. Wait until you actually hear about the Capital."

Terran, still unsure of whether he wanted anything at all to do with the Capital, smiled and waved as they left the room. Laying back on the reclined bed, Terran began to sort through the questions he had.

# CHAPTER SEVEN

ictor sat across from his Captain with his legs propped on the spotless desk. He rather liked the Captain's office. It was a sanctuary where he and Glenn could look out for the rest of the ship.

"Here's the thing, Captain," Rictor continued, "We both saw the video footage from the Gungir, we both know that Naomi is lying, and we both know that she is being used."

"Well, what do you suggest?" he asked taking a sip of tea from the small glass in his hand.

"My initial assessment of the situation is that we should interrogate her until she tells us exactly who contacted her, how she was contacted, and what they have on her." Rictor took his feet off the desk and looked Glenn square in the eye. "However, that is the exact opposite of what we should do."

Glenn sighed, then put down his drink before he began to individually crack his knuckles. It was a nervous habit of his that he didn't let many people see.

"Well, what about a second assessment?" the Captain asked, "I just wish we could be forward every once in a while. I hate all this cloak and dagger nonsense."

"The second idea is to let her continue about her business. We could plant some bugs, find out who she is talking to and then act when we have more definitive information." He nodded his head as he finished, indicating that he thought the idea was the better one.

"And why don't we just tell her we are on her side and try to help her with understanding what we know about Promioth's methods?" The Captain had never been very good at being covert, and it showed in how quickly he tried to get out of situations that required sneaking around. Rictor, on the other hand, could appreciate the art of subtlety. It was why they made such a great team.

"We can't do that, Glenn," Rictor said with a quick smile. "It would be easier if we could, but we don't know how they are communicating with her besides her tablet. If we broach the subject openly, then we could damage any hopes we have of finding out which Envoy is tied up in this, and we could end up seriously hurting Naomi as well."

The Captain stared at Rictor for a long minute. Rictor could tell he was pondering through the various possibilities and strategies, looking for a way out of the deceit. Glenn was an excellent strategist, that was the reason why the Lion's Roar hadn't been overrun with Promioth troops like many of the other Planet Jumpers. He was also honest, which is why he made such an outstanding captain. Although Rictor could give advice from his past experiences, it was Glenn's sharp mind which kept them afloat.

"Do you have any ideas who the Envoy might be?" Glenn asked, taking another sip of his drink.

"Most likely Dagor or Endo," Rictor replied after a brief pause. "Hopefully it's Endo, he tends to lie a lot more than Dagor and uses empty threats. Plus, he has never done any real damage--a bit inept you might say. Dagor, on the other hand, isn't afraid to use violence to get to an end."

Glenn nodded his head in agreement. "Then the best course of action will be for me to plant the bug during the exit interview as she enters her probationary period. Hopefully, we can find out all the information we need and get some help for her before anything goes awry. I hate to bug our own people, but if it is going to be done, I will be the one to do it."

"We have to be as shrewd as vipers in this day and age," Rictor said. "That's what the Teachings tell us."

"We are also supposed to be blameless. Where do you think planting bugs puts us?" Glenn asked.

"It puts us in a place where we can protect this ship. I don't like this anymore than you do, Glenn, but it has to be done."

"I think people often forget what the word 'has' really means." Glenn drank the rest of his tea and set the cup on the desk.

Rictor smiled again as he studied Glenn. While many would be put off by the colossal man, anyone who sat and talked with him for even a brief conversation would see the heart he had for the people around him. There weren't too many men like him, and Rictor was glad he was on their side.

"Well, we'll do the best we can and let the Emperor sort it out when we see him. It's off to work for me; if this consultation is over anyway." Glenn nodded and Rictor stood up from the cushioned chair. "Since we are friends, I will send you a bill with the discounted rate."

Glenn chuckled as he walked with Rictor to the door.

"We have to be careful, Rictor," Glenn said. "If Naomi is compromised, there may be others we have to look out for."

Rictor opened the door. "No worries, Captain, between your smarts and my gumption, we can sort out anything."

The Captain chuckled again as Rictor left the room. However, as Rictor turned and walked down the hallway, he was anything but happy. There was a lot of work to be done if they were to find out everyone who was an agent of Promioth. The first step would be to find out what Naomi did that was different than everyone else. That would mean pouring over hours of video footage. Even then he only had access to videos of the common areas since the private rooms weren't monitored. *It's going to be a long night.*

Rictor entered his small cramped office and booted up the small computer at his desk. Most people thought he was just a supply clerk, and that was fine by him. If most people knew that he oversaw security, they would start asking questions. He had been on other ships that were more transparent about their security measures, and none of them had ended well-- not to mention the less people knew about their security measures, the greater the chance they had to find any more moles. *Our measures didn't help Terran though.* Rictor pushed the thought out of his mind. He needed to focus.

Rictor did a quick search and found the first day Naomi entered the ship. It was a year and a half ago. Rictor turned on the small pot next to his desk, and the aroma of coffee filled the room. He wouldn't rest until he found out how the ship had been infiltrated, and the coffee would help to keep his mind sharp. He pulled a tablet and a pair of ear buds out of his desk. Rictor removed the small earplug from his left ear and replaced it with the ear buds. A little bit of noise always helped him to concentrate, and he didn't want any outside disturbances. Taking a deep breath Rictor pressed "Play" and began to watch the silent video of cheering faces entering the Lion's Roar for the first time. Finding Naomi's face, Rictor let out a soft sigh. Of all the faces and laughter evident in the video, Naomi's face was the only one that was solemn and withdrawn. *We are getting sloppy. How in the name of the Emperor did we miss the pain that she was feeling?*

The video kept playing and Rictor took note on everything that Naomi did on the tablet. After the video ended Rictor played it back to double check; then played it a third time, noting every little detail he could. Feeling satisfied with his notes, he played the movie again and focused on the other newcomers. He didn't keep track of how many times he watched the video, or how many times he watched the next one. Whenever sleep began to creep up on him, he gave a silent command and adrenaline would pump into his system. One of the few benefits to having nanos coursing throughout his entire body was that he never needed to sleep.

The rest of the world faded around him as he focused on videos. He would find out every single person on the ship who was working for Promioth; everyone's lives depended on it.

# CHAPTER EIGHT

Over the next few days, as Terran slowly recovered, he was visited often by his sisters. They brought him news of the ship, told him about friends they had made, and helped put him at ease. Much to his surprise, Rictor visited him almost as often. He filled in some of the details of what happened during the flight. On Sisera Rictor had seemed crude, but on the ship his small quips helped to bring Terran's spirits up and further relax him. The only disappointing circumstance was the Captain not visiting at all. He had tried to leave the room, but his doctor, Angela, had stopped him. With each attempt, she had gently guided him back to the bed patting his hand and telling him all the reasons he needed to rest. It had been immensely frustrating.

As he was planning his next attempt to bypass Angela, the door to his room slid open and Glenn strode in. In his right hand, he held a scepter adorned with a clear orb; in his left, a large duffel bag. He was wearing a light brown jacket that ended at his waist along with the blue slacks and white shirt that everyone seemed to wear on the ship.

"Hello, Captain," Terran said.

"Hello, Terran," Glenn replied, "Today you will move into your quarters, no more of this infirmary nonsense. If Angela wasn't such a terror, I would have had you out days ago."

Terran fought the urge to hug the Captain. Angela had been nothing but sweet to Terran since he had awakened, but the infirmary was driving him insane.

"I can tell the duffel bag is probably filled with clothes, but what in the world is that rod?"

As Terran gazed at the orb, a faint glow seemed to pulse from it then fade.

"This is a V-Sphere. We use it for teaching newcomers about the history of the Capital and to explain what you are getting into. Once we get to your room, all you have to do is touch the sphere, and it will do its thing. We have the rod because you can set the imagery it produces at different heights so you can see the images better. Understand?"

"So, it makes a hologram?" Terran asked hesitantly.

"Close enough. Now get out of bed and get changed so we can get you situated." He tossed Terran the duffel bag and left the room.

Terran changed quickly and found the slacks and shirt combination to be quite comfortable. The jacket was a little large for him in the shoulders, but otherwise fit very well. The material of the clothing was a strange synthetic that was both light and heavily insulated.

He left the room in good spirits even though his body was aching from the bed rest, entering the corridor outside. Doorways branched off in every direction, and the Captain was waiting about halfway down talking to Angela. She was a short woman with peppered hair and a hawk-like face. As Terran approached them, he picked up small pieces of the conversation and noted that it hadn't been so much a talking as a reprimanding. When Angela turned to him, however, she was all smiles.

"Are you sure you are up for leaving?" she asked, patting his hand.

"Yes," he replied. "My whole body aches from the bed rest, and it will be good to stretch my legs." Terran said, trying to fill his voice with as much confidence and strength as he could.

"Very well then," Angela frowned. "You are free to go, but if I see a single hint that something is wrong, I will personally march into your room and drag you back."

Terran laughed at first, but stopped when she and the Captain didn't join in. The Captain gave him a knowing look, and they continued walking down the hall to an elevator. Glancing at the buttons highlighted on the panel to the right of the door, Terran was frustrated to find he couldn't read any of the lettering. The numbers were clear as day, but the words looked mostly like big scratches. *Did I expect to read a foreign language? But, then again, I can both talk and understand people talking to me.*

"Captain, why can I understand you, but can't read the panel?"

The Captain laughed a big throaty laugh and slapped Terran on the back. "I was wondering how long it would take for you to ask that. That is always the first question. On the ship, everything is written in the root language of mankind. It should come easily to you, but does take some time. Now, tap inside your ears." Terran obliged and felt plastic. He took them out.

"Say something."

Glenn flashed a smile, "Tucar, endoin eet lesala."

Terran put the earpieces back in.

"So, what happens when only one is in?"

"You get a rather large headache."

Terran let out a chuckle and tried thinking of more questions. Before he could ask any more, the door slid open again to another long hallway with rows of doors on the left and right. He took Terran to the room at the far end, and opened the door with a translucent key. *That's rather archaic.* Terran entered the room after him and was surprised at how nice it was. Along the entire far wall were massive bookshelves. To his left, he could see a small adjacent area with a private bathroom. The main room consisted of a small resting area complete with a couch and two comfortable looking chairs surrounding a low table. Plush carpet covered the entire apartment and bathroom areas. Along the wall to his right, a window took up the entire wall.

Light poured in from the millions of stars and planets that surrounded them. In the far distance, he could see bright bursts of colors reaching far out across the background. Blues and purples and reds showing themselves in so many different shapes and sizes they made Terran's head spin looking out into them.

"It's beautiful."

"It is," Glenn said with a small smile tugging at his lips. "I never grow tired of seeing the view from New-Space."

"New-Space?" Terran asked.

"Another question that will be answered after the V-sphere has done its work."

"Can we watch it yet?"

"Yes, once we shut the shade," Pressing a small button by the door, the wall below the window rose to connect to the ceiling with a loud click. The room stayed dark for a few moments before the overhead lights turned on and cast a dim glow.

"Now, sit on the couch and don't say a word until it's done." Glenn said.

Terran nodded and did as he was told. As the Captain placed the rod on the ground the sphere began to glow. Terran stared into the orb and saw the same pulsing light that he had seen before. This time, it was more than just a flash of light. An image began rushing toward him. He reflexively drew his head back as the image from the sphere seemed to hit the glass, then explode out from the barrier and fill the room. Terran sat wide eyed as a voice began to speak into his head," In *the beginning there was the Capital..."* A bright light filled the room and in a flash Terran found himself on a terrace overlooking the ocean.

# CHAPTER NINE

ooking across the terrace, Terran could see a vast beach of pure white sand stretching into a long peninsula that extended straight out from his perch. Waves crashed on both sides of the beach trying to swallow the small stretch of land back into the ocean depths. Terran watched as birds darted into the water snatching unsuspecting fish from the sea, and felt the sun basking him in its warmth. *How long has it been since I have felt the full force of the sun?* The salty smell of the ocean washed over him, and he began to grow disoriented from the sheer shock of traveling from the ship to the paradise he found himself. As he was about to tip over, a strong hand gripped him by the arm.

"Hello, Terran," a calm voice said, piercing through the confusion.

"Who are you?" Terran fought through the nausea. "Where am I?"

"You are on a planet called Gundalo, and I have many names, but you may call me Ekundayo."

"What am I doing here?" Terran asked, straightening up and rubbing his eyes. The sun was so bright it hurt to keep them open.

"You are here because I wanted you here," Ekundayo replied, "Sit down and rest."

Terran sat without thinking, and for a brief moment thought he would fall to the floor. Instead, he found himself hitting the soft cushion of a recliner.

"You follow quickly," Ekundayo said with a quick laugh. "You are either very tired or you have been waiting a long time for this."

"Both," Terran said looking up at the man. He was of medium height with long black hair, and his tanned skin contrasted sharply against the stark white shirt and slacks he was wearing.

"Well, to ease things for you, I am going to be upfront and will try to answer any questions I can. You probably won't like many of the answers, though." Ekundayo leaned forwards and patted Terran's knee. "Ask away my friend."

Terran paused for a moment. There were plenty of questions he could ask Ekundayo, but his mind was still recovering from the dramatic shift in scenery.

"Why am I asking you questions?" Terran asked, leaning back in his chair and enjoying the ocean breeze. "What makes you so qualified? If you don't mind me asking, that is."

"I am glad you started with an easy question," Ekundayo said. "I am qualified because I am the Emperor's son."

Terran stared at the man, stunned by his words. "As in the so-called maker of the human race, Emperor? That is a rather hard pill to swallow."

Ekundayo's demeanor didn't waver for an instant. "For the record, he created more than the human race. Secondly, just because you don't believe in something or don't understand how something works does not mean it isn't true. The fact that you are here should be at least a bit of motivation for belief."

Terran considered Ekundayo's comment. Even if it looked like he was at an ocean front property, there was the fact that he got here by staring at a flashing orb. But he wouldn't be won over quite so easily.

"What is New-Space?" Terran asked. If nothing else, he was going to try and get the answers he could cross verify.

"I cannot tell you that," Ekundayo responded calmly. "Not because I do not know the answer, but because you being finite, cannot understand the complexity of something infinite. It would be like a grain of sand trying to understand you. You are so far removed from sand it would be ridiculous to think that it could understand us. To us sand is an unfeeling, unthinking, and altogether lifeless substance. Do you understand?"

Terran felt his anger bubbling with him. "Could you at least try? You said you were going to answer my questions, not dodge them."

"All of space should be seen as consisting of a single point. Coming from this point in a cone are all the possibilities of that dot. That is the concept of time that you perceive. New-Space is the area around that point. Because we live in New-Space we can travel to any point in space or time and interact with the world as you know it. That is a very simple picture of things. Any more details would just cause extra confusion."

Terran sat still for a moment. *I wonder how much time I have here.*

"We have enough time for another question or two." Ekundayo's voice rang out next to him.

Terran's eye widened and he turned to face the man. "How did you do that?"

Ekundayo smiled. "I am from New-Space, not space. Things work differently for me than you."

"Are there more like you?" Terran asked.

"In a sense, yes. If you are asking if anyone is exactly like me the answer is no. You see every person consists of two parts. The body in space and the essence in New-Space. At the end of someone's life either their body will join their essence in New-Space or their essence will join their body in space. Does that make sense?"

"So, it's like a soul?" Terran felt the anger give way to excitement as the itch of his scholarly mind was finally getting the scratch it had been waiting for. It had been eight years since he had had any sort of scintillating conversation and he had forgotten how much he craved it.

"That is a basic way of looking at it, but, yes."

"So, what's up with the ships?"

"The main purpose of the ships is to spread the word of the Emperor before it is too late. Space won't be around forever, Promioth thinks he has grown strong, but forgets it is the Emperor who created space to begin with. Soon, I will be sent to collect the faithful. And the rest will be left to fend for themselves. The Emperor will remove his protection from them and without the sustaining power of New-Space, space will collapse."

Terran stopped smiling. "Well that's not fair. I had barely heard about any of this. Why would I get punished? Don't we get some sort of chance?"

Ekundayo smiled weakly at Terran. "Terran, I visited every single planet that sustains life. I told everyone who the Emperor is and how to live right with him. I gave teachings that would help to lead the way and ships to help them travel to the Capital. And yet, on every single planet, I was refused. If a drowning man refuses help, whose fault is it?"

Terran sat quietly and let the sea breeze wash over him. He looked over at Ekundayo and saw that there where streaks on his cheeks where tears had fallen. He closed his eyes and took deep breath of the salty air.

"If the ships can travel between space and New-Space can they travel in time?" he asked.

"Yes and no. They have the capability to, but I inhibit them. If we allowed that, it could cause...complications."

"Like what?" Terran asked.

"Like trying to go back in time to hurt someone or save someone, perhaps a father."

Terran stared at Ekundayo through gritted teeth. "Well, think of all the good we could do. How many travesties we could stop. There have been hundreds if not thousands of tyrants who have slaughtered billions. Shouldn't they be stopped?"

Ekundayo's smile finally began to fade. "Terran, your people have been given every chance to do good, and they choose not to embrace it. But, we are getting distracted with meaningless discussion. There is something I need you to know."

"And what is that?" Terran was surprised to feel a bitterness begin to well up in his chest. *Why am I getting so offended?* He tried to subdue the feelings, ashamed he had felt them at all.

"Terran, I called you here to encourage you, not to push you away. Times will be tough on you in the future. It doesn't have to be, but I have been watching human nature for a long time now and know it will be so. Don't presume to understand my ways or my father's. We are not so simple as to be defined by the likes of you. The created cannot understand the creator."

"Is that it? Some vague warning that my life will be tough? Hasn't it been tough enough already? Why not just collapse space and be done with us? Do you and your all-powerful father care so little for us you can just push us around until you get tired?"

Ekundayo seemed to change as Terran spoke. His posture stiffened, and he seemed to exude an authority that replaced the casual air he had carried before.

"Terran, you shall be careful when you talk about the Emperor. He is not some simple man who gives in to whims. He is the creator of everything you have ever known. He has given you everything and has asked for nothing but a return of the love he gives you freely. You find this hard to believe because you are but a grain of sand. Understand, Terran, the Emperor does not need your love. He does not need anyone or anything, but he chooses to want your love. You will not understand this until the Capital is reached, but you will be given a glimpse of what is to come. You do not know of pain, Terran. You don't know anything for all that you think you do. Even when something as great as the gift I wish to bestow upon you is presented, you give in to selfish desires."

Terran shrank down as Ekundayo spoke over him. He found that he could not look at the man.

"Terran," Ekundayo's voice seemed more faint this time. "Our time is almost up, but there is one last thing I want you to know."

Terran's eyes snapped open and he saw the world around him growing dimmer except for a bright light coming from Ekundayo's body. "Wait," he said, "I have more questions."

Even through the growing darkness, he could see Ekundayo's smile.

"Then keep looking. Pursue the passions I have given you. Read all that you can about all you can. You need to know how the ships work and how to trust in the unknown. I am calling you to something great. And do not fear, I will only be gone for a little while. If you listen, you will hear my voice."

As Ekundayo finished the sentence, Terran felt a light jerk and found himself back in his room. Glenn was packing up the V-Sphere, which was now dull.

"You need some rest," he said, "It always takes a toll using the V-sphere. We can discuss what you saw and heard later."

As Glenn finished packing the V-sphere, Terran went to the window and hit the small button to open the shade. He had a lot to think about, and he was still wanting to look at the New-Space. Somewhere out there the Capital was waiting.

# CHAPTER TEN

Naomi sat quietly on the couch in her room staring at the table in front of her. Her tablet's screen was dark, the self-deleting message already gone. She hadn't expected to be contacted again so soon. Dagor seemed to be contacting her more and more frequently as of late. At least this time all he wanted her to do was pick up some small electrical wire and place it in a drop location. *How in the world am I going to get any wire when I am stuck in my room?* She gently massaged her temples as she went through protocol in her head.

First, there had been the trial, then it was reviewed by the senior members of the ship--which means she just had to wait for them to contact her and present her with their judgment. At the very least she would get probationary leave, which would place anything she requested under scrutiny. Worst case scenario, she would be dropped planetside and left there to fend for herself. Of course, waiting for the punishment was the worst part. She wished they would just let her know already. It had been a week and a half, and she was growing frustrated.

She got up from the couch and began stretching through her routine. She had been practicing various routines since she had been a little girl and had many of them memorized. They were intended as a sort of martial arts, but she had never used them as more than a calming mechanism. As she transitioned from one pose to another, she began to move around the room.

With each pass around the room, the distractions of the ship and Dagor began to fade away. She put everything out of her mind except for one last point of focus. How would she get some wire? The best answer she could come up with was to start a hobby that would need it. She would have to start a hobby--something that dealt with electronics. To make it less obvious what she was doing, she would have to pick something obtuse or antiquated to throw the Captain's and Rictor's scents off her. Maybe old fashioned radios would be vague enough to throw away suspicion, but prove useful later on if she was dropped planetside.

Naomi caught a sudden movement out of the corner of her eye, and reflex won over control. With a quick step and twist she slammed her palm forwards into the person who had entered her room. The Captain took the hit with a groan and fell to a knee with a gasp.

"Maybe I should shout the next time I enter your room. Even after I have both knocked and waited for three minutes while you twirl about your room," The Captain didn't seem upset, and he got up quickly after a few breaths. Strangely enough, he was smiling.

"I'm sorry, sir." Naomi said, embarrassed for both hitting the man and not seeing him come in. "May I ask why you are smiling?"

"It's just been a while since someone has taken a shot at me is all." The Captain chuckled and motioned toward the couch.

Naomi sat down and became aware of the sweat that covered her arms and face. How long had she been doing her steps? It had felt good to have some control in her life again though. She winced inwardly at the last thought. *Some control she had, hitting the Captain just for standing there.*

"Sir," Naomi said, leaning forwards. "Why are you here?"

The Captain laughed again. "You know Naomi, what I have always liked about you is that you are all about business. You like to know the reasons why people do things and what they want. It is an invaluable attribute in a Voice."

Naomi winced again at the praise. She had become a Voice because it gave her the most freedom aboard the ship. All it took was some memorizing of the Teachings and some good insight into how they apply to modern life. Plus, the practical skills would be invaluable when she left the ship. First aid, self-defense, and even brief mechanical work were all part of the training. *Maybe I am prepared to leave the ship.* The thought hit her hard and she leaned back onto the couch taking long breaths to slow her heartbeat.

"I am here to tell you the decision that was reached about what happened with the young man Terran." The Captain's eyes were focused on her, studying her. She hated it when he did that.

"What was the decision?" she asked.

"You will be placed on probationary leave until further notice. If you show yourself to be honest and repentant of your actions, then this period won't last very long, and we can get things back to how they should be. How does that sound?"

Naomi stared at the Captain for a long moment. He had to know that she had made up the story about Terran, and yet, here he was giving her another chance. *How can he function as our Captain? Why hasn't he been broken yet?* For a brief moment, she wanted to tell him everything. To tell him about her son, about Dagor, and why she had done what she had.

As she opened her mouth to speak however, the image of her son came flooding back to her. *I must remain strong.*

"I will do my best Captain," Naomi's words were soft and barely carried themselves across the sofa. She was surprised to find a tear falling down her cheek. Wiping it away, she smiled at the Captain. "Thank you for this opportunity."

The Captain said nothing for a long while.

"Naomi, I know something is wrong. I don't know what, but I can tell you are not okay. If you need anything, feel free to come talk with me."

Naomi's breath caught in her throat making her cough as a bolt of panic hit her. Naomi couldn't find any words to say, so she sat quietly instead, waiting for the Captain to leave.

Eventually, sensing he wasn't wanted, he got up from the sitting area and left the room. Almost immediately, her tablet lit up with a message from Dagor.

"If you tell him anything, you will regret it. We won't kill your son, but by the time we are through, he will be wishing we would."

Naomi stared at the message and a rage began to storm inside. How many times had they threatened Nathaniel? How many times had she had the chance to see him torn away from her? *Is it even worth it anymore? Is he even alive?* Before she could stop herself, she had grabbed the tablet and sent a message to Dagor demanding proof that he had her son. She sat on the couch and stared at the screen stunned at what she had just done. If Dagor had been bluffing she would be free. If he wasn't...a chill crawled up her back. She steeled herself and pushed the thoughts away. She wasn't moving until she saw something that gave her proof that Nathaniel was alive. She hadn't been waiting long when a new message appeared. It was empty except for an attached video.

With trembling fingers Naomi downloaded the attachment. It played by itself after it finished downloading. It showed a professional looking man in a suit sitting in an office behind an impressive looking desk. His dark red eyes stood out in stark contrast to both his pale skin and his dark hair.

"Hello Naomi," Dagor said with a smirk. "In light of recent events I have decided it is time to show you a demonstration of the power I have. You seem to forget that I own you and your son. So, to help you get off that high horse you are on, I am recording this. Bring in Nathaniel." Dagor spoke the last words into an intercom, then stared into the camera. With a shudder, Naomi realized that Dagor wasn't blinking. The camera twisted just as a door was opening into the room to reveal two large men carrying a much smaller person between them. As they walked closer to the camera, a light fell on the small body they had in between them. One of the men turned the body's head up toward the camera. Nathaniel's face was revealed in the light, covered in bruises and blood. His nose had recently been broken and blood was still pouring out of it onto the floor. He was barely conscious. Naomi could not tear her eyes away from the screen as it slowly panned back to Dagor.

"Naomi, now you understand that I am not a good man. I will hurt children to get what I want. I will double cross, I will lie, and if my subordinates don't do what I say, I will hurt them in the worst way possible. Your son has ten fingers. You have ten days to do what I asked. Message me when you have finished the job."

The video closed, leaving Naomi to stare at the blank screen in her hands. She was too numb to cry. She was too numb to feel anything. She hadn't understood Dagor at all. He wasn't some imp, pitiful and full of himself. He was something far worse. She got up and went to the end of the room. Slow at first, but building speed as she went along, she began her steps again. Tomorrow she would get the wire.

# CHAPTER ELEVEN

Rictor stared at Naomi from across his cluttered desk.

"You want what?" he asked raising an eyebrow.

"Copper wire. Exactly ten feet," she repeated. She hated that she had to ask him of all people, but he handled every requisition order.

"And, why exactly do you want ten feet of copper wire?"

"I am using it for an art project." The lie wasn't perfect, but it would do. She had done some art pieces before and needed to stay away from anything that might seem dangerous.

"Well, when do you need it?" he asked, making a few notes on the paper in front of him.

"Today if possible, I would like to get a head start on it while it's fresh on my mind." She didn't smile or flirt with Rictor, this wasn't the right time for feigning attraction. Plus, if she attempted to suddenly find him attractive, he would immediately know something was wrong. It would be better if she kept the same cold demeanor she always did with him.

"I can make that happen, but you will owe me a favor," he said with a wink, "If you ever need help with anything, let me know. It's what I am here for."

His words jarred something in Naomi's mind. The way he had said he would help with anything. It was just like how the Captain had offered to help.

"Thank you, Rictor, but the wire will be all." She flashed a quick smile and turned toward the door.

"Naomi," he called as she opened the door. "Don't forget your copy of the requisition order."

She hastened back to the desk and snatched the paper from his hand. "Is there anything else, Rictor, or can I finally leave?" She was too tired to put up with nonsense. Last night had been filled with nightmares of Nathaniel's bloody corpse, forcing her awake more than once.

"Just make sure you look over it carefully, and don't fold it." He was positively beaming as she left the room.

The wire would be sent to her room and would take some time to process. In the meantime, she intended to head to her room and rest. The walk was short from Rictor's office, and the darkened ambience of her room was welcome. Her room didn't have a window like some of the others, but a camera mounted on the ceiling could project the surroundings of the ship into her room.

She turned the camera on and lay in bed hoping the dancing lights would lull her to sleep. As she rolled over, a soft crinkle sounded from her pocket. Taking the small scrap of paper out, she studied it in the shifting light. *How often was paper handed out?* Paper wasn't altogether rare to see on the ship, but it wasn't exactly something to be wasted. And, it wasn't usually handed out for something as simple as a resource request. The rotating camera flicked a light across the paper and words appeared for the slightest moment. Curious, Naomi placed the paper on her bedside table. She had only glimpsed a single word 'help', but there was definitely more to it. *What is Rictor trying to say? Is he working for Dagor as well?*

Naomi seriously doubted that train of thought. Rictor could practically be the poster boy for the Capital. Always spouting off quotes from the Emperor or from the Teachings. He was consistently getting onto everyone about the right way to act both on the ship and planetside. Even if it was with a smile, it irritated a good number of people, herself included.

Naomi traced over the area of the paper she had seen the message on. The ripples in the paper from her laying on it gave her some frustration, but she could make out most of it. 'I no about son. Will help.' There were a few more words, but she wasn't able to make them out.

Naomi's heart raced faster as she lay on her back again. What should she do? As far as she knew, Dagor could hear everything she heard and received all the messages sent to her. She wasn't sure if Dagor could see into her rooms, but she didn't doubt it.

The flood of emotions stopped all at once as thoughts of Nathaniel slammed into her mind. What was she doing? Who cared if Rictor knew. He couldn't stop Dagor, he couldn't do anything. He was an irresponsible slob. A pain welled in her chest as she thought about what else might happen to Nathaniel if Dagor even suspected she was plotting against him.

Even still, the thought to be free almost triumphed over her pain. She was so tired of the pretending and the deceit. The paper was calling out to her, to reciprocate a message, to beg for help from him, but she knew she couldn't do it. She had to at least talk to Nathaniel again. Then she could make a decision.

A loud knock on her door interrupted her thoughts, and she hurried to open it. A small spool of wire sat on the floor in front of the doorway.

Taking it into her room, she placed it onto the small table and watched the lights as they shifted colors on the wall.

As expected, a soft tone from her tablet let her know that Dagor had sent her a message. Reading it in an instant, she picked up the spool and left the room. To be honest, she didn't mind the assignments from Dagor when they didn't involve killing people. Usually, it was just a small bit of sabotage. No one got hurt, and it usually only kinked up things for a day or two.

This assignment was cut and dry: drop off the spool in the cargo hold in Box B-7. Then she would get to talk to her son. As she neared the elevator, she practically skipped with excitement. Any thoughts of reaching out to Rictor were diminished by the all-consuming thought of finally talking to her son again. Then, one day, she would have him back with her, away from Dagor. They would go on walks along the coastline and ride bikes, and do things that normal families did. She could almost feel the warm water caressing her feet as they talked about the new friends he had made at school, the girl he had a crush on, or how much he wanted to grow up and be like his daddy. An older, deeper pain grabbed hold of Naomi at the thought of Orion. He had been gone for so long, but the pain was still there.

She could feel the tears forming and forced them down. In just a small bit of time she would see her son. She would smile and laugh and so would he. This was no time to fall apart. The elevator dinged as it reached the cargo hold.

The cargo hold was massive. It took up nearly an entire floor of the ship all by itself. Modeled after an arch, each aisle she passed was almost imperceptibly twisted at an angle towards the back of the room. The rows were about one hundred feet long and twenty-five wide with ample spacing between them. An open area was in the middle to make loading and unloading into the different aisles as easy as possible. As she passed each aisle, she read the small posters on the side of each of the shelves which gave a general rule for what was in each one. Naomi marveled at the sheer number of items in the hold as she made her way to aisle B. There was everything from small transport vehicles to medicinal supplies. She had never seen any supplies being loaded onto the Lion's Roar, but there didn't seem to be a dent in any of their stores. Finally, reaching her destination, she turned down the aisle and began looking for Section Seven. Aisle B seemed to contain food for the ship, she noted, locating the small box marked B-7.

The drop box itself was easy enough to find. Whereas all the other boxes were wooden and plainly listed themselves as food, B-7 was metallic, polished and smooth. The lid of the box was almost indistinguishable from the rest of it. If not for the small tongue of metal missing a padlock, Naomi wasn't sure if she would have been able to know where to lift.

She quickly popped the lid open and tossed in the spool of wire, glad to be done with it. Turning on her heel, Naomi rushed back to the elevator and sent it toward the living quarters. Leaning her head back against the wall, she wiped her palms on her pants. Soon, so very soon, she would see her son. She clutched her tablet as she left the elevator and ran to her room. She didn't care who saw her at this point.

As she reached the door, the tablet in her hands vibrated. She fumbled it back and forth between her hands as she tried to type in the passcode. The message was short, and a smile wound its way easily to her face. As she opened the door, she burst into her room almost laughing for joy. She was finally going to be able to talk to Nathaniel.

# CHAPTER TWELVE

Rictor's hands swayed back and forth to the rhythm of the music pounding into his ears. A smile played across his lips as he glanced toward the monitor then, shut his eyes again. After two weeks of looking through video footage, he had finally found the tip. It had taken combing through the same footage numerous times, as well as all the available files pertaining to the Voices and those who had accompanied them when they had visited Naomi's planet Minodori. The trouble was that no Voice had visited Naomi's region, which meant that one of Promioth's Envoys had to have sent an agent to bring her to the jump ship. Once that had been established, it wasn't too much of a stretch to understand that the Envoy's agent had probably twisted the truth in some way and prevented Naomi's son from getting onto the jump ship. This meant it was a simple hostage situation they were dealing with.

His smile quickly disappeared as the recorded message from the bug they had planted replayed itself in his mind, "Your son has ten fingers. You have ten days to do what I asked," followed by the whimpers of a mother longing to be with her child. *Would it be murder if I killed Dagor?* The thought had pierced his mind on multiple occasions, and Rictor tried to push it away again.

The Capital Bound did not handle their problems by murdering people. Revenge belonged to the Emperor alone. Even so, his hand began flexing itself, and he could feel the adrenaline coursing through his system. He sent a quick page to the Captain about a training session and focused back on the task at hand.

After Naomi, had arrived on the ship, he had noticed that she already had a tablet and an ear piece. Unless someone had seen the footage of her entering the ship during the first hour, there would have been no way to tell the difference between her and everyone else- except for the fact that she seemed to talk to herself. At first, Rictor had thought it was just an odd quirk. He had known quite a few people who muttered to themselves before. However, when it came to Naomi, she never seemed happy to talk to herself. Every single time she began muttering to herself, her face scrunched up as if she were in pain and she would almost immediately distance herself from anyone surrounding her. Not in any overt manner, but she would suddenly decide to take an elevator, skip meals, or duck inside random rooms. The more recent the footage, the better she got at keeping a low profile, but the key was in those first few days. Now, all he had to do was look through the footage and find any other people who randomly scrambled or would cringe for no reason at all. From there he could get a list of possible suspects and figure out how large or small Dagor's network on the Lion's Roar was.

A loud beep from his computer told him that the Captain had responded to his training request. Glad to release some pent-up energy, Rictor left his office and made his way down to the training grounds. Located below the housing floor, the training rooms were designed to help keep the members of the Lion's Roar in top shape.

Rictor exited the elevator and made his way through the many rooms filled with exercise equipment. Some rooms held free weights, others held large tracks, and others were simple rooms with nothing in them. In one such room he found Glenn sitting patiently on the ground with his legs crossed. His eyes were shut, and if not for Rictor's enhanced vision he wouldn't have noticed that the Captain was even breathing.

As he made his way to the center of the room, he could feel his body begin to meet resistance. Glenn had turned on the room's gravity well. Judging by how hard it was to move his body to the inner well, Glenn had probably set the gravity to a full two times normal gravity. Glenn opened his eyes as Rictor finished the slow trek across the room.

"Hello, Ric. You took your time I see." Glenn rumbled the words out slowly and carefully, his mouth barely moving to let them escape. Rictor could see from the way his skin hung that he might have been wrong about the two G's. Chances were that it might be a bit more than he had initially thought.

"Well, I had a whole band of spies and cut throats to take care of. Nothing big though." Rictor smiled at the Captain and began to stretch out his muscles.

A grunt was the Captain's only reply as he labored to move his large form. Beads of sweat began to form as he rose from his sitting position to a kneeling position. A second later he gave out a yell and began raising himself to his feet. His breathing became ragged, and the sweat began to drip off his scarred body as he struggled to straighten from his stooped position. Like a mountain rising from the earth his form began growing taller as he fought to right himself fully.

Rictor marveled at the Captain's strength and endurance. Unlike most of the others who assumed that the Captain just happened to be born the way he was, Rictor knew the real reason. It was what had brought them together as brothers in their quest to spread the news of the Capital. Both bore scars that hadn't come from fighting. Rictor's doctors had just been more careful.

Finally, regaining his full stature, the Captain moved in a slow and determined manner, not letting the decrease in G's cause his body to accelerate more than it needed to. It took fifteen minutes when all was said and done for him to leave the center of the gravity well and, when he had finished, he towered over Rictor with a large smile across his face.

"Well, how many was it?" Rictor asked finishing his stretches.

"Three G's," The Captain's reply came labored and his body gleamed with a film of sweat.

"Well, I suppose you thought I needed a handicap for our bout today?" Rictor asked.

Glenn's laugh resounded throughout the small room defying the padding that lined the floor and walls as he began to twist and stretch his own body.

"No, to be honest it was an accident of sorts. I was trying to think of how I could beat you this time and wandered right in to the center of the room. By the time I had commanded the artificial gravity to turn on, I was trapped.

Rictor stared at the captain confused. The room was hardly large enough for the Captain to be unaware of how close he was to the center of the room.

"Glenn, one of these days you should learn how to think and walk at the same time. You could have seriously been injured. Not even you are immortal."

"Like you?" Glenn's reply was soft, but carried a weight that slammed into Rictor.

Rictor watched Glenn walk around the center of the room to a rectangular case sitting by itself. Rictor hated it when his longevity was brought up. Glenn was the only person who knew about it, besides for the scientists from Yino, and Rictor wanted to keep it that way.

"You didn't have to bring that up," he called across the room. "It's not like I bring up your past all the time."

"The difference between us, Ric," Glenn replied as he opened the case, "is that I have made peace with my past and what I have done. You have not."

He pulled out two training swords. Glenn's was substantially larger than Rictor's because his size, but they were both the same design. Glenn flung Rictor's sword over the gravity well toward him. The flight of it was jagged and disjointed as it left the Captain's hands and then passed through the varying degrees of gravity, but Rictor still caught it easily. Since the swords had guards, on them he had no fear of cutting himself and was too skilled to worry about missing the hilt.

"How about we talk after you're lying on your back?" Rictor called to the Captain. He loved the man like a brother, but often his digging stirred up bad emotions.

Glenn nodded solemnly and walked back around the well to stand opposite of Rictor. They both entered a forward stance and touched the flats of their blades together in a salute. Slowly, each one paced backward three steps and stood motionless waiting for the other to make a move. Glenn moved first. Inching forwards, he kept his sword pointed toward Rictor's chest. Rictor began slowly edging his way to his left, keeping the gravity well to Glenn's back.

His heart rate began to rise as Glenn came closer, then skyrocketed when Glenn lunged toward him-his massive form crossing the small distance between them at breakneck speed.

Rictor dodged to his left, smacking Glenn's sword away with his own, then he thrust his sword forward. A small trickle of blood dripped down Glenn's side as he levelled his sword toward Rictor again, but he didn't seem to notice the blood.

Again and again, Glenn attacked Rictor. Blows came in from all around him, and he danced as much as he parried. Glenn's sword missing his flesh by centimeters with each swing. After each encounter, Rictor would dart his sword out and cut another slit in the Captain's flesh. On and on they danced around the room keeping a safe distance between themselves and the well.

Rictor ducked a high blow and slid the tip of his sword across Glenn's chest. The Captain roared in defiance and grabbed the cross guard of Rictor's blade before he could pull it back. Glenn pulled on the guard, catching Rictor off balance, and then kicked him square in the chest. A loud crack told Rictor that some of his ribs had just broken as he flew backward through the air and landed near the center of the room. The increase in gravity caused even more discomfort and pain in his chest.

He chuckled weakly as Glenn approached, both swords in his hands.

"Well Captain, looks like you might have won this one." The words were hard for Rictor to say as he struggled for breath. "Any chance you could help a fellow up?"

Glenn lowered his weapons and walked over to Rictor with a small smile on his face. "I guess I did. It feels good when it happens."

As Glenn extended his hand to help him up, Rictor snatched it and rolled backward flipping the Captain over his back and square into the center of the room. Rictor landed soundly on top of the fallen man, who tried in vain to lift his friend's weight, magnified as it was by the well. The Captain uttered a small command and the increased gravity was lifted from the room.

"Maybe I should have just left it off the whole time," he said pushing Rictor off.

"It did help you to begin with though," Rictor replied getting up from the ground.

"It always amazes me how fast your body fixes itself," he commented between large intakes of air. "Makes me wish I had some nanobots in me."

"Glenn, you know full well the price I paid for them. I wouldn't wish it on anyone," Rictor's voice grew softer as his muscles began to relax. "We need to talk about Naomi, though. She didn't reply to the message we sent. I am sure she would have seen it."

"She isn't exactly fond of you, for the record. Maybe she just threw it away."

"But, she's smart enough to notice something out of place. That's why I gave her the paper. She had to have seen it. So, the question is, why wouldn't she seek help?"

"Maybe she doesn't think she needs it?"

"No, no, no. She knows she needs help. She practically cries herself to sleep each night. She knows she's trapped and can't get out."

"What if the Envoy finally gave her what she wanted? Also, do we have any idea who it is yet?"

"You mean actually let her see Nathaniel? And I am thinking Dagor. I haven't heard his voice in ages, but from the recording I'm thinking it's him."

"Yes. What if Dagor gave her a bit of carrot before hitting her again with the stick? Just enough to keep her going."

Rictor paused in his stretches and chewed on the thought. Dagor wasn't a fool. He sat back on the ground with his legs crossed. They needed a way to reach her without alerting any of Dagor's other agents.

"Have you talked to Terran much?" Glenn asked, interrupting his thoughts.

"No, sadly not. Have you?"

"Not since the V-Sphere. I think something happened to him while he was watching it. His eyes never focused on the images, and he was speaking to himself the whole time. Something is off. We need to find out what is so special about him and why Dagor wants him dead."

"I am trying, Glenn," Rictor moaned. "I can't force anyone to tell me anything. I am not even sure if Naomi will be able to shed any light on the situation. But, I figure if we can get to her, we might be able to get to everyone else. I can't focus on both Naomi and Terran."

"'If' is a big word, my friend." Glenn stood up and began cleaning the training swords. "The whole ship is in danger while Dagor's followers are on board. It is time we switched tactics. I want you to confront her directly, and that's an order. I will take care of Terran."

Rictor closed his mouth and nodded in affirmation. He didn't always agree with Glenn's decisions, but he trusted his friend. He wasn't sure how he would reach Naomi without Dagor knowing, but he had the nagging feeling he was running out of time.

# CHAPTER THIRTEEN

Terran sat in the crowded classroom and placed his head on the desk. *Why is school so boring?* Of course, the classwork itself was easy--that had never been a problem. His problem was paying attention during lectures and acting interested. He had already read and memorized the textbook that the teacher was quoting, albeit incorrectly, and hated hearing the same information again. *Where is the analysis and critique?* The squirrely man at the head of the classroom began going down a distracted tangent, and Terran fought the urge the scream. Instead, he began drumming his fingers across the desk to calm himself. Many of the students around him turned in frustration at the distracting sound, but turned quickly back toward the front when he showed no signs of stopping.

Kelly, however, flicked his hand and gave him a stern look. "We don't all have super brains, Bro," she whispered, leaning over. "What are you even doing in this class anyway? I thought you were in a different segment all together."

"I was, but I finished early so I thought I would check out the other classrooms. I didn't think you were interested in Metaphysics," Terran shot back. "If I recall the last time I tried talking to you about it, you rolled your eyes and threw a teddy bear at me."

"I was nine, I wasn't quite interested in Metaphysics at that point," she replied. "Do wish I had another teddy bear though, Anna looks like she's about to die."

Glancing across the small room, Terran located his other sister with her face planted on the desk in front of her. It would have been easy to think she was asleep, except for her left hand drawing a small terrier in striking detail.

Terran let his eyes wander across the classroom as the teacher--Jerry might have been his name--kept on with his meandering speech. Most of the students there were taking copious notes trying to soak in all that Jerry was saying. *The fools don't even know how wrong he is.* As Jerry began fumbling over the importance of understanding the limitations of the human mind in trying to understand ourselves, Terran got up to leave the room.

"See you at dinner," Kelly called after him.

Terran smiled back at her and made his way to the door. Jerry kept his monotonous lecture going without paying Terran any attention. As he entered the bright lit hallway, a small figure crashed into him and knocked him to the floor.

"I am so sorry," the figure said bending down to pick up some papers.

Turning over, he saw a slender woman on her hands and knees frantically picking up the papers that had scattered across the hallway. Her uniform was different from the standard white top and blue slacks; she had on a small jacket with several stripes along her left arm, each one having a different metallic sheen.

"It's fine," he said helping her gather her papers. "Where were you going in such a rush?"

Picking herself up from the floor and smoothing out her slacks, she extended her hand and smiled at him.

"I was trying to find someone. My name is Catherine. Sorry for rushing into you," she said.

Terran stared at her smile and lost his train of thought. Her amber hair fell gently around her face to her shoulders and framed her pale blue eyes. She was beautiful.

"Are you going to shake my hand or just stare at me?" she asked pursing her lips.

"Uh, sorry," he called out, shaking her hand. "I'm Terran."

"Terran Neuman?" she asked.

"Yes," he replied. Letting go of her hand he extended the papers he had picked up. "I think these are yours?"

"Thanks." She flashed a grin. "I was actually looking for your picture when I ran into you. Now that you are here though, we can be off." With that she turned and walked down the hall. She turned after a few steps and faced Terran, who hadn't moved.

"You coming are not?"

"Where are we going?" Terran asked, walking towards her.

"To your new classroom. Your aptitude for learning has been noted, and we are proceeding with a learning environment more suitable for someone of your talents."

Terran hid a smile as he basked in the recognition.

"Of course, you were also a major distraction to the other students around you, so don't be too proud of yourself." She winked at him.

Terran found himself unable to talk as they walked down a maze of hallways. He tried to take note of where he was going, but found his gaze being drawn back to the woman walking beside him. She didn't seem to notice his attention, however, and kept up her brisk pace. For someone a head shorter, she could move remarkably fast. Finally, they stopped in front of plain looking door.

"This is going to be your new classroom," Catherine said opening the door.

Terran peeked in. The room was small and sparse with barely enough room for the single table and two small metal chairs that sat underneath a harsh light. There were no windows, the walls were bare, and the floor seemed to blend into the wall creating a chamfered edge.

"Is this a joke?" Terran asked.

"Nope. This room is designed to eliminate distractions."

"Looks more like a prison cell." Terran said

"Well the best way to look at things is the positive way. You can either be a sour puss about getting intensive one on one teaching or you can embrace it." She sat down and gestured to the seat across from hers.

Terran sat down and folded his arms. "You're my teacher?"

"You betcha," she said looking at the papers in her hand. "Now, here is the thing. From reading your profile I see you have a unique memory. Is that correct?"

"Yes," Terran said shifting in his seat. "Why?" *How did they know that?*

"No questions from you just yet. You need you to tell me your earliest memory. As much as you can remember in as much detail as possible."

"That is personal information."

"Look, personal memories have the greatest impact on us, which means we remember them better than abstract concepts. Once we get a baseline going, we will move on to less personal areas," smiled again and leaned back in her chair, notebook in hand. "We can begin when you are ready."

Terran took a deep breath and closed his eyes. He sorted through memories, some bright and vibrant in his mind, some dull. He dug deeper, and the duller memories began to outnumber the vibrant until at last there was one left.

"I remember my father holding me. He is looking down at me, and I am holding his finger. We are in the hospital, he is smiling. He is young, twenty-seven, and my mother is with him."

"He is wearing a suit, minus the tie, and he is whispering to me."

"Do you know what he is saying?"

Terran could make out the words perfectly in his mind, but knew what they really were--how insincere. *What do you know of love?*

"It's just a lie," he said.

"Terran, I need you to try and remember his words. Do you know how old you were?"

"Look, I know what he said, but I am telling you what it really was. I was eight months or so."

"Excuse me?" Catherine obviously didn't believe him.

"Once we get to other subjects, you will understand how deep my memories go." Terran said, fighting the emotions that tried to crawl out of him. Catherine seemed to get the hint.

"Let's move on then."

Terran wasn't sure how long they were in the room. He wasn't sure how much of what he said made sense, but every time he faltered, Catherine would encourage him to keep going. He did get the feeling as time dragged on that what he was doing was important somehow and that made it easier. By the time Catherine had told him to stop, he had grown hoarse and sat quietly waiting to hear what it was all for.

"Well, I must say that your memory is quite impressive. I will send you a schedule for our future meetings tonight. Just keep an eye on your tablet. You're free to go." Catherine smiled at him, then began studying the notes she had taken.

Terran got up from his seat and walked to the doorway. Opening the door, he paused in the doorway. "Why?"

"Why what?" she asked, looking up from work.

"What's it matter about my memories?"

"It was important for me to see the capabilities of your mind as well as understand you as a person to see if you were the right person for the job we have lined up for you."

"So, what kind of job?" Terran leaned against the door frame. *So tired.*

"There is a position that we need filled. I don't have all the details, but the Captain requested you personally," she said walking toward him. "I need to understand who I am going to be working with."

"So this was a test for a special position that only the Captain understands the use for?" he asked as a yawn escaped his lips.

"Apparently."

Terran paused for a second remembering Ekundayo's words before he continued his way. "See you later then." He exited the room and began walking down the hallway. Catherine, seeming satisfied, reentered the room.

After turning a few corners, Terran realized he wasn't entirely sure where he was. He closed his eyes to remember, but exhaustion had begun to wear on him. He pulled out his tablet, hoping to find a contact number or something to help him. An email notification from Catherine flashed across the top of the screen.

Terran tapped it and an attachment pulled up.

Getting to his room, he found his sisters lying on his bed chatting amicably about the different people they had met. As the door closed behind him, they both stopped and smiled at him.

"How was your date?" Kelly asked from his bed.

"It wasn't a date. And how do you two even know where I have been?" he asked.

"I happen to know Catherine." Ana said, sitting up. "What did you talk about?"

"If you must know, she made me talk about memories."

Both girls burst out laughing as Terran pulled a chair by the side of the bed and rested.

"That must have been a rather one-sided conversation." Kelly said. "Did she say anything at all?"

"Not really. For the most part she just sat there and listened."

"She really is a top-notch tutor. She knows a ton about the ship and how everything works. I think she said she was the lead engineer, but I might be mistaken."

Ekundayo's words came back into Terran's mind again. Telling him to learn as much about the ship as he could. "Have you two seen the V-Sphere?"

"Of course," Kelly chirped. Ana nodded in agreement.

"What was it like for you?" he asked.

"Well, you've seen it, too. It doesn't change. It zooms about showing the history of the universe and all that. If you mean purely what did I think about the presentation. I liked it." Kelly brushed the hair from her face and got up from the bed. "We should let him rest, Ana, all that talking must have worn him out."

Ana was too busy staring at her brother to pay Kelly any mind. "You saw something different, didn't you?" she asked him.

Terran smiled weakly at his sister. One minute she could be just as flippant as Kelly and the next she would be as analytical as a machine.

"I did," he sighed. "I will talk about it later though. Kelly's right, I'm awfully tired."

Smiling, he ushered his sisters to the door and locked it behind them. What in the world was going on?  If everyone saw the same thing in the V-Sphere, then what had he seen?

He lay on the bed and tried to rest, but knew that he wouldn't be getting much sleep at all that night.

# CHAPTER FOURTEEN

Naomi stared at the broken tablet by her feet. The screen had shattered from the impact, and blood was dripping down her legs where the glass had dug into her. She didn't wipe it away. One large piece of the screen was still stuck in the tablet, and Naomi pried it loose. It fit easily into the palm of her hand. She was so tired of this double-life, so tired of all the masks that people wore and all the lies they told. For the hundredth time the conversation with Nathaniel replayed in her mind.

It had been wonderful at first. They laughed and talked about the times before they had been separated. He had been covered in bruises, but it was still her boy smiling at her. He had told her that he didn't blame her at all, that he understood she loved him and couldn't wait to meet face to face on Torga. Dagor had stepped in briefly to break the news in a more formal tone; she would be able to stay on Torga with them once they reached the planet. She would no longer be bound to anything besides Nathaniel himself.

She had started crying then. The sheer joy of being reunited with her son was enough to make the pain worth it. Shortly after, they had said their goodbyes until they would meet again, and with a heavy heart Naomi had ended the call. She replayed the video, analyzing every frame of it, rejoicing at the sweet talk she had had with her son. She had been happy, truly happy, for such a short time.

During one of her replays, she had noticed something out of place. When the camera shifted between Nathaniel and Dagor, Nathaniel's face had shifted just enough that Naomi had barely caught it. Naomi had a hard time discerning whether it was the light or something else. With a pain already growing in her chest, she went through each frame of the hour-long call. When the camera began switching between Nathaniel to Dagor, it became evident that something wasn't right. For three short frames, Nathaniel was someone else. A small man still covered in bruises, but much too old to be her son. She had scanned the frames again and again hoping she was wrong, but it was clear as day. Dagor had lied to her again.

Naomi had shocked herself when she had slammed the tablet onto the corner of the table, causing the screen to shatter. Examining her feet again, she put the glass onto the table and wiped away the bits that peppered her skin. She chastised herself for believing Dagor, and again for breaking the tablet. She sat back down and considered her options.

She could just kill herself. The glass on the table would be plenty sharp enough to put her out of her misery. She pushed that thought away. She was not weak or selfish enough to follow in her late husband's footsteps. She would remain strong and fight this out. The pool of anger within her needed to be directed, however, and she needed a target. The obvious mark came to mind. *Why kill myself when I could kill Dagor instead?* A vicious smile spread across her lips. That's what she would do. She would punish him for everything he put her through. For taking Nathaniel away, for making her think he had hurt him, and for making her think he had given Nathaniel back to her.

There was no way, of course, for Dagor to know that she knew he had lied. She had recorded every single communication that had passed between them, and he had never said a word of it to her. Surely if he had known, he would have stopped her. She would have to play along with him then, doing whatever he asked until she could get close enough to end the little imp's life. *No, he isn't an imp. A spider is what he is, sitting on a web of blood and lies.* She would need to practice then. She normally went through her steps as a calming process, but as she went into the first form of the step, she knew it would be different from then on.

Disregarding the blood on her feet, she began to pace slowly around the room. She forced herself to go slower than usual, taking each step for as long as possible as she stretched each of her muscles to the max. After the first pass around the room, she began to increase the speed of the routine. She continued, letting her body take over. Each pass she grew faster and faster until the room itself became a blur to her. Her body didn't hesitate or falter at the increased speed. Years of practicing the routine had given her body an almost superhuman sense of where she was in relation to her surroundings. With her last twirl, she lashed out with the palm of her hand and slammed it into a small wooden chair. The seat of the chair shattered at the force, and her palm continued to the floor. The heavily carpeted floor absorbed the blow noiselessly.

Naomi laughed and stood up from the chair. She would be ready when the time came. Dagor wouldn't stand a chance when she was finally close enough to snap his scrawny neck. A low rumble reminded her that she hadn't eaten yet, and she found herself quite hungry. Revenge apparently worked up quite the appetite. Before she left, she grabbed a small slip of paper from her coffee table. She would need an ally to make sure she could get planetside to be able to take out Dagor. The Captain was out of the question, of course, which only left her former partner. She sighed as she scribbled a hidden note on the paper. It wouldn't be easy, but it had to be done.

Rictor was finishing the small plate of food in the mess hall when Naomi entered the room. Most everyone else paid her no mind and only a few stared at her in suspicion, but Rictor doubted any of them saw what he did. This was not the same distressed woman he had been looking into for the past few weeks. This was a woman brimming with confidence. It was the face of someone who had just lost a great burden.

He continued to watch her as she piled a large amount of food on her plate. She paused for a moment before she caught his eye and smiled. It was not the tired smile that Rictor was accustomed to seeing, but a legitimate smile that changed the air around her. Rictor found himself gesturing at the seat next to him before he could stop himself. Naomi walked gracefully to the table and sat across from him.

"You seem awfully chipper today," he said.

"Well, at some point you have to stop being a victim and take responsibility." She looked down at her plate and hesitated, as if trying to decide exactly what morsel would be devoured first. Making her decision, she began wolfing down a sandwich stuffed with large cuts of meat.

"Do you feel as if we have targeted you?" Rictor asked, eyebrow raised. "We had no intention of victimizing you."

Naomi almost choked on the sandwich as she began laughing. It was a rich laugh and several people from the tables around them turned. Rictor could see the tension relieving itself from Naomi's shoulders and his curiosity grew. Finally, she slumped back into her seat and wiped the tears from her eyes.

"Don't be so naïve, Ric," She took a small sip of water between fading chuckles. "I am referring to Dagor."

"Are you sure this is the time and place for this sort of thing?" Rictor asked looking around the room.

"Don't worry, Ric. None of Dagor's spies are in here. At least, none that I know of." She smiled at him in a knowing way. Rictor had seen it before. People who thought they were in control always wore that look. Brief images of a group of scientists flashed across his mind. Each one had that same smug face. He snapped himself out of the memory and focused on Naomi.

"Well, what is making you suddenly so chummy with me?" Rictor asked.

"I want a favor." She didn't even look at Rictor as she said it, instead she focused on finishing the large sandwich.

"You aren't really in a position to ask favors. Remember, I'm investigating you for almost killing someone?" he said, hunching toward her.

"Well, true. But, I am in the probationary stage, so the investigating part is practically over. And, after all, it's a small favor. I just want to go planetside on Torga."

It was Rictor's turn to laugh. His was considerably shorter, however, but Naomi seemed nonplused.

"You can't be serious. Why would we even consider doing that?"

In response, Naomi leaned over the table and kissed Rictor on the cheek. "I might have a proposition for you." Sitting back down, she began to tackle the salad that had come with the sandwich. Rictor sat, stunned, and watched as she devoured the greens and then polished off her glass of water.

"Naomi, are you feeling okay?" Rictor said, unable to think of anything else to say.

"I've never felt better," she replied. Patting his hand, she left her seat and headed for the exit. When she got to the door, she paused and turned back. "Don't forget, I need that new tablet pronto."

Rictor scratched his chin and watched her exit the room. Something fishy was going on, and he found himself feeling more lost than when he had found out someone had poisoned Terran.

He got up from his seat and took both trays to the trash. As he began to dump Naomi's, he noticed a small slip of paper from under her plate. He pocketed it as subtly as he could and left the room, heading for his office.

He unfolded the paper as soon as he entered the small room and seeing no ink, held it up to the light. A small message appeared. "Cargo Hold One AM." Rictor tore the paper to pieces as he sat at his desk. He would go, of course, even if Naomi was lying through her teeth. He couldn't afford not to. *What in the world had gotten into her?* He typed in a quick request for a new tablet for Naomi. Turning some soft music on to drown out the memories eating at him, Rictor closed his eyes to get some fitful rest.

Naomi lay on her bed unable to sleep. Had she played her hand right? She needed Rictor off his guard, and the kiss had surely done that. She turned the hologram imaging back on and watched the dancing lights for a while. Rictor would be a huge asset to her. She didn't think she would need to go further than a kiss or two in order to get what she wanted out of him. Of course, her story might be enough to persuade him, but there was always the chance she would need to provide some incentive to help him along.

# CHAPTER FIFTEEN

R ictor was standing in the middle of the cargo hold when Naomi got off the elevator. He was standing with his head hung low as if his shoes were more interesting than anything else that could be happening.

"Ric!" she called out, "are you alone?" Of course he was alone. He was far too trusting even when he was suspicious.

Rictor's body jerked as she spoke, and she realized that he had been sleeping while standing!

"Hello, Naomi," Rictor yawned. "I brought chairs, but thought it impolite to sit before you." He pointed beside him to two small chairs sitting next to the end of one of the aisles, out of the way.

"Much appreciated," she said, making her way to one of the chairs. "Did anyone see you?"

"Nope. Most people are asleep in their cozy beds this late."

Rictor seemed at ease. His manner was affable and his tone was light. Did he not realize how serious this all was?

"I am here to tell you the full story," she said taking a large breath.

"Which one?" he chirped, breaking her momentum. "The one where you work for Dagor because your son is under duress? The one where you ask for my help to get your son back once we are planetside? Or maybe the one where you tell me every agent Dagor has on this ship so I can take care of them and what you all were doing for him before someone else gets hurt. I prefer the third."

His tone never changed as he talked. His words flowed effortlessly, flawlessly. They could have been talking about the weather for all his tone implied. Naomi paused for a second to get her bearings. He was the one supposed to be caught off guard, not her!

"How about I tell you three in exchange for two?"

"Or you could just tell me three and if you say anything I don't know, we can discuss two." Rictor reached into his pocket and pulled out a small chocolate bar. "At some point, you have to take a risk, Naomi. For all I know, this is a trap and you're here to kill me." He pulled the wrapper partly off the chocolate and took a bite.

Naomi could feel her temperature rising. *He wants me to take a risk? I am risking everything just to have this conversation.* If he wanted to be childish, she would treat him as such.

"No," Naomi said, "you guarantee two, and I will tell you three. I am taking the bigger risk. I set up this meeting and trusted a buffoon to do the work of a professional. My son could die if this goes down wrong, and I won't have that." *Except that my son isn't in danger, from Dagor at least.*

Rictor's face changed as she spoke until there was no trace of his usual joviality.

"Fine," he said, "If you give me the information I need, I will make sure you get planetside."

Naomi was surprised to find regret welling within her. In truth, Rictor had always been kind to her, and it seemed that at every opportunity she always fought against him. She pushed the feeling down. There was no time for regret when business needed to be done.

She reached into her coat pocket and took out a piece of paper. "Here you go," she said, handing it over to Rictor. "That is a comprehensive list of everyone Dagor has on the ship."

Rictor raised an eyebrow as he unfolded the paper. Then he barked out a short laugh. After he had scanned the sheet, he looked her right in the face and began tearing it to pieces.

"What are you doing?" Naomi shouted, reaching for the pieces. "If anyone can piece that together, we will both be dead. What is wrong with you?" she began scrounging for the pieces. Rictor didn't move.

"Naomi, I know every single person on that list is working for Dagor. It was easy to piece together once I found out how he had contacted you. However, I am going to tell you a secret." Rictor's voice was steady, but there was a weight behind it. Naomi stopped scrounging and looked back at him.

"What is it?" she said as certain fear crept into her. Could Rictor be working for Dagor?

"No, I don't work for your boss, if that is what you are thinking. I am Capital Bound first and foremost." A smile crept to his lips. "Naomi, I am 346 years old."

Naomi stared at Rictor, "What?"

"You see," he continued, "I was created in a lab. The doctors on my planet were looking for ways to extend human capabilities. They wanted to enhance strength, endurance, and intelligence. Well, after years of tests and failed experiments, they had a breakthrough. They successfully created a person who surpassed those capabilities--not to the extent they had wanted, but at least he didn't die as soon as he left the test tube." He paused for a moment, his eyes still locked onto hers. "I have seen everyone I have ever cared about die. I have been whipped, beaten, burned, electrocuted, locked in a room without food for weeks on end, and even went without sleep for two weeks straight. Then I finally escaped the prison I had lived in for 237 years. Some crew from a Capital Bound ship found me and took me in. I have been here ever since."

Naomi remained silent after Rictor finished, unsure of what she should say.

"Do you know why I am telling you this?"

"No," Naomi shook her head. "You would think after a few hundred years that the world would become more gray to someone. For me though, it has just gotten more absolute. You want to kill Dagor, don't you?"

"Yes," she replied. "I do. He is a vile man who needs to die."

"Which means that he doesn't have your son," Rictor said.

"Correct."

"Naomi, I want to help you."

"How? By telling me that killing him won't bring me solace? That it isn't the right way to do things? That we have to let revenge belong to the Emperor? I am sick and tired of waiting. I want my justice now." The bitterness she felt welled up and tears began streaming down her face. "That monster destroyed my life. He has taken everything from me. I will not let you tell me that killing him isn't worth it. He is going to die." She stared at her shoes while she waited for Rictor's reply.

"I am not saying anything of the sort. I am saying that I will help you. Do you understand?"

She looked up and stared into his eyes. An understanding passed between them. "Why?"

"Because if we kill him, think of how many more will have the opportunity to know the Emperor. He is an Envoy of the enemy and he needs to be put down. We will need to work together on this. You have your contacts and methods; and I have the capabilities. We will need to come up with a plan of how we will kill him."

Naomi shifted in her seat. "Before we begin, can I ask you a question?"

"Of course," Rictor said, "Anything at all."

"How did you escape from the labs?" It might have been a stupid question, but there was something there that Rictor hadn't mentioned.

"You have to understand that I was a different man back then. I did things I regret, and I have changed a lot in the lifetimes I have lived since."

"What happened?" she asked again.

"I seduced one of the scientists and convinced her to let me out." His breathing became irregular as he spoke.

"That's not so..." Naomi tried to speak.

"Then I killed them all," he whispered.

"Bad," Naomi finished the sentence before she could stop herself. A moment of silence passed between them, and they held each other's gaze.

"Well," Naomi said, breaking the silence. "Let's begin."

# CHAPTER SIXTEEN

Terran stood up from the cramped chair and stretched his back as Catherine reviewed her notes. It had been two weeks since their first meeting. Two weeks of classes, with no breaks. He had avoided his sisters, not wanting to talk about his experience with the V-sphere. He wasn't sure how much Catherine talked to them, but she never brought it up.

"Well, Terran," Catherine said from across the table. "You passed this test too. That memory of yours is something else. Do you ever forget anything?"

"Only things that aren't important," he said basking in the compliment. "The only problem is that what I find important and what others do doesn't always line up."

Catherine smiled and put his test down. "We have covered a lot of material in the past two weeks, but it has all been review, with a focus more on analysis than learning. Today that is going to change. Do you know how much time we have until we reach Torga?"

"Nope," Terran replied. The thought of seeing an entirely new planet was intriguing. Who knew what the people would be like or what the surface would look like. It excited him, to say the least.

"A month and a half, which means I have a month and a half to cram your head full of useful information instead of useless. But before we begin, there is an important question I need to ask you. You must be one hundred percent honest. Do you understand?"

"Ok," Terran said, unsure of what else he could have said. She did have him stuck in a room.

"Do you believe in the Capital?"

The question caught him off guard and he was surprised to see a look of intensity on Catherine's face. He thought back to Ekundayo's words. It all seemed so unreal to him, but he knew what he had seen.

"Yes," he said, looking back toward Catherine, "and I believe that one day we will reach it, sooner rather than later."

The last part of his question seemed to catch Catherine off guard and she stared at him with a peculiar look on her face.

"You saw something different, didn't you?" she asked, raising an eyebrow.

"What do you mean?" Terran asked feigning confusion.

"What was your favorite part of the V-sphere, then?" she asked as a coy smile spread across her face.

"Ekundayo, of course," Terran said smugly. At least knowing the Emperor's son's name would be beneficial.

Instead of Catherine backing down, however, she rose from her chair. "You did see something else. You're just like my father." Her voice caught for a second, and she sat back down. "What did you see?"

"Your father?" Terran asked.

"Yes, he had a vision from the Capital. Unfortunately, not too many people believe him. If you saw something different as well, people would have to believe him. Now, what did you see?"

"Is your father on the ship?"

She laughed. "Stop dodging my question! What did you see?!"

"Okay, Okay." Terran said. "If you tell me who your father is, I will tell you what I saw."

"My father is the Captain," she said, leaning back into her chair.

Terran's mouth hung open as he processed what she said. "Glenn is your father?"

"Yep. Most people say I look just like him. What do you think?"

Terran stared at her. There was no way in the world she looked like Glenn. She was absolutely stunning and Glenn was...not.

"I am going to have to disagree with them on that one." He said. "You look more like a model than a monolith. No offense to the Captain, but looks aren't exactly his strong suit."

Catherine giggled at his compliment, "I am glad you don't think so. Also, I was lying. No one says I look like him. But he is my father."

"But you gave me a different last name--Lindan, right?"

"Well, people treat you differently if they know you are the Captain's daughter. This way I can get to know people for real before they start trying to act perfect around me."

"So, what did he see?" Terran asked.

"How about this. I will tell you what he saw and heard if you tell me what you saw. Deal?" Catherine extended her hand over the table.

"Deal," Terran echoed, shaking her hand. Their touch lingered for a moment before Catherine pulled her hand back and focused on the papers in front of her.

"Okay, so, when my father got onto the ship he went through the orientation just like everybody else, but when it got time to do the V-sphere something happened. While everyone else saw the history lesson that's so popular, my father had a vision with the Emperor's son. They were sitting by a river in the country side. They both had their feet in the water and fishing poles in their hands. Dad says that the Emperor's son actually looked pretty normal. Just a tanned guy fishing in the river. It wasn't how he looked that convinced him though. Dad described a certain aura of authority the guy had, as if my father had no choice but to do as he said. Not in a domineering way, but it was as if there wasn't anything else he would rather do."

"What did he tell him?" Terran asked.

Catherine shrugged. "I don't know... He says that he was instructed not to tell anyone what was said, just what he had seen."

"So what did he see, then?"

"Now you're asking the right question. My father looked around him and saw hundreds of broken fishing poles. Each one was broken in a different way. Some were missing their lines, some their hooks, and some were snapped in half. Then, when he looked at his pole, a falcon came and snatched it from his hand. My father was going to chase it, but the Emperor's son wouldn't allow it. Instead, the Emperor's son rose to his feet and the river stopped. Hundreds of fish lined the bottom--all different sizes and shapes. My father went to get them, and again, he was stopped. The Emperor's son instead commanded the fish to come out. Some stayed and some came out, and some that tried to come out he threw back in. Then my father said he awoke again. No one on the ship believed him, so they forced him out at the next planet. He waited ten years for the next ship."

"That is not the most encouraging thing I have heard," Terran said.

"Well, it worked out for the better. Besides, not everything is always going to be encouraging. Sometimes you need a warning or push instead." Catherine wasn't smiling anymore, and a somber look had replaced the laughter.

"What does it mean?" Terran asked.

"Not sure," Catherine replied, "My dad won't say much about it. I was surprised he even told me. I'm not even sure who all knows. I don't think it spells out easy times ahead for the Bound, though."

Terran nodded his head in agreement. In his mind, he compared his vision with the Captain's. They seemed unrelated for the most part. His vision seemed straightforward, while the Captain's was metaphorical. His vision focused on himself, and the Captain's on everything but himself.

"So, what did you see?" Catherine asked, interrupting his thoughts.

Since Terran couldn't remember any warning in his vision of sorts, he told her everything. She listened intently, soaking in every word.

"Wow; that is a tough challenge." She said after he had finished. "The good news is that now we know what you need to focus on in studies."

"True," Terran replied. "How much longer do we have today?"

Catherine pulled out her tablet and checked the time. "Negative two hours. We went over again."

"I didn't even notice," Terran said.

"Me neither," she said, smiling back.

"So, how many people have you tutored?" Terran asked.

"Counting you? Fourteen. Why?" she got up from the chair and stretched.

"Just curious," Terran answered.

Catherine looked over at him, and Terran looked away, unable to meet her gaze. "I should get some food," he stammered. "Guess I will see you tomorrow?"

"Or we could go to dinner together," she said.

Terran's heart skipped a beat. "I would be delighted."

"Then let's go; I'm famished!" She walked out the door and didn't pause to look back.

Terran smiled and jogged out of the room to keep up.

# CHAPTER SEVENTEEN

"You're telling me that you never met your mother?" Terran asked.

"Nope," Catherine poked around at her food a bit more.

This was their second date and Terran had asked what he assumed was a harmless question. They sat in the little classroom that had become their hideaway. A tablecloth and dim lighting transformed the room into something special.

"She died when I was born. Dad says I'm just like her, but I think he says that so I can feel close to her."

"Do you?"

"Sometimes. My dad gave me some perfume for my fifteenth birthday that she used to wear. When I do, it almost feels like she's with me."

Terran couldn't help but smile. He had never met anyone so full of hope. She caught his gaze and flashed one back at him.

"What about your parents? You haven't mentioned them at all."

Terran's smile faded. "You don't really want me to talk about mine, it would ruin the mood."

"I do, really. I would like to know where the genius of Terran came from. Did you get it from your mom or dad?"

"Neither," he said, a little sharper than he intended. "My father was a coward who abandoned my family and caused us to live in squalor, and my mother is an idiot who is waiting for him to come back to her. As if he didn't almost kill us by leaving us to rot."

He regretted the outburst immediately and looked down at his food. He waited for her chair to scrape the floor, to hear her footsteps walk away, for her to abandon him. She deserved someone better, not someone so damaged.

He heard her chair scrape the floor and his heart sank. Even if he had expected her to leave, it still hurt. Before his pity could worsen, he felt her arms around him. The subtle smell of cinnamon surrounded him and he breathed in deeply.

"I'm sorry, Terran," her voice shook.

*Is she crying?*

He felt a tear fall onto his shoulder, which made him feel even worse. He hugged her back. "It's okay."

"No, it's not okay." She whispered. "Fathers are meant to protect their family, not abandon them."

"You don't have to cry. It's not like you did anything."

In response, Catherine hugged him harder.

"You deserve better, Terran. You need to know that there is someone who cares deeply for you and no matter what will be there for you. No matter how bad your dad was, the Emperor will see you through."

Terran gently pushed her away. Her make-up had run, but in that moment Terran knew she was the most beautiful woman in the world. *More like the universe.*

"Thank you, Catherine." Terran smiled at her and wiped a tear from her cheek.

"Terran, I want you to know that I am always here for you. If you ever want to talk, I am just a phone call away."

"I know." He suddenly became aware that many people in the tables surrounding them were staring and his cheeks became warm. "I should go."

Catherine looked at him, confused, then glanced around the room.

"Ok." She squeezed his hand then, picking up her tray, left the room.

When Terran got back to his room, he found a surprise. The Captain was sitting on his couch reading a small book with two steaming cups in front of him. As the door shut behind him, the Captain turned and smiled. A small chill ran down Terran's back.

"Hello Terran." Glenn spoke lightly and patted the cushion next to him on the sofa.

Terran went down to the couch and sat next to him. The large man seemed even more intimidating than he had before.

"Let's cut to the chase," Glenn said. "You are interested in my daughter, and she, for some reason, is interested in you. True?"

Terran had no doubt that lying would be the absolute worst thing he could do at this point. "I can only speak for myself, sir," he stuttered. *Is he going to threaten me?* As the Captain reached for the two steaming cups, Terran noticed how hard it was for the fabric of the Captains shirt to hold his bulk.

The Captain chuckled as he handed Terran one of the steaming cups. "With an answer like that, you may be smarter than you realize." He winked as he took a sip.

Terran followed suit. The cup was filled with a spiced tea. As he drank it, a gentle fire seemed to spread through his body. He finished the cup quickly and set it down. The Captain seemed surprised as he continued to sip his.

"Do you know what that was?"

"Some sort of tea, it seemed like." Terran replied growing a little wary.

"That's because it takes a lot of spices to make poison taste good."

Terran paused, his hand unconsciously reaching for his throat. "Poison?" he asked in a whisper, his eyes growing wide. "Why?"

The Captain was quiet and continued to drink from his cup, then he snorted. Before he could stop himself, he began chuckling. Then the chuckle became a great roaring laugh. He swatted Terran on the back, almost knocking him off the couch, as he continued to let loose. Terran was terrified.

"You are a freaking lunatic!" he exclaimed getting to his feet. "What is wrong with you?"

The Captain's laugh faded slowly as he wiped tears from his eyes. "Sit down, Terran," the Captain said. "I was just fooling with you. It was just a simple tea. I am not the type of man to poison someone."

"You know, telling someone who has been poisoned before that you had just poisoned them is not a good joke." Terran sat down, thoroughly put off.

The Captain's face turned thoughtful for a moment. "I suppose you are right. Sorry about that, but I couldn't resist. You want to date my daughter, and most people have the idea that I would kill anyone who tried. Just thought I would play that up a bit." He chuckled again as he set his own cup down.

"You are okay with it?" Terran asked.

"Of course I am. She is a grown woman with a solid head on her shoulders. I have full trust that she knows what she's doing."

Terran relaxed as he leaned back into the couch, and wished he had some more tea. "So, what are you doing here then?"

"Well, if you and my daughter are going to be involved, then I want you to be able to protect her. You ever been trained in defense?"

Terran felt his pride deflate under the Captain's gaze. "No sir, but..."

The Captain raised a hand, cutting him off. "That is why I am here. I am going to train you. You will report to me at the gym area at the beginning of every day. Is that understood? If you and Catherine are going to be planetside, you need to be able to protect her. She has had her fair share of training, but you need to be able to guard her back. That's why we send people out in teams. Not everyone is a friend to the Bound, but that doesn't mean we don't give them the opportunity to hear the message."

Terran toyed with the idea in his head of training with the Captain. It seemed almost surreal to think of an average man working out with the giant, but there was nothing to lose.

"When do we start, sir?" Terran asked.

"Tomorrow," the Captain responded. "Also, call me Glenn. Now, I have to go take care of a few things, but I expect to see you bright and early. Understood?" The Captain got up and headed for the door.

"Yes Capt--err, Glenn." Terran felt awkward at the new familiarity, but suspected it would get easier in time.

"One last thing, Terran," Glenn said from the door. "If you are in any way unfaithful to my daughter, it would not end well with you." Before Terran could respond, he had left the room.

Catherine had told Terran that her father would pay him a visit, but he hadn't expected it so soon. Terran lay down on the couch and sprawled out. He had six hours before the first set and knew he needed to rest, but his heart was beating too fast from the meeting with the Captain and the dinner with Catherine. Although it had hardly been romantic, and there had been plenty of people at all the other tables; it had felt special to him.

Closing his eyes, he focused on the thought of her. He could still smell her perfume and picture her in his mind with acute detail. Not even his sisters knew just how well he could remember things. It went far beyond just words. He could replay whole days in his mind if he tried hard enough.

He opened his eyes and got up from the couch. Opening the shade of the window and commanding the lights off, he allowed the light from New-Space to flood his room. He lay back on the couch and watched the lights dance in a hypnotic rhythm around the ship.

As Terran replayed the whole day back through his mind, he couldn't help but smile. For the first time in a long time, he felt happy. With nothing but pleasant thoughts churning through his mind, he set an alarm and closed his eyes.

# CHAPTER EIGHTEEN

Rictor stood in front of the door leading to Glenn's office. The last time he'd been there, he and the Captain had parted ways jovially, laughing. This time, Rictor doubted there would be any laughter at all. So much had changed in such a small amount of time. Still, this had to happen. Glenn had a right to know. Mustering up his nerve, he knocked on the door.

"Come in," Glenn's voice carried easily through the door.

Rictor opened the door and entered the room. He stopped midstep when he saw Naomi sitting across from Glenn. That was not a part of the plan. Rictor continued toward the chair next to Naomi, scrambling to come up with something to say. What all had she told him? Why was she even there? She had been against telling him anything to begin with.

As Rictor sat down, Naomi spoke up. "Sorry to catch you off guard, Ric, but after our talk I decided that telling the Captain our plan would be the right move."

Rictor paused for just a brief second as he studied both of their faces. "And you are okay with this, Glenn?"

"Don't see why not. Saving a boy's life is the right thing to do. I would do just about anything to save Catherine if she were kidnapped by someone like Dagor."

Rictor had the sudden urge to throw Naomi through the window behind Glenn. Lying was the wrong move. She had no idea what she was doing. "Well, Captain, I'm glad we have your approval. Has she told you the full plan?"

"Oh, yes," Glenn said as he rummaged through some pieces of paper in front of him, "Basically, she is going to contact Dagor, offer to meet him in person to give you up as a hostage, follow along to his compound on Torga to get with her son, then you will fight your way out and make it to the jump ship back here. That about it in a nutshell?"

"Yes, sir," Rictor replied. He was surprised she hadn't seemed to change the plan at all behind his back. "Is there anything you would change or recommend?"

"That is exactly what the Captain and I were talking about when you came in," Naomi said. "But I think we were about to come to the agreement that the plan was actually pretty solid, because your...unique capabilities."

"We don't need to sugarcoat it, Naomi," Rictor said, "I have the best chance of not dying, plain and simple. Plus, with a smaller team, there is less of a chance for anyone to get hurt."

"Exactly." Naomi nodded.

"How many do you think you will need in total?" Glenn asked. "It definitely can't be just the two of you."

"It has to be," Rictor said quickly. "If she shows up with anything more than her and a hostage, Dagor won't show."

"Well, have you two figured out the story of why you would follow her to an undisclosed location once we land?"

"We have," Naomi said. "People are going to assume we are an item and just want some alone time."

Glenn rubbed his chin as he looked from Rictor's face back to Naomi's. "Is that what the kiss was about in the cafeteria?"

Rictor coughed, but Naomi filled in the silence quickly. "Yes. It was meant to show the beginning of us becoming an item. If you are worried about the squabbling, we will keep it up. Now we can just call it a couples' quarrel."

Although Rictor disagreed with her methods, he was impressed by Naomi's quick mind. She was able to spin almost anything to make it beneficial to her.

Glenn was quiet as he glanced back and forth between the pair. "It looks like you all know what you are doing. Naomi, I would usually suggest you get some training from Rictor, but I know first-hand that you can throw a good punch." He smiled at her and Naomi blushed at the comment. "You two have my blessing. Feel free to use the resources you need to get Naomi's son. You are dismissed."

Naomi and Rictor got up from their chairs and headed out the door. As it closed behind them, Rictor grabbed hold of Naomi's hand and tugged her down the hallway. She smiled and followed him wordlessly. A few interested groups passed by, and Rictor heard his name mentioned more than once. At least this would start the rumor mill going.

When they had reached a room Rictor knew would be empty, he opened the door and gestured for Naomi to enter. Closing the door behind them, Rictor turned back to Naomi and said as calmly as he could, "What was all that about?"

Naomi smiled back at him. "That was me ensuring that the Captain both agrees to help us and isn't aware that we plan on killing someone. Knowing the Captain's gung ho nature about the Capital's rules, it seems rather odd that he would agree to an assassination."

Rictor ground his teeth. "I could make him understand. We are friends, practically brothers. I could convince him that this was the best way to handle Dagor."

Naomi's face hardened. "If that was so, then why haven't you convinced him before?"

Rictor paused, trying not to raise his voice. "Glenn is a cautious man. He doesn't like to make rash decisions and is very particular about what he views are the needs of the ship. There wasn't a proper time to tell him until now."

"That's a load of crap," Naomi shot back.

The handle to the door began turning and Rictor pulled Naomi close to him as the door opened. A soft yelp escaped from the young woman who was about to enter the room and she shut the door. Naomi pushed herself away from Rictor.

"You might have a problem with my methods, but you can't tell me they don't work. We have a cover, a plan, and Glenn's backing. What more do you want?"

Rictor did not have an answer. He knew that what they had just done was wrong. He could feel it in his core. Rictor sat in one of the desks of the small classroom they were in. His shoulders slumped as he ran his hands through his short hair.

"Do you understand the consequences of what you did, at least?" he asked in a whisper.

"It doesn't matter. I am staying on Torga. My troubles with Dagor have nothing to do with the Capital. It is purely personal." Naomi stood in front of him with her shoulders back and a proud look on her face.

Despite himself, Rictor found himself smiling. Even with everything she had been through, she was still proud. She refused to be beaten down. "And what of me? What if I wanted to be a part of this "Capital business" as you call it? What if I sincerely believed in it. What if I wanted to keep on the work we have been given? Doesn't that mean anything? We need to be a team. We need to stick together. How can we do that if you do stupid things like meeting with Glenn without me?"

"Sometimes, Ric," Naomi replied as she put her hand on his shoulder. "You have to eliminate the variables. You and I are in this because we need to be. The more people we add, the harder it becomes to keep it quiet. No one can know until it is too late to stop us. Dagor has spies everywhere. What would he think if you, me, and Glenn started meeting? I can't be hooked up with both of you."

Rictor brushed her hand from his shoulder and made his way to the door. "I know, Naomi, I just don't want to lose the only friend I have."

"It could be worse," Naomi said joining him. "It could have happened already."

Rictor gazed into her eyes for a long time. They were sad and lonely, longing for warmth. He gently drew her face toward his and kissed her.

Naomi pulled away slowly and flashed a grin. "You're a pretty good actor, Ric. It almost feels like you were wanting a real kiss there."

Rictor watched her leave the room and cursed himself. *What in the world am I doing? She is dangerous, obviously troubled, and we are planning on killing someone together. That is not the basis of a relationship.* He watched her walk down the hallway. *She is beautiful though.*

# CHAPTER NINETEEN

"Dodge!" Glenn roared as he swung a massive fist at Terran.

Terran frantically worked to do just that. Instead, Glenn's fist slammed into Terran's stomach.

He fell to the ground, gasping for air.

"Terran," Glenn said reaching a hand toward him. "You are improving, but you need to be faster. It's all in the reflexes."

"I...know," Terran gasped from the floor.

Glenn grabbed him and pulled him up. "If you extend your arms to the ceiling, you will get more air."

Terran did as he was told. After he regained his breath, he went back to his starting position. It had been a week and a half of training so far. Each day, Glenn would take him to one of the exercise rooms and either punch and kick him in various places or wrestle Terran into submission.

His body was covered in bruises, and it ached when he moved, but it was worth it. To be able to spend time with Catherine, it was worth it. She never really made a big deal about his bruises, and she hadn't seemed surprised when he had walked in with them. While overflowing in mercy and kindness, she apparently lacked sympathy.

"Now, dodge!" Glenn roared again as he tried to sweep Terran's leg. This time Terran was a bit more ready. He jumped over the leg and landed with his knees slightly bent and his fists up. Glenn finished the sweep then came at him with two quick jabs. Terran dodged them by ducking underneath. As Glenn's knee crashed into his sternum, he learned that was a bad move.

The worst part of the whole experience was that he could tell that Glenn was holding back. The man was a paragon of fighting prowess. He even looked the part. Glenn stood over him again without a shirt, revealing that the scars he bore covered his torso as well. He reached down to help Terran back up and Terran took his hand. *Is there any part of the man that isn't scarred?* As Glenn turned back to his starting position, Terran got back into another stance.

Glenn, however, kept his back toward Terran. "You are improving, Terran. I was concerned at first. Most bookish types don't take well to any type of meaningful labor. Their bodies are soft, and they prefer to keep them that way. Tell me, why do you so readily accept this training?"

Terran smiled. Glenn had a certain way of talking that seemed so out of place on a ship in New-Space. Really, it was everything about him that was anachronistic. His manners, his insistence on fighting, his way of thinking. It was all completely backward from everyone else on the ship.

"Well, like you said, I need to be able to protect Catherine," Terran said.

"But why take me up so readily? Why give it so much enthusiasm and energy? You have not complained or seemed bitter. If I didn't know better, I would say you enjoyed getting punched." Glenn's voice was thoughtful as he turned to face Terran again. "Why?"

Terran's smile disappeared as he thought back to Sisera, of the countless times he had lost food his family had needed because he couldn't defend himself, of the innocents gunned down by the gangs. He hadn't been able to protect his family, not really. It had all been luck.

"The reason I am so enthusiastic," Terran replied, his voice low, "is because I have already seen what happens when you can't protect who you care about. I know how easily it is to lose something dear, to watch as people I love go hungry because I was weak. It will not happen again."

Glenn looked Terran up and down for what seemed like an eternity. He walked over to Terran and placed a hand on his shoulder. "We are done for the day," he said quietly. "Go see Catherine. I have some things to take care of. You did well today."

Terran left the small exercise room and headed for his own. The small compliment from Glenn had meant a great deal to him. In a way, Terran idolized Catherine's monolithic father. He was smart, strong, and commanded the respect of everyone on-board, but still seemed so grounded. Most of all, he just seemed like a good person. He genuinely cared about everyone around him. He was someone to aspire to.

Terran met up with Catherine after a long shower and a small bite of food. She was standing by the table in the small classroom reading a comically large book when he entered. It was almost three feet tall and spanned almost six feet fully opened.

"Reading a book on giants?" Terran asked with a grin.

"Not exactly, but close," she smiled, making a small note on her tablet. "This book is going to be your focus until we reach Torga."

"You expect me to focus on one book for three weeks? Remember who you are talking to? I barely spend more than a week on a textbook before it's memorized and indexed." He tried not to sound boastful, but it seemed ridiculous to ask him to only read one thing for three whole weeks.

"Terran, this is probably the most important book on the ship. You need to focus on it. Besides, I can guarantee you haven't seen anything like it." She walked over and hugged him gently. "How was the training today?"

"It was fine." Terran said, caught off guard. Catherine never asked him about the training with her dad. "Why do you ask?"

"Just curious," she said sweetly. "Are you in the dodge stage or has he gone a different route this time?"

Terran laughed, "So I take it I am not the first one to go through your dad's training?"

"Nope, but you are the first one who seems to take it well. That means brownie points from my dad. He respects a man who can take a hit."

"So, does that mean he likes me? It's kind of hard to tell with him."

"Yes, he does. Which is a good since I don't want to lose a boyfriend and a student at the same time. That would not look good on my resume."

Terran hugged her again despite the growing pain in his back and abdomen. "Well, I'm glad I can help."

"Good." She said, resting on him for a moment. "But we really do need to study this book."

Terran let her go and walked to her side of the table. The book was lying open to a page on schematics. It showed a long oval broken down into separate rooms with a small diagram in the top right corner showing different levels. Terran paused for a moment as what he was staring at sank in.

"Are these the schematics for the ship?" he asked.

"Not just for this ship. It has the schematics and piloting instructions for most of the ships in circulation. Of course, that only covers the first half. The second half is something just as interesting."

"And what is that?" Terran asked in disbelief. What could possibly be more important than the ship's schematics?

"The star maps and travel paths for all of space." She waved towards the maps in a flurry of motion. "These detail the paths of the ships within space."

Terran reached out to touch the book, but Catherine slapped his hand away. "Do you realize what this knowledge means? If the Envoys got a hold of this type of information, it would be disastrous for the Bound."

He paused as he considered what she had said, "I understand."

"I am trusting you, Terran. My father and I have talked a lot about your gift and the best way to utilize it for the Capital. We believe this is it."

Terran let the words sink in. "Okay," he said softly. "Don't worry, Catherine, I am not going to betray you or leave. This ship is quickly becoming the best thing to ever happen to me."

"Good," she said pecking him on the cheek. "Now you study this while I go make a report to my dad. Just don't tear up anything."

As she left, Terran bent down to examine the drawing. Luckily, Catherine had taught him how to read the old language when he had first started tutoring under her. The script was small, but legible. As he continued to study the large schematics for this ship, a small question kept trying to worm its way into his mind. Why did Glenn and Catherine want him to learn about the ships?

# CHAPTER TWENTY

Catherine stood outside her father's room waiting for the door to open. It had been a few minutes, but she didn't mind. It was a relatively new development anyway. He used to answer the door so quickly that a rumor had started that he would wait by the door and wait for someone to knock. She missed those rumors.

The door opened and her father motioned for her to come inside. The room was larger than the others. It had plush carpet and an extended living area following the same color scheme as the rest of the ship. The only trace that someone lived in the room was the steaming cup sitting on the small coffee table by his bed. The strong smell of cinnamon and others spices filled the air.

She sat down on the large couch in the living area and propped her feet on the small table in front of it. Glenn sat down beside her, sipping his tea. He was drinking a lot more of it these days.

"Hello Papa," she smiled at him.

"Hello, little mouse," he smiled back. "How is everything going?"

"Good. I showed Terran the maps and schematics, and he is bound to be on board. Is it getting worse?" she asked as her father polished off the tea in a quick gulp.

"Oh, it's not so bad. Just getting old, is all." He put the cup on the table quickly, but not before Catherine noticed the slight shaking of his hands.

"Just making sure," she said straining to keep the sorrow out of her voice. "What's next?"

"All we have to do is be patient," he told her patting her hand. "We have good people on this ship working on the problem. With any luck this will be over by Torga."

"Are Rictor and Naomi still planning on killing Dagor?" A shadow fell across Glenn's face as she asked the question.

"Yes, child, unfortunately they are. I will be speaking with them both soon. I might be able to talk some sense into them." He began to pop the knuckles on his left hand as he talked. "They will lose themselves if they follow through with their plan. Not to mention we would lose the trust of Torga. Are we willing to doom an entire planet to satisfy a blood thirst? We cannot let that happen."

"But wouldn't it be better to be rid of Dagor? He is a top agent of Promioth. He is vicious, cruel, and power hungry. Why not just let them act out as rogue agents and clear ourselves of the blame?" Catherine asked.

"Do you know how I was described before I came to be Capital Bound?" Glenn asked after a brief pause.

"No." Her father rarely talked about his past. He usually preferred to focus on the future. Of course, that wasn't looking too bright for him either. She cursed herself for her morbid thoughts and tried to focus as her father talked.

"I was called the Keeper. It was said that when men entered the arena, it was I who determined their fate, not any gods. I was renowned for struggling against odds stacked against me and winning, which usually meant that a lot of men died. Tell me, would it have been better for me to die?"

"Of course not, Father, but you weren't against the Bound." She barely got the words out before he continued.

"We are all against the Bound, up until the moment we decide we aren't. One day I will stand in front of the Emperor and I will be judged for what I have done. I am just trying to spare others of that same fate. Do you understand?"

"Yes, sir," she said lowering her head. Glenn's hand reached out and pulled her toward him so they were sitting side by side.

"Enough of this pessimistic talk. How are you and Terran?" His eyes brightened as he asked the question, and he gave her a toothy grin. It had been a long time since she had seen him smile like that.

"We're good," she said as she blushed. "Thank you for taking it easy on him."

"He is a good man. He just needs some help in the right direction. You two need to take it slow until he figures out who he really is. It will be hard for him."

Catherine matched her father's smile to hide the fact that her mind was racing. Her father had the uncanny ability to read into people. He always knew who was genuine and who was just trying to fake it on the ship. "And who is he?" she asked, genuinely curious.

"You know I cannot tell you. He is important to the cause. That is the most I can give you." He kissed the top of her head. "Sorry, little mouse. Even someone like me must answer to a higher power, and I was told what I am allowed to speak of."

An awkward silence hung between them. It had always bugged her that she had not been able to see something spectacular like her father. She had watched the V-sphere countless times trying to dig in and experience something radical like he had. All she had to show for it was an acute knowledge of the history of the Capital Bound.

"I told him about your experience with the V-Sphere." She said, breaking the silence.

"How did he take it?" Glenn asked.

"Pretty well. He had a different experience than you did, but similar in that he talked with the Emperor's son as well."

Glen nodded as she spoke. "That is enough. Terran will share his vision with me in time. It is his story to tell."

"Okay, do you have any other orders for me before I go?"

"No, just enjoy yourself and stay safe. Remember, Terran needs guidance and it is up to us to give it to him. There is a reason I chose you to look after him instead of Rictor."

Catherine got up to leave. "Duly noted; if you need anything let me know."

"Of course I will, little mouse," Glenn kissed her on the forehead, and she left the room hiding the tears that had started to form.

# CHAPTER TWENTY-ONE

Terran and Catherine stared at each other over the starship lexicon.

"The point I am trying to make is that I don't understand what the big deal is," Terran said for what felt like the hundredth time.

"The deal is that there is more to becoming a Voice than just passing the test," Catherine shot back, throwing her hands up.

"But that's stupid. Anything they try to teach me in a classroom, I can teach myself," Terran said again. He had made the same argument before. Each time he would use different words to say the same thing, but neither he nor Catherine seemed to be willing to budge.

"It's more than just textbook knowledge," Catherine shouted at him, "you can't get people to trust you just because you know all the answers. To most people that just makes you look like a jerk. Kind of like when you are being childish and stubborn." Catherine's face flushed red as she finished.

Terran had many responses for Catherine, but instead he turned and left the room slamming the door behind him. He was not going to just stand there and be berated by some sheltered girl. As much as he liked her, he had never met anyone who could be as irritating.

Terran was halfway back to his room when his tablet started vibrating. A quick glance told him that Kelly was wanting to meet up and talk. Terran ground his teeth and sent back a text, telling her he was on his way.

Even if he wasn't in the mood to talk to anyone, family was family. She was waiting for him by the door to his room. Sitting with her eyes closed and her head leaning on the wall, she almost seemed to be sleeping. He walked over to her and nudged her with his foot. She swatted his foot in retaliation, but did not move or open her eyes. A little lost on what else to do, he gently kicked her. She reached over and pinched him on the thigh.

"Ow," he yelped. "Why in the world are you sitting outside of my bedroom?"

"When did you make it a habit to kick pretty girls who are all by their lonesome?" Kelly asked tilting her head to the side. "Or do you just pick on me because I am the prettiest?" Although her voice was chipper, her puffy eyes betrayed her.

Terran forced a chuckle and extended his hand to pick her up from the floor. *What could possibly have happened to make her cry so hard?* Kelly could be the warmest ray of sunshine in the midst of winter, it seemed out of place for her to be sad. She took his hand and stood up.

They entered his room and she went right to his bed, forgoing the couch. She jumped onto it, spinning in midair, and landed on her back. Kicking off her shoes, she sprawled across the mattress.

"Terran," she said staring at the low ceiling of the room.

"One sec," he responded, climbing into the bed beside her and resting his head on a pillow. Terran gave the voice command to open the shade, and colored lights from New-Space began pouring into the room. They drifted all around as if dancing to an unseen rhythm.

"First off," she said in a small voice, as if trying not to interrupt the lights. "Your room is way more impressive than mine. Second," she paused and took a big breath. "I think I want to be a Voice for the Bound." The words came out in a staccato as if rushing before she could stop herself.

Terran stared at his sister. "What? Why?"

"I already told Anna, and she said that I was crazy, that fourteen was way too young to do something like that and that they probably wouldn't let me do it anyway. Then I told her they had already accepted me, and she flipped out and left the room going who knows where. And now I'm struggling because I really feel like I should do this, but now I'm not so sure. I just have always felt so useless and this is the first thing I really think I would be good at." She finished the confession and was silent again.

"You do know everything that a Voice does, don't you?" he asked.

"Not you, too, Terran. I thought you at least would believe in me."

He could almost hear the tears filling her eyes. "It's not that I don't think you could do it, I was just curious what part of being a Voice attracted you to it."

Kelly let out a few more sobs before regaining her composure. "Really, it's all of it. The medical training, the diplomacy, helping people to experience all the joys and wonders that we have. I know it won't be easy, but I really feel as if I could do some good for a change. I know I'm not as smart as you or Anna, but I should at least be able to try."

Silence filled the room broken only by her intermittent sobs. Terran turned to see tears in her eyes and wet streaks across her flushed cheeks. His heart hurt to see her so distraught. *I need to talk to Anna at some point to see why she doesn't want Kelly to become a Voice.*

He sorted through the different thoughts in his head, trying to figure out the right thing to say. A part of his mind told him that this was part of a plan by Catherine and Glenn. That they had somehow plotted this all out and were using Kelly against him. None of that changed the fact that she was in his bedroom, was crying, and he had never been able to tell her no.

"You should do it," he said brushing a tear from her cheek. "Tell Anna that I will be in the class with you to make sure you aren't rushing into any dangerous situations."

There was a break in her breathing. "Really?" she asked between sobs.

"Really," Terran replied pulling her to his side. "And you have never been useless, Kelly."

"Yes, I have been," she said. Terran was surprised at the bitterness in her voice. "You were constantly risking your neck for us, and all I could do was sit in the room. I couldn't even help at the house. All I did was eat food and take up space."

"That's dumb," Terran said, rubbing her arm. "Without your wisecracks and shenanigans, I would have fallen apart years ago."

"Wisecracks and shenanigans never brought in food." Her reply was nasally after crying so long.

"They brought me home." Terran kissed the top of her head. In truth, he doubted if Kelly or Anna would ever really understand what they had done for him. Each day he had walked in darkness, seeing the worst in people. When he had finally come home each night, Kelly and Anna had always been there to remind him of who he was.

They sat in quiet as he waited for Kelly to respond. He stared at the lights and his eyelids began to droop. Each time the shade opened, he knew what to expect, but he was still amazed at how beautiful they were. A soft snore brought him back to reality. He gently let Kelly's head down onto a pillow and made his way to the couch. Pulling out his tablet, he sent Catherine a quick message telling her he would do the class as long as Kelly was in the same one.

A response came almost immediately. He was to go to a new classroom at the end of the week to go through the certification course. He put the tablet away and settled in for the night. If he had been played, then they had chosen the right way to do it. Something told him that everything was going to be all right, but he pushed the thought away. He had gotten too comfortable on the Lion's Roar. He needed to remember what he had learned on Sisera. No matter how nice their intentions were, people would always use each other.

# CHAPTER TWENTY-TWO

The day of the certification, Terran and Kelly found themselves in a spacious classroom filled with other members of the ship. They found their way to their seats, and shortly after a small woman walked into the room and stood in front of the large desk. She carried a V-sphere and a pole which she began to set up once she had looked briefly over the class.

After the sphere was set up, she gave the command to dim the lights and the V-sphere started to glow. Without warning, a universe exploded from the sphere and covered the room in a soft light. The image turned slowly, and Terran was surprised to see that the images didn't just cover the walls, but floated freely in the air as well. He reached out to touch a star and it floated unhindered through his hand. Everyone else in the classroom barely gave the images the time of day, but Terran was transfixed. He saw with a smile that Kelly took the time to try and squish a few of the stars between her fingers. A voice called from the V-sphere as the images continued to swirl.

The voice was androgynous, flat, and overall unappealing. It started off saying that the message it was going to tell them was life changing and that they all had to pay strict attention to pass the exam. It carried on and on about the weight of importance of its message, but Terran kept getting distracted by the beautiful imagery around him.

He was particularly transfixed by a set of small planets that revolved around each other as they in turn revolved around their central star. Again and again he saw beauty and wonders as he scanned the room. The other students were all busy taking notes from the V-sphere, but Terran knew he would be able to answer any question they would ask him. A test hadn't been invented yet that he couldn't ace.

The voice died down eventually, and Terran was saddened as the stars faded away. The small woman appeared again and took the V-sphere down and sat behind the desk. She cleared her throat and began speaking.

"Hello, everyone."

Her voice carried through the room and Terran was surprised by its tone. Although the woman appeared to be in her late fifties, her voice was strong and rich.

"Today will be a very important object lesson. Now, who can tell me what is the greatest thing to keep in mind about becoming a Voice?"

There was a large amount of paper rustling as students surveyed their notes. Various students raised their hand quoting different phrases that the V-sphere had spoken. Each time their answers were rejected. Terran raised his own hand and waited to be called on.

"Yes," the woman asked looking toward him.

"To ensure that only the best and most qualified students are selected; otherwise they could botch everything up." He smiled as he finished. No one else had said it, and the V-sphere hadn't either, but it was obvious. Only the best people could take the message of the Capital to the other planets.

"Nope," she said flatly. "Anyone else?"

"Wait," Terran called out. "How is that not the answer? It is the most important thing to consider. You don't want any old yokel to be the face of the Capital. Think of the damage it could do."

"You, sir," the woman replied as Terran finished, "have an overinflated sense of self. The role of a Voice is not to be the 'face of the Capital' nor is it a position to be desired for our own sake. It is one that you are called toward and must respond to. Remember that. Anyone else?"

Terran clenched his jaw as he heard snickers from a few of the students around him. This whole thing was stupid anyway. He just needed the test and it would be a cinch.

"I think I might know," Kelly's voice rang out.

"Oh?" The woman smiled as she spoke. "And what would you say is the answer?"

"Well," Kelly stood and cleared her throat. "I don't think anything the voice from before actually said mattered." A couple of students started murmuring as she spoke, but the woman shushed them.

"Carry on," the woman said.

"It's just, the message that the voice was talking about was important and I think it is good to know all the rules and stuff, but it was hard to keep focused on it because was so monotonous and boring. It was like it wasn't even interested in what it was saying. I just feel like whoever made the V-sphere should have picked someone who was more excited about what they were saying. Then they could have delivered the same message, but in an effective way. We need Voices that resonate with our hearts, not just our minds."

The woman's smile broadened. "Now that is a fine answer. Very fine indeed. You may sit down." Kelly sat down looking pleased, and Terran felt a small stab of jealousy.

"It is not enough to know about the Capital and what we are doing. To become a Voice, you need to be able to remember the feeling of it. The feeling you experienced when you first learned about the Emperor. You can't lose that. If you do, it won't matter what you say, no one will pay attention. If you don't believe it yourself, then you shouldn't be here. That is all for today, I will see you all tomorrow same time and place."

"What should we call you if we have questions?" a student called out from the front.

The woman turned and smiled. "Nothing, I am just a Voice." With that she turned and left.

"Well that was dumb," Terran said turning to Kelly. "What kind of a question was that? It was stupid."

"Just because you didn't get it right doesn't mean it was stupid," Kelly said packing up her small notebook. "It just means you weren't paying attention. I don't think it will count against you," she added, seeing his displeased look.

"I just hope the rest of the class isn't as big a waste of time as this." He said getting up from his desk. "I don't see the point in all this listen-to-your-heart type of stuff."

"That's because you don't get it. You should probably take some time and make sure you really get what all this is about."

She left him standing by his desk and walked out. He gritted his teeth and watched her leave, followed by everyone else in the class. As the last person left, his anger at the Voice gave way to frustration.

*Do I really know why I am pursuing all this? Am I just biding my time?* He wanted to talk with Catherine about it, or Rictor, but instead he found himself going to the small classroom he knew would be empty.

As he sat at the table looking back over the schematics of the ships he began to wonder if his heart was really in it at all.

# CHAPTER TWENTY-THREE

Naomi shifted her weight back to her left foot. Her tablet was blank in in her hand. She needed to call Dagor. It would be suspicious if she didn't give him an update on how things were going. She ground her teeth trying to figure out the best approach to the conversation. She had written a few notes down to try and pick out exactly what she would tell him, but the exercise had been useless. She still had no idea what she would say. Time was running out, and she needed to reach out to him. Drawing a breath, she sent the email she had drawn up concerning Rictor.

She dreaded hearing Dagor's voice. The familiar chill crept up the small of her back causing her to shudder. She could feel the tension mounting in her shoulders as she waited for the response. She set her tablet on the small bookshelf that lined Rictor's office and sat down. She had cleaned up the office while he was away to keep from thinking about the phone call she would have to make. As the chore had progressed, it had been a good way to get her thoughts in order. As she had tidied up the desk and random stacks of papers, her own thoughts had been tidied up as well.

She closed her eyes and rested her head on the wall behind her. How long had it been since she had checked in? It wasn't like Dagor to not use someone.

"Hello, Naomi," Dagor's voice wormed its way through her ear piece.

"Hello, Dagor," Naomi said trying to keep the revulsion out of her voice.

"It has been quite some time since we have chatted. To what do I owe the pleasure?"

As he spoke, the video he had sent her began replaying in her mind. The anger she had felt watching it began to return as well. She forced it down and kept her composure.

"I wanted to thank you for letting me meet with my son once I get to Torga. So, I have been trying to get close to the Captain's right hand man. Surely you know of Rictor."

"I do," came the response.

"Well, I have been drawing him close, and he has promised me that I will be able to come planetside. On the condition that he accompanies me, of course."

"I had heard that you two were getting closer. What do you expect to get from this favor you are bringing me?"

"I want to make a simple trade, is all." Naomi didn't have to fake the nervous waiver in her voice. This needed to go their way. "I would like to trade Rictor for Nathaniel."

"Interesting," Dagor's voice oozed with easy confidence. "Didn't I tell you that you and your son would be reunited? Surely you don't think I would go back on my word, do you, Naomi?"

"Of course not, it's just that you said I would be reunited with my son... But I was hoping this trade would ensure that it would be permanent. I am done with all the plotting and scheming. I just want to be with my son."

Naomi waited patiently for a response, but there was no answer. She had just begun to think that Dagor had gotten off the line when his voice erupted into her ear.

"Very well, Naomi. If you give us Rictor, you may leave us in peace. No more plotting and scheming. But I want you to know that if this goes wrong, your son will die."

A short burst of static told Naomi that the call was over. She took the small earpiece out and placed it in a small metal box. Then, after a few deep breaths, she began pacing the office. Rictor entered a few minutes later, carrying a small tray of pastries and two cups. A small rumble from her stomach reminded her that she hadn't eaten yet. She reached out to get a sip from one of the cups and found it empty.

"Forget something?" she asked, shaking the cup.

"Nope, it is time you finally tried coffee. I can't believe you haven't tried it."

He bent over next to the coffee pot and began setting up the machine. She really didn't have any desire to drink coffee, but it would make him happy. *And why do I care if he is happy?* Naomi cursed her thoughts, frustrated that they had even occurred. Keep it about business. Emotions would cause her to make mistakes.

They sat quietly eating the pastries as the smell of coffee began to fill the office. Rictor tried to make some small talk, but Naomi found herself keeping quiet more than usual. She really did hate all the plotting and scheming they had been doing. She wished for simpler days, when her only concern had been taking care of Nathaniel. They had been stressful at times, working to provide for him, but nothing like the cloak and dagger they had been at on the ship.

A small beep from the coffee pot alerted them that the coffee was done. Rictor poured the mixture into two cups and handed one to Naomi. She took a small drink and set it on the desk.

"Well?" Rictor asked.

"It's awful," Naomi grimaced as she spoke. "Almost as bad as talking with Dagor."

"I doubt it. It's far less oily," Rictor smiled and passed two small packets to her. "I prefer mine black, but I guessed someone as sweet as you would need some sugar."

Naomi rolled her eyes and poured the packets into the coffee. A quick sip from the cup confirmed that a little bit of sugar made all the difference in the world.

"Dagor is in with the plan," she said between sips. "He will most likely attempt some subterfuge or other, but we should be able to find an opening."

"I wouldn't worry about that," Rictor said taking a bite out of a pastry. "There are more than a few gadgets on this ship that will help make sure we can get to him."

Naomi traced a finger around the rim of her cup. Today, it seemed Rictor had no problem with what they were doing. He was unpredictable to a degree. At some moments, he almost seemed to enjoy the planning and at others Naomi could sense that he wanted nothing to do with it.

"How certain are we that you and I are going to be on the same team again?" she asked. "The last time it happened, it didn't go well."

"Well, Glenn trusts me to keep an eye on you, so I think we are safe there. Speaking of your attempted murder, do you have any idea why Dagor wanted you to kill Terran? I have been meaning to ask you and was waiting for the right time."

"I have no idea. The kid is brilliant for sure, but I suspect there is more to it than that. There are plenty of smart people on the ship, one more wouldn't hurt."

"Have you talked to him at all?" Rictor asked after another bite.

"No, I was asked to speak at the end of the certification this round, so he is bound to try and talk to me there. He still thinks it was an accident?"

"Most on the ship do. Glenn and I made it clear that it was just a misdiagnosis that caused the problems."

"How often do things like this happen?" Naomi asked. There was something off about what Rictor had just told her.

"What do you mean?" he asked, finishing his pastry.

"How often does the ship or someone on it get attacked, and only you or Glenn knows about it?"

Rictor just smiled in return. "Naomi, don't you worry about that. Glenn and I have it under control." A small beep sounded as he was reaching for another pastry.

"You late for something?"

Rictor groaned and got up from his seat. He began scrambling around the room, opening drawers. "Where is the extra outfit I keep in here? Did you clean my office?"

Naomi grew wide eyed as he spoke. "Did you just now notice? Didn't you wonder why you actually had someplace to put the tray?"

Rictor paused for a second, then shook his head. "Never crossed my mind. But back to you moving my clothes, where are they?"

Naomi walked over to a small chest in the back of the office and took the clothes out. "You need better organization in here. It's a mess. Almost as bad as you are."

Rictor grinned as he grabbed his clothes and turned to leave. Pausing again, he turned back and kissed her on the cheek. "We need to be convincing to people, Naomi. Gotta get into the practice of showing affection. It pains me to have to kiss a beautiful woman like yourself, but I am willing to take one for the team."

As he left the room, Naomi sat down and began eating another pastry. At first, she had resisted the few affections that Rictor had tried showing in public, but he was right. Dagor would be asking his other spies to check in on them at any moment. They would need to be convincing. If they weren't affectionate in private, it would seem more awkward when they were in public.

A small part of her told her that she didn't exactly mind being kissed, and Rictor wasn't bad at it all. *It's been seven years since Orion died, surely it's okay for me to enjoy myself.* She pushed the thought away. She needed to focus on the mission. Maybe after everything was done she would consider letting someone in, but not now.

Naomi took another bite of pastry. If she was going to be stranded on Torga, there were worse people to be stranded with than Rictor. He was a survivor, just like she was. *He's not too bad to look at either, if only he wouldn't talk quite so much.* She set the pastry down and picked up the tablet. The certification classes would be ending soon and she needed to write the graduation speech.

Thoughts of the young man she had poisoned came back to her. He would undoubtedly have questions. Maybe she would be able to just give the speech and leave, or even give the speech remotely. Anything would be better than facing that young man again. She let the thoughts go and tried to focus on the speech. She would take it one day at a time. She would get through this. As she was writing, however, the familiar guilt came creeping back to her. She could call herself a survivor, but really, she was just a murderer.

# CHAPTER TWENTY-FOUR

Rictor entered the exercise room for his routine spar with Glenn when an extra person in the room surprised him. Terran was here too, and Glenn was instructing him on the proper techniques of grappling with someone on the ground.

"You trying to muddle up his brain up with all that technical jargon?" Rictor called from across the room.

Terran looked at him with curious eyes, but Glenn just waved him over.

"One of these days you will actually be on time, Ric," Glenn said.

"And one of these days all your scars will magically vanish." Rictor retorted with a snort. "Let's face it, I will always be fashionably late, and you will always lose beauty pageants. It's the lots we drew in life."

Terran's face went from shock to horror as Rictor was talking, but Glenn just barked out a laugh and swatted Rictor on the back.

"Terran, don't look so mortified. One of the greatest secrets of the universe, apart from faster than light travel, being able to know the foundation of space, and coffee, is that you have to accept what you can't change." Rictor smiled at him.

"But insulting someone isn't the same as accepting the truth." Terran said, scrunching his forehead. "That's just mean."

"It's okay, Terran," Glenn said. "Rictor, I need to talk with you and Naomi after the Voice certification tomorrow. Terran, you may join us as well."

Rictor gave a sharp nod.

"Should I bring Catherine?" Terran asked.

"Did I say to?" Glenn retorted.

"No, sir."

"Well, are we sparring or what?" Rictor asked, trying to break the tension.

"No," Glenn said. "I am rather tired today, Ric. Now that you are here, would you be able to help Terran learn a few holds? I have some things to attend to." He left without waiting for an answer.

A brief silence fell between Terran and Rictor. "What did you do?" Rictor asked, eyes widening. "Either you spit in his tea this morning or you did something to Catherine."

"I didn't do anything," Terran said, kicking a small tote bag. "I'm just struggling a bit with this."

"With what?" Rictor asked, kicking the tote back.

"Everything!" Terran shouted. "It's not easy being forced fed all this information and not being able to get any answers. It's not fair. He expects me to memorize all the information about all those stupid ships and the star maps, but won't tell me why. I am supposed to become a Voice so I can go planetside, but I can't just become passionate at the drop of a hat. I need answers. I need reasons. I haven't had either since being on the ship. Even after the talk with Ekundayo, I still have a ton of questions."

"Who is Ekundayo?"

Terran looked at him and then blushed. "When I saw the V-sphere something weird happened and I had a vision."

"And you have a hard time believing in all this even after you have had a vision?" Rictor sat down on the floor and patted the space next to him.

Terran sat down next to him. "It was a single experience that can't be validated. Maybe it was because of the after effects of the medicine or bad food. How do I know it's real?" Rictor noted a quiver had entered Terran's voice.

"Because you know it is," Rictor smiled. "That's how belief works. There isn't a set amount of facts you should know before you trust it. You either do or don't. Having a vision would be a boost though."

Terran stared at the floor. "How long did it take before you knew for certain?"

"I think a part of me knew before I admitted it," he confessed. "I had a lot of issues when I learned about the whole thing. I had questions too--still do, in fact. But I have peace about things now. I don't need answers to everything because I can't understand everything. The finite cannot understand the infinite. Understand?"

Terran gave him an odd look. "That's basically what Ekundayo said."

"Seems like a smart guy." Rictor stood up and began stretching. "The real question here is what made you start doubting in the first place?"

"Well, during the first Voice class the teacher said that only people who truly believed should be telling people about the Capital. It was just hard on me because I have so many questions about everything."

"Understandable," Rictor said putting a hand on his shoulder. "But you have to take what people say with a grain of salt. We're all trying to figure out what we're doing here. We have the Teachings, sure, but there are a lot of gray areas. In those instances, you go by your own convictions."

Terran scrunched his forehead. "The Teachings?"

Rictor gave him a blank stare. "You don't know what the Teachings are?"

Terran shook his head.

"How in the world did you not learn about them?! Have you even looked through your tablet?"

Terran shook his head again. "Sorry," he said.

"The Teachings were sent out by the Capital to make sure we had some guidelines to go by in this crazy life of ours."

"That sounds like it could be helpful."

Rictor let out a small laugh. "Terran, I do believe you are getting a sense of humor."

"Well, you can blame my sisters for that."

"Speaking of them, how are they?"

"Good, they both seem to have found their place on the ship. Kelly is trying to become a Voice as well and Anna is helping operations."

"And you?"

"I have no idea. Glenn has some plan for me, but neither he nor Catherine will tell me anything. I just wish he would give me a hint or something."

"You mentioned star maps before, what exactly is he having you do?"

"I'm not sure if I am supposed to tell anyone."

Rictor raised an eyebrow at him.

"Terran, I just helped you through an existential crisis, plus I am basically Glenn's brother. There isn't a single person on this ship as committed to the Capital as me. I am the least threatening person on this ship."

Terran scratched his chin, hesitating for a moment, but Rictor knew he would tell him. Even if it was just to get it off his chest, Terran needed to talk about this.

"Catherine has me studying navigational star maps and the specs for every known Capital-issued vessel."

"What?" Rictor raised an eyebrow. "That is quite peculiar."

"I know," Terran threw his hands up. "At first I was excited, but after thinking it through, I didn't think it made much sense. The star maps maybe, but why would we even need to know the specs of the other ships?"

"Because he doesn't know what ship you will be on." Rictor muttered. *Is Glenn leaving him on Torga?*

"What was that?" Terran asked.

"Nothing," Rictor lied. "Let me talk with the Captain, I will see if I can pry something out of him for you."

"Thanks, Ric."

"Anytime."

"So, do you think I should finish the certification?"

"You basically have finished it, haven't you? You only have a few days left. What's the harm in sticking it out?'

"I could fail it," he said.

"True, but you won't."

"Why do you say that?" Terran's eyes seemed to be begging him for confirmation.

"Because you really do believe in all this. You just have to let some things go before you can admit it."

Terran laid on the ground. "I just wish there were more 'yes' and 'no' types of questions."

Rictor laughed. "Welcome to the real world. There is a lot more gray than people think. And a lot more that's black and white. Really, it's just confusing since everyone has their own opinion that they just know is right. That's the bottom line."

Terran got up from the floor and extended his hand. "Thank you, Rictor."

"No worries, Terran." He patted the younger man on the back. "How about you just take the rest of the day off?"

Terran looked thoughtful for a moment, then shook his head.

"I have some things to work out still. I might hit the treadmill and pound out some frustration."

"Suit yourself, I am getting some lunch. If you need anything, Terran, let me know."

"Will do. Thanks for the pep talk."

"It's what I'm here for."

Rictor left Terran lying on the ground and headed for the elevator. A small part of him was hurt by the news that Terran had shared. It wasn't that Glenn had some plan in the works, but that he hadn't made Rictor a part of it.

# CHAPTER TWENTY-FIVE

aomi stood behind the podium and surveyed the small group of people in front of her. Terran was there, she noted, and so was his sister. Both wore the same uniform she was wearing. A sharp blue jacket with matching pants, shiny black shoes, and a simple white shirt. Naomi's jacket, unlike theirs, had three stripes along the right shoulder--indicating she had graduated the course. Their new jackets were laid out on a table in front of the podium, each one having a corresponding name embroidered on the left breast.

She hadn't worn her uniform since Sisera, but it felt good to have a sense of place. It was familiar. As she continued to survey the small group, she locked eyes with Rictor in a back corner. He was wearing the same blue uniform; and although it was faded, his name stood out in stark contrast to the light fabric. It was an official Voice uniform, which threw Naomi a bit. She hadn't been aware that he had gone through the training. She should have known better, of course. If he had been around as long as he said he had, it only made sense that he had done the training.

*What if Rictor lied to me about his age, the labs, everything. What if he's just leading me on?*

She re-read the small cards in her hands. No time for distractions. She took in a deep breath and began her speech. It was full of little anecdotes and jokes mixed with serious warnings and equally serious encouragements. The soon-to-be Voices laughed when they were supposed to and grew serious when they were supposed to. Once she had finished, she received a standing ovation. Fierce clapping assaulted her as she stepped from behind the podium and made her way back toward Rictor.

The graduates rushed forward and passed the jackets to each other, immediately putting them on and tossing aside the old ones into a marked bin. As she approached Rictor, he mimed clapping his hands together and gave a solemn nod before breaking into a smile.

"That was masterful." He said, scratching his short beard. "If I didn't know better, I would say I wrote it myself."

"You wish," Naomi leaned against the wall next to him and looked back over the group.

Terran stood away from the crowd wearing his new jacket. He was peering through the group with mild interest, and his gaze drifted to where she and Rictor were standing.

"Oh, no," she said, "he is definitely going to walk up here and talk with us."

No sooner had the words left her mouth than Terran began walking towards their corner.

Rictor placed a hand on her shoulder and gave a comforting squeeze. "What you did when Dagor had control over you is not who you are. Terran is a good kid. Besides, we both know you can take care of yourself."

Naomi frowned at the reassurance. It was true, of course--she could take care of herself, but she didn't like the idea of hurting people. Except for Dagor. He was the exception. She didn't have time to retort back at Rictor, however, as Terran had closed the small gap and stood in front of them.

"Congratulations," Naomi said, extending her hand. "You passed with flying colors. You really are as smart as everyone says."

"Thank you, Naomi," he said taking her hand with a firm shake. "For everything. Without you I wouldn't be here. I want you to know that I understand what happened on the ship."

Naomi froze, and she felt Rictor's grip tighten ever so slightly. "How do you mean?" she asked as pleasantly as she could.

"Well, we were running late and sometimes when you rush you make mistakes. I understand that. I forgive you for almost killing me. That's what I am trying to say. Maybe if we get some more Voices, we won't have to rush so much next time."

A whirlwind went through Naomi as she frantically searched for what to say. "Thank you, "she said, not faking the relief in her voice, "I feel awful about everything that has happened to you because of me."

"Well, just make sure it doesn't happen again. Rictor, take it easy," Terran smiled, extending his hand to Rictor.

"I'll pass," Rictor said, amusement evident in his voice. "Wouldn't want to overextend myself."

Terran just chuckled and turned to walk away.

"Terran," Naomi called out.

He turned back to her with a raised eyebrow. "Yes?"

"I hope we can work together in the future."

"It would be my pleasure." He gave a brief wave and headed back to the group.

"Has no one told him what really happened?" she asked without looking at Rictor.

"Believe it or not, we can keep secrets on the ship," Rictor said with reservation. "But I am a little confused about that as well. He seems different today, not quite so serious. It's good, maybe, but I can't help but think that something is wrong."

"Or we could both be paranoid," Naomi said as she turned toward him. "Both of us have so many secrets it's natural for us to think everyone else should too."

"One thing I have learned, Naomi, everyone has secrets." Rictor's eyes studied Terran as he mingled with his sister and they began laughing with friends.

*Oh, to be carefree and young again.*

"We still meeting with the Captain today?" she asked.

"Yep, at two o'clock." Rictor said as he looked at his mobile. "We have about thirty minutes."

"Well, let's get going then. We can grab a bite to eat first." She walked past him, then turned and kissed his cheek. They needed as many people as possible to see them together. A few whistles and hollers from the small group let her know she had timed the kiss correctly.

"I am rather enjoying this playacting," Rictor said, "Random kisses from a beautiful woman are always welcome."

"You have much experience with that before?" Naomi asked.

"Being kissed? Yes. By someone as beautiful as you? No."

Naomi's heart skipped a beat at his reply. "Ric," she said, stopping in the hallway.

He turned and smiled. It was a genuine smile, more reserved then the one he usually wore. *Remember who he is. He's the slob with a dirty office and childish attitude.* That's right, Rictor was not some knight in shining armor. *But he is doing everything he can to help you. He is working non-stop for you.* She did not have time for this right now.

"We can't get tangled up in this. It would just make things complicated. We can't afford to let feelings grow between us."

"Are you saying they already haven't?" He took her hand.

Blushing, she took a few steps away.

"Let's just grab some food and meet up with the Captain." She walked more quickly toward the cafeteria, leaving Rictor behind. *We are just acting.*

She had to wait for him at the door leading into the cafeteria and they walked in together holding hands. She could feel the people staring at them and knew they were playing the ruse well. *Maybe we are acting too well.*

They each grabbed a sandwich from the food line and sat down at an empty table.

"How's the plan going?" she asked.

"Good," Rictor replied. "We have everything loaded into our assigned jumping vessel, and I included some extra goodies to keep us safe."

"Ric, we need to talk about you wanting to keep on with the Bound."

"Not right now," he interrupted. "Let's just enjoy the time we have."

"Pushing the problem away isn't going to fix anything."

"I will cross that hurdle when we get to it. Until then don't worry about it."

He reached out and placed his hand on hers. He began gently stroking her hand and she would have been lying to herself if she wasn't happy to push off reality a few more minutes.

# CHAPTER TWENTY-SIX

Glenn sat in his office staring at the clock. In a few short minutes the small debriefing was going to take place. He had just finished another round of talks with the governments of Torga, and things were getting complicated. More and more planets were growing hostile towards the Bound, which was making going anywhere difficult. Of course, the ship's AI plotted their course for them, but still, he was surprised the planets they visited weren't more congenial. Sisera had been a nightmare, only allowing one dropship per continent. Torga, at least, had allowed them to send down ships to each of their Pods and visas to stay for a full year. There had been a time when a year was practically a minimum.

Promioth had been doing his job well and most planets wanted nothing to do with him. If it wasn't for the tech and expertise the Bound could offer, most planets wouldn't have let him send a single ship planetside. He took a sip of tea and felt some of the pain in his joints dim. He knew he didn't look it, but he was getting old. He shifted in his chair and felt his hip grind in the socket. The cartilage had long since been worn away.

He stood, despite the groaning of his hips and knees, and walked to the back wall. A soft command shifted the wall to a screen of New-Space. Soon he would be at the Capital. The others on the ship didn't understand yet. That was ok, it took a certain viewpoint to really understand how it all worked together. Rictor would have it the hardest.

The door opened behind him and a gentle smell of cinnamon tickled his nose. The perfume was a small token left over from her mother. Catherine didn't wear it often, but he always appreciated when she did.

"Hello, little mouse," he said without turning.

"Hello, Father,"

He heard her sit down, and the door opened again. This time he did turn, and saw Naomi and Rictor enter. They took their respective seats together and waited patiently for the rest of the group. More people filed in and took the seats around them. Terran sat next to Catherine and the two shared a smile. Kelly and Derek sat together talking in hushed voices.

"I am going to cut to the chase," Glenn said. "We are ahead of schedule and will be dropping planetside in three days. Terran and Catherine, Rictor and Naomi, and Kelly and Derek, each group will receive one drop ship filled with basic necessities and the bartering items that Torga requested in exchange for visas. You have all been picked because you have shown both aptitude and have a genuine interest in spreading the news of the Capital. Each of you will be sent to a different approved region of Torga to talk with as many people as possible. You will be planetside for a full year.

"We will have one pick up of interested individuals every three months until we leave, which Emperor willing, will be in about a year. I am working to extend the visas, but there is no guarantee it will work. Due to the geography of Torga, we will be rotating your assignments at the end of each interim period. Individual reports have been sent to your mobiles for you to review that will cover your station, employment, and requirements. Any questions?" He paused--as much out of need as he did for their benefit. He shifted his jaw and felt the pops at the joints.

"Aren't some of the leaders a little young?" Naomi asked, glancing at Kelly.

"We pooled the best from whoever was interested, regardless of age or circumstance."

"But it just seems a little irresponsible to send a fifteen-year-old girl planetside." Naomi retorted.

"I can understand your concern. But I didn't make the choices I did without consideration. Do you have any particular ideas for replacements?"

Naomi hesitated. "No, sir."

"Your concern is noted, but we must do what we have to. Any other questions?"

Reading no more concern from the pairs, he dismissed them. He stood tall until the last one had left the room. When the door had shut behind them, he walked back to his chair, using the desk to prop himself up.

His hand shook as he took another sip of the tea and sent a prayer to the Capital, hoping he had made the right choices. Things were about to get very different for everyone. He closed his eyes and his vision flooded his mind.

The familiar sights and sounds came back to him easily. The soft rush of wind through the trees. The murmuring of the river quietly stirring in its bed. The young man who sat with a simple rod in his hand and his feet in the water. Glenn walked up beside him and put his own feet in. Goosebumps appeared and he shivered slightly as the cool water soothed his aching feet.

"It will be hard," the young man said.

Glenn stayed silent and enjoyed the rays of sun on his back.

"Sadly, many will die. You have been given the burden of preserving those who must carry on. Can you do it?"

"Yes," Glenn said, his voice young and vibrant.

"For what it is worth, I am sorry to put you through this. However, there will be a great awakening because of it."

"Could you stop it?" His younger voice asked. It was a foolish question of course, but he had asked anyways.

"Of course." The young man looked pained for a moment, then smiled. "But I need you to trust me. This is the best way. Those on the ship who know me already, I will embrace. Those who do not, are poisoning the rest. They have all heard and made their choice."

Glenn sat in silence again for a moment. "Thank you." He still wasn't sure why he had said his thanks, but he had.

The young man placed a hand on Glenn's knee. "You cannot tell anyone what will happen to the ship. I am telling you because you must know. Not even your daughter."

He stared, wide eyed, at the young man. His mind had been full of doubt. With everything that he had been through, and had done, the thought of every marrying someone had never crossed his mind. Pictures had shot across his mind, different women of various ages, as he had tried to picture what his daughter would look like. He never would have been able to guess how beautiful his daughter would really be.

"You will, and you will name her Catherine, for she will be pure in a sea of darkness."

"Is there anything else?"

"Yes. I need you to know that no matter how hard things get for you I will be with you. I am all that you need. You need to make sure your daughter knows me. Lead her to me when the time comes."

"I will."

"Good bye, Glenn," the young man said, "I will see you soon."

The memory faded and Glenn opened his eyes; according to the clock, he'd been lost in his mind for close to two hours. It'd only seemed like minutes. Heaving a sigh, Glenn drank the last of his tea, grimacing as the now-cold liquid hit his taste buds, then dialed the phone.

"This is operations, Heather speaking." The voice was stressed, fake happiness trying to overcome frustration.

"Heather, this is Captain Glenn Denner. Have you finished your sweep of the ship for any irregular electrical impulses?"

Heather didn't respond.

"I repeat, have you finished the sweep?"

"I'm sorry sir, but no. We are still on the third floor, sweeping the rooms."

"What is the estimated time of completion?"

He could almost hear the panic in her breathing and cut her off before she could find an excuse. "Just try to get it done please, as fast as you can."

"Yes, sir!" He hung up and spun his chair to face New-Space. There was a chance this was the time he had seen in his vision, but just in case, he was going to do everything in his power to stop Dagor from getting his way.

*Maybe I should check the jump ships, just in case.* He glanced around the office, then pulled out a small leather pouch from his jacket pocket. Then, from his desk, pulled out his spiced tea, and a bottle of water. He poured the powder into his tea mug, followed by the tea leaves, and water. The water boiled instantly as it touched the white powder, helping the tea leaves to steep. He took a sip and felt the familiar warmth spread throughout his body. The aches and pains subsided ever so slightly and Glenn reclined in his seat.

Pulling out one of his drawers, he took out a large tablet and set it on his desk. As it turned on, it displayed the results from his last physical. Angela had been shocked at the deterioration she had seen, but Glenn had known it would happen sooner or later. He began cracking his knuckles as he read through the report, feeling the metal plates attached to each bone. You could only do so much to the human body before it started to reject things. Angela wanted to try surgery, just like the doctors before her had, but it never worked. It was always easier to fuse things together than rip them apart. He sighed and shut off the tablet, tossing it in the drawer and went to shut it. A brief flash of light reflecting off something inside hit his face and he paused, taking out a small box hidden at the back of the drawer.

It fit easily in his palm, and he fingered the worn velvet coating that covered it. Catherine deserved to have it. Especially if anything were to happen to him. He placed the box in his pocket and drank the rest of his tea. With a last glance towards New-Space, he headed out the door.

# CHAPTER TWENTY-SEVEN

Terran rushed through his room, shoving the last few items he needed into the backpack he had been given for the trip. He could remember every formula he had ever learned, but somehow always seemed to forget something when he was headed on a trip.

Even as a child, he had been forgetful in this one small way. His father had always chided him gently about it while wearing his lopsided grin. Terran paused in the middle of the room. When was the last time he had a pleasant thought about his father? He tried thinking back, but gave up. It didn't matter, the man was gone and they all had new lives. Well, except for Mother.

A small ping came from his pocket taking him away from his reverie--a message from Catherine telling him to hurry up. He smiled and texted her he was on his way. They were actually going planetside. His heart began beating faster. He had been rather uncomfortable in the Captain's office with everyone else there. Even more so when Kelly had shown up with some random guy he had never met. *Derek, that was his name.* He would have to talk to Kelly about that later.

If only Anna had chosen to go down with them planetside, it could have been a family vacation of sorts. He knew that Operations would be her best fit, but he was still going to miss seeing her. Of course, he was going to be partnered with Catherine, so that was something to look forward to. They had reconciled since their last argument and Terran knew he was finally beginning to understand what it meant to pursue the Capital.

Zipping up the pack, he slung it over his shoulder and left the room, heading to the cargo hold. The thought of being on the Gungir again caused an influx of emotions. On the one hand, it would be exciting to head back onto the planet, but on the other hand he had almost died the last time he was on the ship.

He made it to the elevator and pressed the button to head down to the cargo hold. He tried to keep his breathing calm as the elevator descended. *I'm going to be fine. No one is going to stick me with any types of needles. Just stay calm and try to relax.* The elevator dinged and the doors opened, revealing Catherine standing with a broad grin on her face.

"Hey, you ready?"

"Yep." Terran replied as the tension left his shoulders. This time would be very different. He smiled and reached for her hand. In a few short minutes, they passed the U-shaped rows of supplies and arrived at a wide steel door.

Catherine input a number into the keypad to the side of the door and it opened, revealing a room larger than the first. The bay for the ships was rectangular and held four ships of the same style as the Gungir. Terran stared at them with his mouth open. They were beautiful. Each one the same crimson sheen as before, seeming to burn before his eyes. The same fierce lion was emblazoned on the front, roaring in defiance at some imaginary foe. Terran could almost hear them.

He looked to see Catherine's reaction to the ship, but was dismayed to find her looking at her tablet.

"You know, you can really kill a mood," he teased.

"Well, I grew up around these ships, so there's that." She said without looking up. "Besides, one of us has to understand Torgal culture and the appropriate things to do."

"Rictor doesn't seem to care too much about those things." Terran said as they continued walking to one of the ships.

"Well, we can't all be Rictor now, can we?" She winked at him and entered the hangar.

They walked in silence to the second ship on the left and were about to walk in when Terran heard Kelly yelling from across the room.

She was running toward him wearing her brand-new Voice uniform, and threw her arms around him in a bear hug before he could ask her what was wrong. They stayed silent for a moment, then pulled away.

"I just wanted to say bye is all," Kelly said, forcing a smile.

"Well, you chose a grand way to do it." Terran said hugging her again. "Don't worry, everything is going to be ok."

"I know." She sighed. "I just can't stand the thought of losing you again, and then I couldn't stop thinking about what happened the last time you were on a ship like this, and then I basically started having a panic attack and had to see you."

Terran kissed her on the top of her head. "I will be fine, Kelly. Catherine is here, and circumstances are quite a bit different from before."

"I know, just tell me you will be okay. I need to hear you say that we will see each other again."

"I will be okay and we will see each other again," he mimicked. "Now, go back to your ship and brief yourself on the details of Torga. It will keep your mind off me."

She smiled and turned to leave then turned back and gave him another brief hug. She left him on the boarding platform and walked to her ship, but Terran had caught sight of tears as she turned away.

"Your sisters really look up to you." Catherine said from behind him.

"We're all pretty close." He was still staring at Kelly. *When did she grow up?* He remembered her as the small girl that barely stood up to his waist. Now here she was, scared for him. Wasn't it supposed to be the other way around?

Without talking, Terran and Catherine made their way through the back of the ship. They walked through a small cargo hold filled with various boxes of supplies, into the small medical section, where the restraining chairs were located, then they walked through the empty passenger compartments, until they finally reached the bridge.

"Is it really just us going?" Terran asked as he surveyed the small room. The front of the Gungir was visible through the large panel of reinforced glass. Small workstations lined the walls around a central chair in front of a monitor. Two small seats lined the wall to the right of the door.

"Yes," A rough voice said behind them. Terran jumped, not expecting to hear Glenn's voice. "Terran, I need to talk with you for a second, if you don't mind."

Terran followed Glenn back through the door into the passenger cabin. Catherine dutifully stayed behind and sat in the central chair. The monitor flickered on as the door closed.

"Terran," Glenn said in his usual soft tone.

Terran turned to look at him and was surprised to see a burning intensity in the man's eyes.

"I need you to promise me that you will look after my daughter and that you really did study those maps and understand them." The command came out barely as a soft growl.

Unable to find his voice, Terran nodded in agreement.

"That's not good enough, Terran. Look me in the eyes and give me your word."

"Yes," Terran squeaked, wanting desperately to look away from Glenn's eyes, but unable to tear his gaze away.

"Good." Glenn smiled, and suddenly the intensity was gone. He was his usual self, standing tall and firm like a mountain. "Take this and give it to Catherine when you land. It is important." Glenn handed over a small box.

Terran took it and stood motionless, unsure of what to do.

"You need to remember," Glenn said over his shoulder as he began to turn away. "We were both given a gift. It will be hard to understand for now, but trust in the Emperor's son. See you soon."

As the giant of a man walked away, Terran felt a distinct sense of sadness. As if he wasn't sure he would be seeing Glenn again. Shaking the thought from his mind, he walked back into the cockpit, tucking the box into his pocket. Catherine had already booted up the ship's main computer, and diagnostics covered the window as the ship powered up.

"Well, are we ready then?" he asked, fingering the box in his pocket. It was small and covered in a soft fabric, maybe velvet.

"Yes sir." She gave him a halfhearted salute. "We will be lifting off in fifteen minutes, which means we should buckle in."

They made their way to the small seats on the side of the room and sat down. Their hands intertwined and Terran knew he should be feeling something else. He should be elated. He should be ecstatic that he was about to visit another world. Yet, between Kelly and Glenn, the only feeling left inside of him was one of dread. Something was wrong.

# CHAPTER TWENTY-EIGHT

Naomi and Rictor were both in their seats when Glenn walked into the cockpit. He loomed over them, his face expressionless.

"I know what you are planning to do." He said looking directly at Naomi.

"Glenn, we already..." Rictor was cut off as Glenn held up his hand.

"I need you two on the ground. I advise against your plan to kill Dagor. He is just a pawn in the grand scheme of things. Focus on what the Emperor has taught us and stay true to him. Our lives are not about revenge or providing justice. Our lives are for the Emperor alone."

"Glenn, we have talked about this before. For the sake of the people of the Bound--" Rictor started.

"Rictor--" Glenn interrupted, but Rictor kept talking.

"--We need to take him out. How many people have Promioth's envoys killed? How many people won't reach the capital because we were too scared, too hurt, too weak to stop them. For once, we are going to fight back. I will not stand by and watch innocent people die."

Glenn looked square at Rictor, and Naomi thought she could see tears in his eyes.

"I am sorry, friend, but it seems I have failed in the friendship I have treasured most." Glenn said. Tears began running down his cheeks. "I hope that one day, you will find the first love you had for the Capital."

Naomi avoided looking at Glenn completely. He waited for a moment, then left the cockpit.

A silence hung between the two of them as the ships started to whir, then slowly began lifting off the floor of the cargo hold. Naomi closed her eyes and tried to push away what Glenn had said from her mind. The sides of the cargo bay opened and each ship slipped out the Lion's Roar into the blackness of space. The onboard computers quietly adjust the angles of reentry so that each ship would land on the correct set of rails.

"How dare he say that to us," Naomi declared. A fierce anger suddenly welling up inside her. "Who does he think he is? He doesn't know us. What right does he have to look down on us so much? And don't you dare say some smart-aleck remark, Rictor." Rictor closed his mouth and leaned his head back against the wall instead.

"Dagor has put both of us through so much pain and trouble. He has hurt so many people it's unbearable. He deserves to die." Naomi crossed her arms, finished with her rant.

"There might be another way." Rictor said quietly. "Maybe we could imprison him or get Torga to put him away."

"No," Naomi said sharply. "The plan is already set in motion. We won't have the resources to take him hostage. Death is the only way."

Rictor shut his eyes and didn't reply. Naomi rested her head as well and tried to sleep. It probably wouldn't work. She hadn't really slept at all for the past few days. Images of the Nathaniel-impersonator kept appearing in her mind. Dagor had threatened everything she held dear in her life. She would make him pay.

The ship landed with a soft thud and decelerated at what would have been an alarming pace if Rictor had not been expecting it. Of course, it would have been disastrous without the ship's shield dampeners weakening the forces on the ship. When it had finally stopped, he and Naomi made their way to the small cargo hold and began getting ready for their meeting with Dagor. The preparations were quick. Rictor equipped himself with a small pistol and a small saber. The blade could be turned on and off so all Rictor needed was to keep the small handle hidden. It was a bit old fashioned, weapon-wise, but in a close-quarters fight it could prove useful.

Naomi went ahead and sent the message to Dagor saying they would be ready to meet up and then got the rider ready. It was a simple hover craft that seated up to six people, plus some cargo. It was meant more as a loading utility than an actual vehicle, but it would work.

They fully lowered the end of the cargo bay revealing the desert planet, Torga. Bright sunlight reflected off sand that stretched out for miles in every direction causing heat waves to distort their vision.

Naomi pulled up the map that Dagor had sent to her tablet and they both got into the rider and began making their way toward the meeting point. An uneasy feeling began growing in the pit of Rictor's stomach, but he knew it was too late to stop.

They rode in silence across the desert. They didn't see one living soul. Of course, the whole population of the planet lived underground, but Rictor thought there might have been cactus or something to mark the landscape. Instead there were sand dunes, sand dunes, and more sand dunes. Without the map, it would have been almost impossible to find their way. As it was, the map guided them easily enough and they had no difficulty reaching the meeting spot.

It was one of the few landmark locations on the planet. They parked next to the edge of a chasm that spanned for miles in either direction. About thirty feet wide, the chasm released a steady stream of warm air that caused the sand to dance and swirl in eddies around the edges. Naomi's tablet pinged and the message from Dagor told them he would be there near sunset.

"Are you ready?" Rictor asked.

"Yes," she seemed confident, but Rictor heard the subtle tremor in her voice.

"It will change you." He said softly.

"What?"

"Killing a man. It changes you. The first time I killed someone, I took showers every other hour or so for the next two days. I just kept imagining his blood was still on me."

Naomi stayed silently. "Why did you kill him?"

"I was told to by the scientists. They put another man in my cell for a time. Then without warning they stopped giving us food. They told us that we could only get food if one of us killed the other. He attacked me on the forty-second day in my sleep. I woke to him choking me and I threw him off me. His head hit a bedside table and cracked open. The scientists just watched him bleed out. I tried to help him, but I couldn't do anything."

"There is a difference, Rictor," Naomi said from underneath the canopy. "You felt guilty because you didn't intend to kill. I do plan on killing Dagor and I doubt I will feel any amount of guilt."

Rictor sighed, and turned away from her. She was so full of hatred. Maybe it would be better when he was out of the picture. Or maybe she would fall apart without a purpose. Rictor had a feeling it would be the latter.

"We should rest while we can," he said. "And don't forget to stay hydrated."

He closed his eyes and tried to feign sleeping, but the warm sun and the unfamiliar weight of gravity caused him to drift off slowly without even knowing.

*His heart was racing. Blood covered him. He stared at his hands and then at the bodies lying all around him in the narrow corridor. White lab coats stained red, bodies broken and twisted, and she was there. On the other side of the bodies, looking at him like a monster. Had she screamed? It didn't matter, she did now. She ran back down the hall, and he let her. He looked back at the bodies, a grin spreading over his face. He was free.*

# CHAPTER TWENTY-NINE

Rictor awoke to a loud whining in the distance. Naomi was asleep on his shoulder, and he shook her awake as he scanned for the source of the sound.

The sun had traveled most of the way across the sky and was beginning to set behind the horizon. Red and orange hues danced across the sand, turning it into a patchwork of color. Rictor paid the beautiful display no attention, instead focusing on trying to find where the whining was coming from.

Finally, he spotted a small shadow zooming toward them across the sand dunes. He grabbed a pair of binoculars and looked again. The shadow was comprised of two riders, each one with the symbol of a lion on the front of their hulls.

Pulling out his mobile, Rictor found multiple messages from both Kelly and Terran asking him to check in. Had he forgotten to send the confirmation message?

"What's that noise?" Naomi asked, getting up from the air rider and stretching out her back.

"It's the other teams headed toward us to make sure we are okay," he said, turning and kicking the air rider. "How did we forget to send a confirmation message?"

There was a pause as what he said went through Naomi's mind. She spun around to look at him. "Rictor, this is bad. They can't be here when Dagor shows up. This is bad."

"Of course it's bad," Rictor said, struggling not to yell at her. "We need a plan. They will probably ask why we aren't anywhere near our rendezvous point for entry underground. What are we going to tell them?"

Naomi looked at him and drummed her fingers on the side of the air rider, then she smiled and dropped her tablet into the sand. She ground it in with her foot a few moments then picked it back up and tossed it into the rider. "You need to do the same to yours. We will tell them I was looking at both tablets, dropped them out of the rider and the maps got corrupted. We came here because it was the closest land mark. Then we get them to send us a new one, and we go on our merry way with them none the wiser. We call Dagor and tell him we need to meet tomorrow--simple."

Rictor looked at Naomi for a moment, then nodded. A simple plan was better than none.

Terran and Catherine stepped out of their rider, and Kelly and Derek did the same. They made their way to Rictor and Naomi, who sat on the side of their vehicle with the tablet between them.

"Everything OK?" Terran called to them as they grouped together.

"The map got corrupted and led us here. We thought we had sent a message to you, but apparently, it never sent. We were waiting for a reply when we accidentally fell asleep because the blistering heat and gravity." Rictor smiled unwavering at Terran as he responded.

"Ah, well, that's awkward." Terran said taking his tablet out and locating the map file, quickly sending it to their tablets again. "I thought we would have to search along the chasm for your bodies or something. Really thought something was wrong here."

"Everything's OK." Naomi said with a smile. "Just a simple but embarrassing mistake. A lesson to you younger teams that communication should never be assumed; always double check."

"Noted," Kelly said with a quick smile. "I'm just glad you guys are all right. I was super worried."

Catherine, Rictor noted, did not seem to completely buy in to the excuse. Her expression remained doubtful, though she didn't speak up.

"Well, let's get going," Terran said, turning toward her. "We have a lot of ground to cover, and if we plan on getting underground before the night chill comes, we will need to use up the battery getting to our entry point."

Catherine locked eyes with Rictor, and something about her gaze reminded him of her father. He looked away. It wasn't judgement that filled her eyes, it was pity.

"OK," she said, finally turning away.

"You might not want to leave just yet." An odd voice called out.

Rictor spun and looked all around, but couldn't find the source. That voice should not have been there. He wasn't supposed to be there.

The small group turned back toward Rictor and Naomi, and from behind them a sharp whine erupted from the chasm. Four medium sized vehicles flew into the air and settled softly in front of them, blocking their escape.

Dagor stood in the back of one of the squat vehicles behind a turret. Each of the four vehicles had one, and each one was pointed at the small group. Dagor had a large smile on his face.

"You thought you could outsmart me?" he laughed. "You two are idiots of the highest order. The rest of you are just blind fools."

"Dagor!" Naomi shouted. "The deal was a trade. I brought you Rictor; you promised me my son. Anyone else being here is just an honest misunderstanding."

"I decided I wanted them all," he scoffed. With a simple hand motion, he signaled toward the other vehicles and all four powered off. "You have been such a good pet, I have a gift for you. Do you see that little dot above us? Way up there, like a guardian angel?" Naomi glanced up and could see the dot darting across the sky. "Do you know what that is? That is your wonderful ship, the Lion's Roar."

A sinking feeling began growing in Rictor's stomach. He reached for his pistol, but one of Dagor's men caught sight of him and fired. Rictor fell to the ground with a yell and grabbed his shoulder. Blood poured onto the hot sand, and it sucked it up greedily. It had been a long time since he had been shot. He did not miss the feeling.

"Tsk, tsk," Dagor said with a smile. "It's impolite to interrupt. The gift I am giving you, Naomi, is one of absolution. I am freeing you from the bonds of a double life. Now you will be free to live the life you choose. If you survive tonight, you can do anything you want. I'll tell Nathan you said hello." As he finished the words, the small blip in the sky exploded.

A primal scream wrenched itself from Naomi and blended in with the screams from both Terran and Kelly. Rictor lay on the ground, stunned by what had just happened. Catherine stood still, her eyes were fixated on where, moments before, her home had been.

"You're welcome," Dagor said in a bored tone as he dusted off the arm to his jacket. "I want to thank you as well for providing the wiring for the bomb that was used. Without you, all those people would still be alive--and that would have caused problems."

Naomi couldn't contain herself any longer. She charged toward Dagor's rider. No shot was fired at her, raising a flag of suspicion in her mind, but she took the advantage anyway. As she reached Dagor's rider, she leapt onto the side and kicked out against Dagor. Her leg passed through him and she fell, momentum twisting in the air. She hit the far edge of the rider and began to slide off onto the sand, but her ankle caught the handrail that ran along the top of the vehicle--and with a sickening twist, she felt her ankle break. One of the passengers on the vehicle yanked her foot clear of the handrail and Naomi fell to the ground, moaning in agony.

Dagor's cruel laugh rang out through the night. "You stupid woman! Do you really think I would be here in person? You're a bigger fool than I thought. Blow up the riders and leave them to rot. By the way, your visas were revoked, so getting underground might be a problem. Have a nice night."

As the hologram cut off, the turrets opened fire on the group's air riders. Each rider wavered for an instant, then crashed to the ground as the engines were decimated by the barrage of bullets pounding into them.

As the turrets died down, Dagor's air riders simultaneously rose from the ground and drove away, leaving the group in the growing darkness. The temperature rapidly began to drop as the sun sank behind the far horizon, and with a growing fear Naomi realized they were going to die. She tried to stand on the sand, but her ankle buckled under her weight. She crashed to the ground as a sharp pain shot up her leg. With no other option, she began crawling back to the others, letting out soft whimpers along the way.

"Please help me," she croaked.

Catherine turned toward her, and Naomi saw tears flowing freely down her face. On all their faces, tears were streaking down, disappearing into sand at their feet. In the gentle moonlight, their sobs echoed a silent dirge for those who had lost their lives.

"You did this," she said.

"I'm didn't mean..." Naomi whispered.

"You did this!" Catherine screamed.

"Yes," Naomi's voice cracked, barely audible.

Catherine picked a bloody gun up from the ground and leveled it at Naomi's chest.

"Please do it," Naomi said as her last strand of resolve broke. "All I have done is cause pain. Just end it now. Please. I want to die."

"Catherine, don't," Terran said from Rictor's side. He had a small med kit open and was attending the wound in Rictor's shoulder. Rictor was trying to push him away, assuring him that he was fine.

"Terran, she deserves it. Look what she did to us. She killed dad, and Anna, and everyone else I have cared about. She has lied to our faces since the day she arrived. She is a wolf in the fold, a rabid dog to be put down before someone else gets hurt."

"It won't bring your father back," Terran said softly as he sterilized a needle and began to inject Rictor with a small syringe.

Catherine turned toward Terran and her rage focused fully toward him. He had barely enough time to look back toward her as she sprang on him. They fell back and Catherine began pounding on his chest. Tears fell onto him as each fist made contact. Terran caught her arms and sat up, still holding her. She struggled against him, then put her face on his neck and gave in to distress. They held on to each other, Naomi forgotten.

Kelly was sitting by the man who had accompanied her. He was lying face down on the sand. A stray bullet had pierced his skull and the sand around him was stained red. Kelly was staring at her hands, covered in his blood. She had stopped crying and seemed to be in shock.

"So much blood," she said, "so much blood." She repeated the words, rocking gently, seemingly unaware of the world around her.

A soft moan escaped from Rictor's mouth and Naomi pulled herself to him. His eyes flickered open as she lay beside him.

"That did not turn out how it should have," he groaned.

"No, it did not," she said trying to think of a way to elevate her ankle.

"Do you think he actually blew up the ship?"

"Most likely, the ship was where it should have been for this time of day."

The sun finished its descent, covering them in darkness. No moon broke the horizon, leaving them in the darkness with only the faint light of stars to see by. A coldness grew over Naomi and she knew if she slept she wouldn't last the night. She closed her eyes anyway and wished for the night to swallow her.

⸻ ❦ ⸻

She awoke to a warm ray of sun hitting her face. Terran and the rest of the group lay asleep under thermal blankets. Naomi found one over her as well. The smell of smoke attacked her already dry mouth. Sitting up, she saw a man sitting on a small metal stool around a fire with green flames that seemed to come out of a bed of glass cubes.

She yelped, then covered her mouth. The man turned towards her and smiled, motioning for her to join him by the fire on one of the other stools that lined around it. She limped over and sat on a stool. As she drew closer to the flame, the smell of roasting meat made her mouth water. A small rodent was skewered on a metal rod that was rotating itself above the fire.

She stared at the man and struggled agains the pit forming in her stomach. There was something familiar about him, and it set her on edge. If only she could place it.

A small grunt caused them both to turn. Terran sat up, rubbing sleep from his eyes. He glanced toward the fire and his eyes grew wide.

"Dad?"

"Hello son," The man replied. "Quite a mess you've put yourself in."

# CHAPTER THIRTY

The last remaining members of the Lion's Roar sat around the small fire, picking at the strips of meat that Terran's father had cooked for them. Terran stared at him, eyes narrowed to slits. Fist clenching and unclenching, he rose and opened his mouth to speak, then sat back down. Where to begin?  He ran his hands through his hair. The other members remained silent, sending sideways glances at him, concern on their faces. He got up and took a step toward his father but choked on his words again and sat down. He tried to breathe, but he couldn't focus over the sound of his heart beating. Too fast. A thousand questions ran through his mind and tried to force themselves out of his mouth at the same time. He swallowed, trying to get something, anything out.  His father just stared at him. His face calm and steady.

He hadn't changed much since Terran had seen him last. His prominent features were made even more so in the harsh sunlight. He wasn't wearing a

Capital Bound uniform; instead, he wore a light jacket over a gray t-shirt and a pair of jeans. He was getting wrinkles around his mouth and eyes and his dark hair was peppered with gray, revealing his age.

"What are you even doing here?" Terran forced the words out in a growl.

"I came to help, Terran," he replied gesturing toward the meat.

"Oh, you brought us some meat and blankets," Terran shot back. "That makes abandoning your entire family totally OK. It might have been on the line if you had only brought one or the other, but you brought both so I actually feel indebted to you."

"Terran..." Kelly began.

"No," Terran cut in. "Don't you dare defend him right now. Do you know what I have had to do because you left? Do you know what I sacrificed? You forced a twelve-year-old boy to become the head of family. I wish I could just punch you right in that smug face of yours."

Terran's father hung his head as his son berated him. "Terran, leaving was the hardest decision I have ever made in my life, but I am not going to defend myself to you. I thought you had been provided for. I left you everything."

Terran paused for moment and tried to push the anger away, but it came roaring back. "You left us with nothing." He hissed.

"Terran, I can't change the past, but I am here to help you now. Deep down, you know I'm your best shot. Let's move on towards surviving our current situation. If you want to punch me or fight me or even kill me when this is done, then fine, but for now, let's take care of what we need to survive." His father replied, voice even. "From what you have told me, you have lost your main interplanetary vessel, but still retain your jump ships. That's gives us a little good news amidst a lot of bad. We can take my craft and load it with some supplies that would benefit one of the Pods. Once we are underground it will be a lot easier to find Dagor's work station and then we can get back to doing the Emperor's work on this planet and the ones to come."

"Wait, you mean you have an interplanetary ship?" Kelly asked, as she bit into a large chunk of meat.

"Long story short, I have been here about a year and half searching through the Pods looking for Dagor's work station. There are only two out of the eight left, so there is a fifty-fifty chance it will be in the Pod we are headed to."

"I have a question of particular importance." Rictor said suddenly, causing Kelly to literally jump from her seat and turn around. He was standing upright, no sign of the bullet wound evident. Naomi was folding up the thermal blanket beside him. She tapped his leg when she finished and he helped her to her feet.

"How are you not dead?" Kelly asked.

"It's rude to interrupt, dear," Rictor replied to Kelly with a grin before turning to face Terran's father. "What's your name?"

"Peter," he answered.

"That's not your name," Terran called out.

"It is the name I go by now," his father replied in a neutral tone.

Terran felt like throwing a rock at him--to lash out in some way. He scanned the area around him and caught site of Catherine. Her eyes were still puffy from the night before. She hadn't eaten or said a word all morning. Terran's frustrations diminished as he looked at her. Here he was throwing a tantrum because his father was alive, and Catherine had just lost hers. Terran sat down and put his arm around Catherine's shoulders. At first there wasn't a response, but soon she relaxed, leaning onto him.

"How are we getting to the underground Pod?"

"The rider I have can seat six comfortably," Peter said. "The supplies we trade for your entry will need to be small, but valuable."

"We have some medicines that would probably be of use," Naomi said, limping besides Rictor as they made their way to the two empty seats left.

"We aren't taking her," Catherine said staring daggers at Naomi.

"I didn't kill your father, Catherine; Dagor did."

"You provided the wire for the bomb, didn't you? You stupid, selfish woman. Was your son worth more than the lives of everyone on that ship? I can't even fathom how you would justify your actions in your mind. You are responsible for their deaths, Naomi; I will never let you forget it." Catherine was breathing heavily when she finished.

Silence settled over the group.

"Is there something I should know about?" Peter asked.

"Dagor had my son under threat of torture and forced me to slightly sabotage the ship at times. The repairs were usually pretty quick, and no one ever got hurt, at least not until Terran. One of his requests was for me to get him some wire. He apparently got someone to build him a bomb."

Everyone's eyes snapped to Naomi at the mention of Terran's name.

"I knew it," Catherine shouted. "Someone tell me we aren't going to work with this snake? All she does is spew venom from her mouth, infecting the people around her. We can't take her with us."

"We need her expertise," Peter said. "In fact, I need each and every one of you- no exceptions. The Emperor's son has called us to this time and this place. We are going to band together and get through it. I don't care if you don't like each other, you are going to work together. Is that understood?"

"Why?" Terran asked. "Why should we listen to you?"

"Because Ekundayo sent me," Peter said with a smile.

"How do you know that name?" Terran asked, eyes growing wide.

"He told it to me," Peter replied. "There is a lot we need to talk about, Terran."

"Who is Ekundayo?" Kelly asked. "Is that like some super important person only known to you two?"

"I hope not, Kel." Peter said smiling at her. "Ekundayo is one of the names for the Emperor's son. It happens to be the one that he told Terran during his vision."

"How do you know about that?" Terran asked.

"We should get going, Terran. We can head to your jump ship and pick up the medicine and I will explain some things to you along the way."

Terran hesitated for the briefest moment before giving his father a quick nod. "Where is your rider?"

Peter smiled and pulled out a small phone from his pocket. After tapping on the screen for a few seconds, the rider materialized a short distance from the group.

"Did you just teleport that from your ship?" Kelly asked, eyes wide. "That's awesome."

"Sorry, Kel, it wasn't teleportation. It was actually cloaked." He gave her a wink. "Let's head out, Terran."

"Don't murder anyone when I am gone," Terran whispered to Catherine as he kissed her on the check.

"No promises," she grunted.

Terran stepped into the rider and sat next to his father who passed him a pair of goggles.

"This is an older model. It doesn't have the same force fields that your models had. Wear these to protect your eyes from the sand and sun."

As the rider lifted off the ground, Terran spared one last glance back at the group of survivors they were leaving behind. Hopefully, they would all still be there when he got back.

# CHAPTER THIRTY-ONE

Rictor watched as Terran sped off with his father and then turned to Kelly and Catherine, "So, that was a bit awkward."

"How can you be so calm next to that killer?" Catherine asked.

"Catherine, this is not a good channel for the pain you're feeling right now," Rictor said stepping toward her.

"And you, how in the world did you heal so fast? You should be dead. What are you, some kind of robot?"

"Something like that." Rictor said, his smile flickering for just an instant. "Seriously Catherine, stop. I knew your father longer than you have been alive. You don't think I'm grieving? You don't think I have that same rage and anger burning inside of me? Naomi is not the right target for that pain you are feeling. She was being used. Dagor is the enemy. Glenn will have justice when we take Dagor out. Heck, even Terran's dad seemed on board with taking out Dagor."

"I wonder how he found us," Naomi asked. Sitting on a stool, she extended her leg and gritted her teeth through the pain.

"If he was looking for Dagor, he probably followed him here," Kelly said, kneeling beside Naomi and gingerly lifting her leg to inspect her foot.

Rictor watched, impressed, as Kelly began to take off Naomi's shoe and dress her ankle.

"When did you pick that up?" Naomi asked, grateful for the help.

"Well, while everyone else was apparently plotting against each other, I spent my off time taking emergency first aid classes. I got through most of them and earned a few certificates, but not enough to be part of the medical team. I don't like blood." She talked as her hands expertly wrapped a gauze bandage around Naomi's foot. Then taking a small rectangular device out of her side bag she affixed it to the bandages. The bandages seemed to swell then meld together, forming a hard cast. Naomi's face visibly relaxed after it was done.

"Thank you," Naomi said softly.

"It will take a while before it actually helps fix your foot, but should help to prevent any more damage," Kelly said. "I am going to look through the other cars' emergency aid kits and pick up what is left. We don't know what kind of facilities these pods will have."

Rictor sat next to Naomi and put his hand in hers. She didn't pull away. They had all been through so much, and it was Kelly, the youngest among them, who seemed to be the most at ease. Maybe it was a coping mechanism, but Rictor could see that she had moved past the shock, somehow pushing herself through what had just happened.

"Are you two really an item?" Catherine asked from across the fire.

Neither replied to her. Rictor looked at Naomi, and she averted her eyes.

"It's complicated." he said.

"So, what was your plan after you killed Dagor anyway? Were you two going to just live here on Torga?"

"Something like that," Rictor said, finally looking at Catherine.

She looked like a mess. Her usual composure shattered, she had a glazed look in her eyes.

"You should have told us the plan." Catherine said.

While she might not have gotten her looks from her father, she had his intensity. Rictor found it hard to meet her gaze.

"Why?" he shrugged. "We would have just spent more time deciding if we would act at all, rather than actual planning."

"You both missed so much," Catherine said, shifting her focus back to the eerie fire.

"Excuse me?" Naomi said, a little put off. "What did we miss?"

"Well for starters, the fact that the other Envoys would probably hunt you down for the rest of your lives. Second, Torga would probably throw you out the first chance they got. Third, you would most likely have put the rest of us in danger. If you had talked with the rest of us we could have helped--somehow."

"We see that now," Rictor said. "What we need to do is focus on how we are going to proceed. The past is the past; we need to move on."

"First things first," Catherine said. "We need to be honest with each other. I need to know more about you two. There has been a lot of cloak and dagger going on, and if I am going to trust you I need to have a reason to. I'll update Terran when he gets back."

"Well, ask away," Naomi said trying hard to fight the pain still throbbing in her foot.

"Ric, how did you heal so quickly? Really? I know you and my father trained together and we both know what he was capable of. I assume you have some sort of enhancement like him?"

"Not quite like him. Your father had a lot of physical enhancements, carbon threading in his muscles and the such. Mine is all nanos." Rictor replied. "I was injected with them when I was young."

"Naomi, how long have you been working for Dagor?"

"He reached out to me and acted like a Voice for the Capital, so I guess ever since I got on the ship and he told me he kidnapped my son."

"Do either of you even believe anymore?"

"Yes," Rictor said. "I never stopped."

"I don't think I ever started to," Naomi said. "For me this was about personal revenge, not some grand crusade."

Kelly came back and sat beside them. Her side bag filled with salvage from the riders. "I have a question as well."

"What?" Rictor asked.

"What are we going to do about Derek?" Her voice quivered as she said it, and the rest of the group turned and looked at the dead body lying in the desert.

"Burn him," Rictor said. "It's a custom here on Torga since they don't really want their dead underground with them."

"Should we do it now?" Kelly asked.

"Probably," Rictor replied.

They spent the next hour building a make-shift pyre for the body. It consisted mostly of scraps from the riders and what flammables they had with them.

"Should we say something?" Kelly asked staring at the body lying in front of her.

"Only if you think so," Rictor said putting a comforting arm around her shoulders.

"Derek was a good man," Kelly began. "We didn't know each other well, but the Captain chose him to come with us and that has to mean something. When we got on the jump ship, he had a small bag of candy that he gave me. He said it was a welcoming gift. He really believed in all of this and gave his life for it. We can only aspire to do the same. To hold onto our belief until the point of death." Tears began to stream down Kelly's face. "This pyre is not just for Derek, but for everyone who died on the Lion's Roar. For Anna and the Captain. For the people who wanted to make these worlds' better places and to shine a light in the darkness."

She tossed a few of the glass cubes onto the pyre using a piece of scrap metal and it caught fire, engulfing the small structure.

"This fire represents the passing of those dear to us and as a message to Dagor. We are burning away our past lives so we can focus on a goal that will save the lives of the people who come after us."

"To burn Dagor to the ground," Catherine's voice cut in.

"To burn Dagor to the ground," Naomi replied.

Rictor stared at the women from across the pyre. *All of this because I couldn't send a simple message.*

# CHAPTER THIRTY-TWO

Terran sat in silence as his father drove the rider to Rictor and Naomi's jump ship. A part of him was excited to see his father. It made sense it had been the Capital that had stolen him away. He should have seen it earlier, but there were pieces that still didn't connect. What happened to the money? Just because his father had left did not mean all his money should have disappeared.

The jump ship appeared from behind a large sand dune and his father slowed the rider as they approached it. The weak shield around the rider prevented the small sand particles from breaking through, but it was still hard to speak over the whine of the engine. His father cut off the engine and the rider settled onto the sand below.

"Did you ever miss us?" Terran asked as he took off the large goggles.

"Every day," he said. "I never thought I would see you again. It was the hardest part of being one of the Bound. I knew I would miss so much of your lives; your graduations, your weddings, your kids. I would miss everything that a father dreams of for his children. But how could I say no to Ekundayo?"

"Why did you take your money with you? Do you realize how hard that made our lives? I never even finished school." There was no shouting between them, just soft words.

"I left everything to all of you. I didn't take a dime with me. I'm afraid someone from the bank probably took it. Corruption was always a large problem on Sisera."

"Why did you change your name?" Terran asked.

"The ship I joined had the requirement that we receive a new name. A symbol of putting our lives behind. Peter was chosen for me. I have been called Peter for so long now, it's just my first response when people ask."

A different silence filled the void between them. It was getting harder to justify all his anger, but it didn't just want to leave. It wanted to fester and build. He just needed a new target. That one was easy enough, Dagor would fit in nicely. But, what would happen when Dagor was gone, would it just disappear or look for someone else?

"So, now what? Don't take this the wrong way, but calling you dad is a little weird for me now."

"I understand. You're a man now, so that is how we should proceed. Call me Peter and I will call you Terran."

"OK," Terran said. "Well, let's get this done. Hopefully, the others aren't fighting too much while we are gone."

"Kelly has grown so much," Peter said before Terran could get out of the car. "I wasn't expecting how hard it would be to see you all, and to hear that Anna is..."

Terran was surprised to see that tears had formed in his father's eyes. The man sitting next to him looked so different from the father he remembered. On Sisera, his father had been neat and clean. He had worn a pressed suit every day to work. His hair had always been neatly trimmed, even his fingernails had been immaculate. That last detail had always stuck out to him.

The man in front of him was far removed from that memory. His shaggy hair hung around a face with light tan lines where goggles would rest. Shallow wrinkles were evident around his eyes and forehead, and his hands were dirty. Terran smiled as he realized that the fingernails themselves were still pristine--not quite as trimmed and neat, but clean. Maybe he wasn't so different after all.

"Hey, we're Capital Bound, remember? We will see Anna eventually, and we have plenty of time to catch up. Also, Kelly never gave up on you, neither did mom or Anna. Really it was just me who was angry."

"Will you forgive me?" He gaze was concerned.

"Yeah, in time. I just need to get my feelings sorted out."

"Well then, let's get the last of the supplies and, if possible, another rider. The more supplies the better."

They both got out and walked to the jump ship. *I wonder if they are all named Gungir.* He would have to ask Rictor or Catherine. He pushed in the pass code on the back of the jump ship and the cargo bay door opened. Terran peaked inside and froze. On the other jump ships, there had been lots of medical supplies, food stuffs, and some light vehicles, but they hadn't really been filled. This jump ship was filled to the brim. Long metal crates lined both sides of the hold with their contents stenciled on their sides. The containers held everything from food and medicine, to precious metals to weapons. There were two additional riders sitting in the middle of the ship.

"What in the world..." Peter said, eyes wide. "What in the world were they planning?"

"I am guessing we should go ask them," Terran replied. "Let's focus on getting the needed supplies. We can decide as a group what we will do with the rest later."

"My thoughts exactly," Peter smiled at him and grabbed a box to head out.

Terran found himself smiling as they loaded Peter's rider the rest of the way and started in on one of the spares. Even with all the trouble that had happened, at least there was some good left. One particular box stood out to Terran, and he made sure to load it onto his rider.

When they had finished loading the supplies, Terran stepped over to the side panel and changed the locking sequence.

"What are you doing that for?" Peter asked.

"I was thinking that if Dagor really had infiltrated the ship to the extent I believe he did, then he probably has access to our passwords and tablets as well. So, changing the password is easy enough. And we have replacements for the tablets."

"You do?" Peter asked.

Terran pointed to the small box he had loaded onto his rider. "That's a box of mobile phones. It will take some guessing to get them to work on this planet's network, but we should be able to figure something out. One of us is bound to know something about electronics."

Peter smiled at him and got into his rider. "You have grown into a real man, Terran. It will be an honor serving beside you."

Terran got into his own rider, uncomfortable with the praise. As happy as he was in this moment, the events of the last night still weighed on his heart. He should have seen that something was wrong. *I won't miss anything again. I will be sharper, smarter. I will keep us safe.*

They sped out toward the rest of the group over the sand dunes of Torga and Terran's mind wandered. Even with everything his father had told him, there were a few pieces missing from the puzzle. How had his father talked with Ekundayo? Had he had a vision as well? Did he have a crew? There was a lot Peter hadn't told them and before Terran fully trusted him, he would get his answers.

# CHAPTER THIRTY-THREE

The rest of the group were huddled underneath the canopy of Rictor's rider when Terran and Peter pulled up to the site. As Terran's rider settled on the ground they walked over to inspect everything he and Peter had picked up.

"What's up with the mobiles?" Rictor asked, picking up the small box.

"I figured if we switched to the backups, it would be harder for Dagor to see our messages."

"Smart."

"Someone has to be." Terran flashed a grin at Rictor, who seemed genuinely surprised at the comeback. "Why did you have all of the extra supplies loaded onto your jump ship?"

"You know why," Rictor said, distractedly looking at another box.

"I just need you to say it." Terran urged.

"Because I wasn't leaving Torga, and if we took the supplies, it would give us a buffer. Some nice padding before we could get situated."

Everyone looked at Rictor, who grinned sheepishly.

"Believe it or not, I am more than a pretty face."

"Regardless," Peter cut in, "it's irrelevant now. We need to focus on the task at hand. As much as the Envoys would like you to believe, they can't travel between planets. Each one has his own area to govern, either from the light or the shadows. We need to figure out how we are going to draw out Dagor and take care of him."

"Can we get out of the heat first?" Naomi's voice was weak and her face looked flushed. "It's starting to get to me, I think."

"Kelly, you and Catherine head out with Terran. I will take Naomi and Rictor. Understood?" Peter gave out the orders easily.

Surprisingly, everyone looked to him before moving. Terran gave a slight nod and everyone climbed into the respective riders. Peter handed out goggles to his group, and they headed out.

There were several distinct differences between the newer riders and the older models. The most substantial was the shield, which prevented sand and grit from getting in. The riders traveled around sixty miles an hour and that, combined with the high wind speeds, meant that the small particles could cause some substantial damage to the vehicles or their passengers. The shield also came with a noise dampener, which meant talking was possible.

"Well," Catherine said.

"Well, what?" Terran asked.

"What did you and your father talk about?" she asked.

"Yeah, did you find out why he left?" Kelly chimed in from the back.

"He left because he joined the Capital Bound. He left us a substantial sum, so he didn't understand that we had to live in the Outskirts on Sisera. Petty corruption was his guess. And don't call him my father. He lost that title years ago."

"You should be grateful yours came back," Catherine muttered.

Terran took a few deep breaths. He would have to be more careful with his words. At least for a little while.

"It's just weird for me," Terran continued. "He hasn't been a part of my life for a long time, and now he is. It's hard for me to separate my feelings for him. I am still struggling with hating what he did, even if I understand why."

Catherine reached over and held his hand. "I think all of us are trying to understand our feelings. We should probably take some time to sort through things when we get underground."

"I agree," Kelly said. "If we do anything now, it won't be for the right reasons. If we act out against Dagor, it needs to be for the right reasons."

"Is justice not a good reason?" Terran asked.

"I don't know, Terran." Kelly said flopping back onto the seat. "I am just as new to this as you. I just don't like the idea of killing people. I thought we were in the business of saving them."

Terran chewed on his lip, thinking about Kelly's words. There might be a way to not kill Dagor. Maybe they could find a prison to hold him. If he really was the string puller of an entire planet, it didn't seem like it would be an easy task.

"Some men have already chosen their side, Kelly." Catherine said, not turning to look at her. "Dagor has hurt so many people, he has attacked the Capital for so long. Do you really think a man like him could be redeemed?"

"I don't know, but if we start putting limits on the Emperor, how can we say we really believe he is who he says he is? Either we take him at his word, or we don't."

They rode the rest of the way in silence, following the rider in front of them dipping slowly over the sand dunes. Terran had the thought that it would probably feel like riding in a boat. He had never done it himself, but based off pictures he had seen had a good estimate of what to expect.

As they crested over a large dune, Terran jerked on the wheel of the rider to avoid crashing into Peter's, which was sitting on top of a large metal door leading into the earth. The door was made of two large interlocking half-circles. A constant stream of air seemed to shoot all around the doors preventing sand from being able to settle on them.

Terran was about to shout over to Peter when the doors began to slide apart, and a loading platform was revealed. Peter drove his rider to park in the middle of the platform, and Terran parked his beside it. The doors above them rumbled shut, casting them into blinding darkness.

Soft lights appeared all around the loading platform and with a soft creaking it began sinking further into the ground. The walls of the shaft seemed to be made of steel, but it was impossible to get a good look at them in the soft glow.

Peter's rider settled softly on the ground, and he walked over to Terran.

"Just let me do all the talking," Peter said in a soft voice. "I have dealt with these types before. They are untrusting of outsiders. The fact that I have been to other pods is bad enough. If they ask you anything, just act like you can't understand them."

"OK," Terran said hesitantly. That was an awful lot of trust to ask of someone, but he wasn't sure if they would be able to get in any other way.

"Relax," Peter said smiling for the first time and raising his voice. "We were lucky to escape from Pod Three, weren't we? I was sure our family would have been executed."

"Right," Terran said understanding the implication. No doubt the people from the pod were trying to listen in.

Peter walked back to his own rider, and all three of its occupants began laughing at something Rictor seemed to have said.

"I have a bad feeling about this, Terran," Catherine said, squeezing his hand.

"I know, but this is the only option we have. We just need to keep up our spirits, and we will be fine."

It was impossible to figure out exactly how slow they were moving, but the ride down the shaft seemed to take hours. As the time ticked away, Terran began drumming his fingers on the steering wheel. He opened his mouth to ask Catherine what she thought about Peter when there was a sharp jolt, and the lift stopped. The wall in front of their riders slid open, revealing a small loading area with several vehicles parked. While some of them had the same hovering capabilities as the riders, the vast majority had rubber tires on them.

"What was the tech level supposed to be here?" Terran asked Catherine as he turned on the rider to park it with the other vehicles.

"Supposedly, advanced." Catherine said, looking at the vehicles. "Maybe it's limited to advanced in only a few areas?"

"Guess we will find out soon," Terran said with a grimace. What sort of backwards people would still use tires when they had hovering tech?

Kelly remained unusually silent as Terran parked the rider next to Peter's, and everyone got out. They stood awkwardly beside their vehicles as they waited for some sort of instruction. The little hangar was bare on all sides. There were no markings on the walls or the floor, nor were there any noises; no humming, no hissing, no clanking--just silence. Terran began to wonder if the place was abandoned, when without warning the door behind them slid shut, and a smaller opening in front of them slid open.

The door in front led to a straight hallway about six feet wide and barely tall enough for them to step into, causing Rictor, the tallest of the group, to duck ever so slightly as they entered. This time the door slid shut behind them instantly, and a soft hiss escaped from the walls around them. Nozzles appeared from small openings in the walls and aimed themselves at the party.

The group froze and turned their head toward Peter. He remained calm and smiled again.

"They want to disinfect us is all, probably."

"From wha--" Kelly was cut off as the nozzles began shooting a mist into the hallway, and they were all thrown into a fit of coughing.

# CHAPTER THIRTY-FOUR

Kelly let out a yelp, and Peter grabbed her, wrapping her in his arms. She buried her face in to his chest as the spray continued to fill the room. Rictor stood patiently, watching as looks of unease passed between the adults of the group. He had been planetside more than a fair number of times, and did not find the disinfection alarming at all. However, he wasn't without sympathy for the poor girl. It was a lot to take in, and no one had probably told her the details of going planetside before.

Naomi stood by him and remained quiet. She was holding his hand and tracing her thumb over his. While most would see it as a tender gesture, she was actually talking to him in shorthand. It was an easy shorthand, consisting of dashes and dots in various combinations.

*Trust?* Naomi wrote.

*Yes.* Rictor replied.

*Stay with group?* she asked.

*For now.* Rictor replied.

He wasn't sure of what they would do once they took on Dagor and shut him down. He was glad that Peter seemed to have the same agenda that he and Naomi did. He wasn't positive that Peter would be OK with killing Dagor, but he wouldn't be able to stop them. Dagor would not get the drop on them again.

The misting stopped and the nozzles retreated behind the walls. A thin dust covered their clothes, an antibacterial agent of some sort, and Rictor tried to brush it off his sleeve, it didn't budge. The door they had been facing opened, revealing a tall man and two armed guards. He was handsome with shoulder-length blonde hair, light blue eyes, and pale skin. Rictor expected they would be seeing a lot of pale skin beneath the surface. The two guards looked like identical twins. Each one had harsh features, the same pale-white skin, and dark brown eyes. All three were wearing black shirts with camo pants tucked into boots. They had what looked like assault rifles trained on the group.

Rictor slowly scratched his chin. There was something off about this place. He had read the file and knew for a fact that there was supposed to be some high-level tech here. So why did they try to hide it? *Maybe they think we are here to try and steal it?*

"I am Lieutenant Laus," the man in the middle spoke in an authoritative tone. His voice was deeper than Rictor had expected. "I want to thank you all for coming to visit Pod Seven. Now, who is your representative?"

"I am," Peter said, stepping forwards. His voice had shifted as well. It seemed to waver, as if it were on the edge of turning into a whimper. *What game is he playing?*

"Why are you here?" Laus asked frowning.

"We escaped from Pod Three and stumbled upon this pod by accident. We are seeking refuge. My family has been hurt, and we just want some rest."

Laus's eyes shifted slightly toward Rictor and Naomi. Her foot was still wrapped in the soft cast that Kelly had made and his own shirt was covered in dried blood. It was a good thing he hadn't changed.

"What can you provide in exchange for entry?" Laus asked, turning his gaze back to Peter.

"We brought high level medicine with us, as well as some minerals," Peter replied, shrinking down from the man's stare.

"How did you escape?" Laus asked. A hunger had appeared in his eyes at the mention of medicine that made Rictor uneasy. He let go of Naomi's hand. He needed to be ready if anything was about to happen.

"My son worked in engineering, and we climbed up through an exhaust duct. We paid a survey team to leave us two riders and used those to drive over."

"Why is his shirt bloody? Scans don't reveal any injuries."

"We were ambushed by a small group of guards and had to fight them off. His wife got her ankle broken and he lost his brother. That's who the blood belonged to." Peter didn't miss a beat with the story, and Rictor was impressed. He played the part of weary traveler looking for asylum perfectly.

"All right. If you have any weapons, drop them to the side and you may enter." Laus gestured behind himself.

Naomi and Rictor both tossed their guns into the center of the floor. He kept the saber, however, since it was soft-coded to his DNA. They wouldn't be able to use it at all, unless they knew what it was and how to reset it. With the level of tech they were displaying, it was worth the risk. He might have endangered them all, but he was not just walking into what seemed to be a military base without some form of self-defense.

"Is that it?" Laus asked, seeming unimpressed with their two guns.

"We aren't violent," Peter sighed and his stature seemed to fall even more. "And we are willing to work; we just need some rest and safety."

Laus smiled and his features softened. "All right, first you will need to head to the infirmary. We need to make sure you don't have any foreign diseases on you that can spread to our community. Once those are isolated, then you will be assigned a home. After a short introductory period, you will be placed in a suitable work environment. Sorry for all the distrust, but we don't get many visitors that aren't spies or assassins. Pod Seven is always willing to help those in need, so you can rest assured that you are safe. Please, follow me."

The group followed Laus out of the disinfection room and into another hallway made of metal. It had a brushed, matte looked to it that prevented the light from two lines of LED's running parallel across the ceiling from reflecting. The hallway ended in a t-intersection with two large arrows pointing in either direction. Indecipherable text meant to direct traffic loomed above each arrow.

Laus led the way to the left and signaled his guards to drop back. As they passed by, Rictor could have sworn he heard something whir. He glanced around at the rest of the group, but no one else seemed to have heard it. If what he had heard was real, it meant that Torga was as advanced as they were supposed to be. Worse, that they were good at hiding it.

They stopped in front of another door, and Laus pushed a button beside it. The doors opened to reveal a windowed elevator. He heard gasps escape from everyone but Peter and Laus as they stepped inside.

The pod consisted of symmetric rings falling to the earth below, connected by several shafts vertically that Rictor assumed were elevators. Each level had several walkways, like spokes spanning the central void to large circular pads in the center which held parks or gardens. Gauging by the machines and the people he saw, each ring was roughly two miles in diameter. The engineering required for the system was incredible. He had read about the system of the pods in the brief they had received, but it was another thing entirely to see it. Machines flew around the different levels within the inner diameter, seeming to take care of the maintenance and cleaning of the various levels. At the sight of it all, Rictor knew he had been right. The guards that had flanked Laus had been androids.

The elevator began its descent and Laus turned to study the group. In a flash, he pulled out a gun and leveled it at them. Rictor noted that the design was similar to a rustic semi-auto pistol, although a battery pack had replaced the clip. Yes, these people were a lot more advanced than they let on.

"So, now would be a good time for the truth," Laus said. "I can tell none of you are from Pod Three. The looks on your faces confirm that. Not to mention we are going the wrong way. If you were from Pod Three you would have been able to read the signs."

Peter smiled. "Just wanted to get you alone is all."

"I'm not afraid to shoot you," Laus said. "Now, who are you really?" His pistol began to whine as it charged.

"We are here to kill Dagor. That's all you need to know," Rictor said.

Laus paused and surveyed the group with a look of confusion.

"You?" he asked. He reached into his pocket and placed a small, circular device on the window, it hummed briefly, then went silent. "You have no intel. You know nothing about this pod. I caught you without trying because you can't even read our language. The woman is obviously injured, the girl is scared to death, and you don't have any weapons. What makes you think you could take on Dagor?"

"Blind determination." Rictor said with a smile.

Laus looked at him, then back to the rest of the group. "Do you have any real skills that would help you? Surely you have to have something."

"What makes you so interested?" Terran asked.

"Because I am trying to determine if I am going to let you live or if you will be a hindrance. Dagor isn't exactly loved in this Pod. He has a lot of enemies, including me. So, once again, how do you plan on taking him down?"

"We don't have a plan," Rictor spoke out. "We were hoping to get in, get situated, then come up with a plan. It will probably be something with explosives. We do have unique skills that will help us in our endeavors. We just need somewhere to rest for a bit."

The small device on the window began humming again and Laus cursed. "Okay, you are going to go to my apartment and we are going to discuss these 'skills' you have talked about. If any of you try anything funny, I won't hesitate to shoot."

The group nodded in agreement and Laus pressed a button on the elevator. It began its descent again. As they started their journey, Rictor looked above them to the hallway and saw three suspicious men in military garb staring at the elevator. *This is going to be a lot riskier than we thought.*

are terrified of saying anything against him for fear of their own lives or the lives of their families." Laus paused for a second and took another breath. The telling of the story was obviously something he wasn't enjoying reliving. "We have lived in fear for a long time, under one man turned bad, and then under this tyrant. It is time for us to put an end to them, once and for all."

"So, did we just get lucky to meet you instead of one of his replacements? Also, won't he know you helped us since his androids were right by your side?" Rictor asked.

"How did you know about them?" Laus asked, then sighed. "It doesn't matter. I can find replacement bodies for each of you and as far as Dagor knows, I have killed tons of people for him. As for why you met me, it's my job. Every army needs a recruiter."

"What do you mean by replacement bodies?" Kelly gave a visible shudder at the question. Laus, for this interruption, seemed to share Kelly's sentiment.

"As part of my military service, I have access to bodies that Dagor has disposed of. All I have to do is change a few records and no one will be the wiser."

"So how will we strike against him?" Terran interrupted.

Naomi glanced over at the young man and was surprised to see how much older he looked in such a short amount of time. In her mind, she always pictured him as an optimistic youth looking forward to the rest of his life, as he had been on the Lion's Roar. It was a ridiculous thought, since the first time she had seen him, he had been covered in blood and smelled like cheap liquor. Worry lines already forming creases on his face, making evident where future wrinkles would root in. He seemed to have aged in years instead of months on the Lion's Roar. Of course, after everything that had happened to him, it wasn't hard seeing why he looked more worn.

"Trying to infiltrate and locate Dagor's office for an assassination is going to be too difficult. So, my thought is that we just blow it up."

"What?" Terran asked. "Why?"

"You see, according to most of engineering plans, there are ten levels to this pod. However, according to some plans that a spy of mine found, there is an eleventh level where Dagor has housed himself. Unfortunately, the plans don't have individual rooms labelled, so it makes precision strikes hard to attempt. Not to mention, we only have one shot."

"How do we know the plans are trustworthy?" Catherine spoke up.

"My spy was murdered the day after he delivered them. That seems like a good indicator that the plans are trustworthy." Laus seemed to bristle as he spoke, anger entering his voice. "Look, even if Dagor isn't on the floor when we blow it up, it's where his production facilities for the androids most likely are. Either way, we can hurt him."

"So, what has stopped you acting before now?" Catherine's voice was hard. "If I had access to the man, or woman, who had killed the people dear to me, I would make them pay as quickly as possible." Laus looked at Catherine with a confused expression.

"Just because I am in the military does not mean I have access to Dagor. I have been planning this for the past six months, waiting for the right time to strike. I have been gathering resources, intel, and coming up with a plan that will work. So, forgive me if I don't share your rash concept of running in without a thought, but I expect my plan to work. When it does, Dagor will be blown out of this pod and straight into hell."

Catherine lowered her gaze, chastised by the response. Naomi, however, felt a chill creeping up her spine as a memory replayed in her mind of a little dot in the distance bursting and fading out of existence. She would not be a part of another plan to execute hundreds of people on another person's will.

"No." She said, barely audible.

"What do you mean no?" Laus asked. "It is the easiest way to get rid him."

"No." Naomi repeated, getting to her feet.

"Why are you getting upset? It's not like we are going to--"

His words were cut off as Naomi punched him square in the face. Laus fell backward onto the floor and began cursing, pressing a hand to his cheek, already starting to swell. The group sat, stunned, as Naomi stood up and walked out of the small apartment.

She turned left and began walking. She didn't care where she was going, she just needed away from Laus and his plan. It was too much for her, too much like what Dagor had asked her to do. She couldn't do that. *No, I won't do that.* She found herself by the elevator and made a rash decision.

Getting into the elevator, she pushed a button with a green mark by it. She had noticed that this level had a symbol like a small egg on the wall. There was a matching button on the elevator itself. If she kept track of the symbols, she would be able to maneuver around the complex.

The door opened and she turned to see where she had stopped. The wall had the same green mark as the button and Naomi smiled to herself. It wouldn't be so hard here. She followed the walkway and was surprised to see that it ended abruptly into a wall. There was a smaller door off centered with the wall and what seemed to be a larger door for vehicles. Naomi crept over to the smaller door and paused before reaching out for the handle.

This level could be anywhere in the complex, but it didn't matter. She just couldn't think about killing anyone or anything right now. She took hold of the handle and gently opened the door as slowly as she could manage. Warm air hit her as soon as the seal on the door had been broken. Naomi was shocked at the smell overpowering her. *Is that grass?*

She threw open the door and stepped into paradise. A lush garden lay before her. Rows and rows of different vegetables lay carefully arranged. Men, women, and children could be seen picking the vegetables and carefully treating the precious crops. Looking up Naomi saw that UV lights basked the crops in artificial sunlight. Metal stairways led both up and down to alternate levels. The smell of wet earth flooded Naomi and she stood with eyes closed soaking it in.

"Excuse me, miss," a high-pitched voice called out beside her.

Naomi looked down to see a small girl, around seven, with a small basket of fruits and vegetables.

"Did you pick all those yourself?" Naomi asked, squatting down to eye level with the girl.

The girl had short brown hair and big blue eyes. Her skin was a healthy ruddy color and dirt streaked her face, although the yellow uniform she was wearing was rather clean.

"Yes ma'am," the girl said, face beaming. "Momma finally let me pick some for myself."

"Are you going to eat all those?" Naomi asked smiling.

"All except for the plum." She said.

"And why not the plum?" Naomi smiled.

"Because my momma saw you come in and told me that I should give it to you." The little girl smiled back at Naomi. "I really like plums, but momma said you looked like you might need it."

The little girl handed Naomi the plum and headed back into the garden toward one of the stairways leading to the upper level. A plump woman, evidently the girl's mother, turned toward Naomi and motioned for her to come over. Taking a bite of the plum, Naomi obliged.

# CHAPTER THIRTY-SIX

The woman, whose name was Mirie, sat with Naomi under an apple tree enjoying the shade. A small blanket was laid out underneath them with a small spread of fruits and vegetables. Various other workers were resting underneath other trees with friends and family, each group sharing the crops they had been tending. The little girl, Tessa, was staring intently at a bee buzzing between some of the blooms on the tree they were under.

Mirie had the same short brown hair Tessa had, but her eyes were a muddy brown that almost matched the color of her hair. Her skin, tanned from working under the UV light, made Mirie look like she was cast of bronze. The light blue jump suit she wore stood out in stark contrast to her dark skin, although that had several dark brown patches from where she had wiped her hands.

"So, you are one of those Bound people huh?" Mirie asked, keeping her voice down and her eyes on Tessa.

"Yes," Naomi replied, taking another bite of the plum. She wasn't sure why she had poured her heart out to Mirie, but she had. She hadn't intended to. It had started with Mirie asking how she was doing. When was the last time anyone even asked me that? And Naomi hadn't been able to stop. This random woman was the only she would be able to confide in, without judgement or fear. Who else could I talk to? The girl who's father I killed or the one who's sister I killed? Now, she was at the mercy of a random woman. Of course, if Mirie couldn't be trusted, Naomi was prepared to do what needed to be done. The mission couldn't be jeopardized.

"Well, everything will be all right dear." Mirie said, patting her softly on the arm. Naomi breathed a sigh of relief and flashed a weak smile at her. "When I lost my Yuren seven years ago--that was my husband--I thought the world was ending. I wouldn't leave the apartment, I would ignore Tessa, and I barely ate. I became a shadow of the person I was before. I blamed everyone else for what I had become. Then one day some people came by and told me that if I didn't change, I would lose Tessa. They would find a place more suitable for her. I was still in shock at this point by the loss of my husband, but it brought me back. As much as I had loved my husband, I knew my love wouldn't bring him back. However, my love could keep my daughter with me. So, I changed. I started working the fields with Tessa on my back and kept my eyes forward. Now, seven years later, I think of how childish I was."

Naomi smiled politely at Mirie. The anecdote was tender, but not exactly applicable to her situation. Mirie caught the uncertainty, and smiled.

"What I am saying is that you can't be a prisoner to your past. Focus on the present. If you don't change, what you have now will be taken away and it will only be yourself to blame."

"What does that have to do with you know who?" Naomi asked, resting her head on the tree.

"Well, I don't know much about your morals or anything of that sort, but I do know what I would do in your situation."

"What's that?" Naomi asked glancing over at the woman. Mirie was still watching over Tessa with a scrutinizing eye.

"I would protect what I love. I would blow Dagor back to whatever hole he crawled out of."

"But, wouldn't innocent people die?" Naomi asked, biting her lip. "I don't want to be responsible for any more deaths."

"I see your point, but by letting him live, it could be seen that you are killing more people than if a bomb were to go off."

Naomi paused for a moment, considering. "Thank you, Mirie. You have given me a lot to think about. I should probably head back to my friends and help them figure out what we need to do."

"Okay dear." Mirie said with a smile. "Stay safe, and if you ever need someone to lend an ear, you know where to find me."

Naomi gave a final wave and made her way back to Laus's apartment uninterrupted. She could hear heated discussion coming from behind the door, but couldn't quite make out the words being spoken. She knocked and waited. Laus' opened the door and motioned her into the apartment. She walked in and sat down by Rictor. Terran was standing now, a concerned expression on his face. Catherine looked like Naomi had felt before she had left. The other two men seemed more contemplative than anything else. Kelly was staring at a wall with an impassive expression on her face.

What in the world happened when she was gone? Laus came and sat back down in his previous spot.

"Where did you go?" Laus asked. He stood quietly by the door, pistol out.

Naomi heard a soft click and knew that Rictor had released the safety on his sword.

"To the fields, on the level with the green triangle."

"Did you talk to anyone?"

"Just a woman." Naomi replied.

"Did you tell her about us, or anything about the plan?"

"Of course not," Naomi said, insulted he would think she was so simple. "I am not going to risk endangering all of our lives simply because I don't think we should kill an entire pod of people. I just needed to blow off some steam. And before you ask, no, I didn't see any robots."

"What you did was stupid and reckless. You didn't even hear the whole plan. You need to trust me. There are structural points that would cause the eleventh level to implode under the weight of the ten above it. There might be a few injuries, but nothing on the scale you were thinking." Laus sighed and put his pistol away. "If we are going to work together, you need to know that I am not like Callas, or Dagor. I want what's best for Pod Seven, and Naomi, if you ever hit me again, I will turn you all loose in this pod and let you fend for yourselves against Dagor. We'll see how long you last. Is that understood?"

"Yes."

"Now, back to our discussion."

"What did I miss?" Naomi asked.

"We were just talking about when to execute Laus's plan for Dagor." Rictor said. "There has been some debate on the timeline of the events being proposed."

"What are our options?" Naomi asked.

"The first option is to strike within the week," Rictor said, reclining against the wall. "Our second option is to give it more time, about a month was suggested. That would give us the most time to figure out how to minimize innocents lost. If there will ever be any."

"How do the votes stand?"

"Kelly, Laus, and Terran are wanting to wait the full month. While Peter, Catherine, and I want to strike sooner."

"Do I get a vote?"

"Yep," Rictor's voice wavered just enough that Naomi turned to see the concerned look on his face. She gave a slight smile back.

"Well, it would be safer to just strike within the week before he notices us, right?"

"Not quite," Laus said, rubbing his eyes. "I have to notify my contacts to set up a few things in advance, which means if we are going to do this, I need to notify them tonight or tomorrow. I will be putting close friends in incredible danger if we don't follow through."

Naomi shuddered at the thought of willingly putting more people into danger. If they could avoid causing any unnecessary harm to the people of this pod, then that is what they would do.

"I vote to wait the full month then. If we can avoid even one unnecessary death, it will be worth it."

There were no smiles or cheers at the decision Naomi made. Instead Laus stood and went over to his bed. He reached into the mattress and took out large rolls of paper secured with rubber bands. Undoing the bands, he rolled them out along the floor. A large schematic for a level of the pod was shown in striking detail. They all crowded in to look at the drawings. There were several scribbled notes along the outer rim of the drawing and large red circles were drawn at different junctions.

"This is the eleventh floor," Laus said, "It houses Dagor's central suite, but is mostly used to create the automatons he employs. The thought process is to place charges alongside the reactors in the factories to cause a chain reaction throughout the entire floor. It should decimate any androids on the floor, as well as Dagor himself. We are still doing recon on Dagor's movements. He doesn't really keep a standard schedule, making it hard to figure out when he will be in his office. Any questions so far?"

The room was silent, so Laus carried on.

"We have seen that the androids are entering the main sections of the Pod via the elevators. This means that there are obviously entrances to the eleventh floor from the elevator shafts. The elevators themselves stop on the tenth floor, but the shafts should continue down to the eleventh. Our objective for the next month will be to figure out how to get down to the eleventh floor discreetly. Once we can get to the eleventh floor it's a piece of cake. We just place the four charges and get out."

Naomi glanced around the room as Laus finished. Everyone was so serious, and even Rictor's usual smile was replaced by quiet contemplation.

"What's stopping Dagor from seeing us walk around the Pod for the next month? Are we supposed to just stay in this room?" Kelly asked.

"Finally, a good question," Laus replied, moving toward his bed again. He took a thin box out of it, and laid it on the floor. Several transparent masks lay in the box and Lau handed them out.

"These masks will cause your face to look restructured and have a built-in voice manipulator. It can't change speech patterns, but the first two should be enough to fool any observer or recognition software."

"These are amazing," Terran said as he toyed with the material. "Where did you get all of this?"

"I have been planning this for a long time." Laus replied. "I have been slowly gathered materials and information using my position in the military. I know it may not look like much, but you have to understand Dagor does not like the idea of people hoarding up these kinds of things. There is one last thing that we need to consider."

"What's that?" Terran asked as he slipped the mask over his face. His hair poked through the top and at first his face just seemed obscured by the translucent material. Then his face began to ripple as though it were under water. Slowly a new face began to emerge and solidify before them.

"You all need to learn to read," Laus said.

# CHAPTER THIRTY-SEVEN

The Bound spent the next week going over plans and reading lessons. Most of them took to it easily enough, Terran could read the language in two days, and Kelly shortly thereafter. Catherine took a whole week before she could navigate around. Naomi, while struggling, seemed to be grasping it. To say that Rictor was struggling would have been an understatement. Even with all his advanced physical prowess, learning new things was burdensome to him. One of the downsides of an extended lifespan was that he got pretty settled about things. He tried to put his best foot forward, no matter how much Laus berated him for not "getting it".

Rictor stood up from his cramped position in the corner of Laus apartment and stretched out his back. The evenings here were nice. He and Naomi would walk through the various levels talking with people and trying to get some useful information and finish the evening with dinner at Mirie's.

She lived on the fourth floor, like all the physical laborers, with her daughter. The apartments were smaller than Laus's, but Mirie had somehow made it into a home. Even then, something felt off about the situation. He had been having headaches recently, and could only remember bits and pieces of their nights. Of course, they never really talked about anything important, but still, it troubled him. Naomi had suggested they go to Mirie's tonight, but he had other plans.

No one in the group really understood what he was capable of. Not even he knew his full potential. The only person he had ever confided in had been taken from him. In a way, he had lost both a brother and a father when Glenn had been killed. Tonight, Rictor was going to do something drastic. He couldn't let anyone else get hurt. He had been made for missions like this. There had been a number of years between him escaping his cell and being saved by the Bound. Tonight, he would need to borrow the skills he had developed during that period.

Slipping on the mask to contort his features, Rictor left Laus' apartment and headed toward the elevator. It dinged and opened to reveal two men in stained jumpsuits talking adamantly about coolant for the Pod's generators.

Rictor joined them in the elevator and pressed the tenth floor. Hopefully, no one else would get in the few floors between where they were and the main generator level. Luck was with him, and they arrived uninterrupted on the ninth floor. The two men left without a second glance at Rictor and the door shut behind them.

Rictor held still for a second scanning for cameras, He gave his nanos a mental command and switched the available spectrums. *Nothing.* What he did see was a slightly recessed corner of the elevator. After closer examination, he could pop the square out and climb out onto the roof. He gently set the square back in place and looked around for a handhold.

The walls were almost sheer metal with only small rungs to one side allowing any foot hold. There weren't any cables for the elevator; instead, it seemed to rely on four tracks that each corner fell into. Rictor was trying to figure out how the tracks worked when the elevator jolted slightly and dinged, letting him know that the tenth floor had been reached. Rictor quickly set the corner of the elevator back in place, then reached over and grabbed onto the rungs. Extending his arm behind him, he checked to make sure he had plenty of clearance. Looking down he could barely see the solid floor beneath him. He gave another silent command, and the world was illuminated green. With a clear view of the floor, Rictor saw that the bottom of the shaft extended about fifteen feet below the elevator.

A few moments later, small sparks shot from one of the tracks and the elevator began raising itself back up the shaft. Rictor clung to the rungs and let it pass. Then, he placed a small proximity alarm between the rungs to give himself some warning when it came back down. After double checking that the alarm was set, Rictor climbed down to the bottom of the shaft. Glancing around the floor, he noted there were no obvious doorways.

Undeterred, Rictor got on his hands and knees and began crawling along the floor. There had to be a way. If what Laus had said was true, then the only way the androids could have gotten onto the higher levels was through the shafts. It would only make sense that an entrance would be in each one. *Unless we were wrong and there is only one entrance.*

Rictor turned and sat on the floor by the rungs. There were four shafts going through each level. He was in the southern most shaft currently. It wouldn't take long to scout out the others, but Rictor had a feeling that there was more than one entrance. *There has to be.* A loud beep from above warned Rictor that the elevator was coming back down the shaft. He hurried to the rungs and looked up toward the elevator. Most likely it would stop at the tenth floor, but just in case it did come down, he didn't want to be caught between an elevator and a hard place.

Rictor changed his lenses so he could see into the elevator as it drew nearer. The light inside of the elevator began blinking. Rictor stared at the light: on, off, on, off. Suddenly, Rictor passed out.

He paced around his cell, waiting for his dinner. A small red light flashed and a plate of food was pushed through a slot in the door. He went to the metal table that sat in his cell and began to eat. The scientists were watching him. He could feel them. The clear walls and ceiling of the cell guaranteed that they would be. He ate his meal in silence. When he was done, he waited by the door. The red light flashed again and the slot opened. He pushed the plate through and went to his bed. He would get out someday.

He was brought out of his trance by a sudden flash of light and a hiss. Something had happened in the elevator. *What had happened?* He opened his eyes to the see the frame of the elevator inches from his face. He jerked back and his head slammed into the rungs. His arm, looped through the rungs, had saved his life. Rictor rubbed his head and tried to focus. The lights, they had been blinking, and had triggered something. *An old memory, maybe? I almost died because of an old memory.* The realization that the elevator was on the eleventh floor suddenly became very clear. Focusing the nanos in his eyes, he barely caught a glimpse of a door closing behind four people in the elevator. The elevator started again and ascended past him, Rictor took a moment to breathe. He untangled his arm from the rungs and began walking around the shaft, looking for clues. There was nothing-no handle, no space, no interlocking joints. Nothing. Spreading out his hands, Rictor began to slowly make his way away the wall, relying on touch instead of sight. After a few moments of searching, he encountered a small ridge. It was barely noticeable, but it was there. He traced it around the wall and wasn't surprised to find that it formed a tight rectangular shape.

Rictor cursed. For all his seemingly infinite energy, he had missed his opportunity. All because some light had triggered, something. Rictor scratched his head again. *Guess I can add that to my list of setbacks from the nanos.* Of course, he wasn't positive it was all the nanos. It could have been the conditioning. Either way, he should probably head back and check in with everyone.

He climbed back up the rungs and waited for the elevator to come back down the shaft. When it finally made its way back down, and was empty, he climbed back into it and rode it up to Laus' floor. He might not know how it worked yet, but he knew where the androids were getting in. Rictor walked quickly to the apartment, struggling to keep the image in his mind. One of them would know how the door worked. Laus would have something, or would be able to get it.

As he opened the door to Laus' apartment he was shocked to find everyone huddled together looking worried.

"What's up?" he asked.

Naomi looked up from her seat and charged toward him. Rictor braced himself, unsure of what he had done, instead of hitting him, Naomi reached her arms around his chest and held him close.

"While this is entirely appreciated, I am unsure of why I am getting hugged and why everyone looks so solemn."

"Where have you been?" she whispered.

"I was looking for a way into Dagor's level. I was only gone for a few hours."

The entire group looked up at him with curious expressions.

"Rictor," Naomi said, "You have been gone for twelve hours."

Rictor cursed himself and eyed the small group. *Well, they were bound to find out eventually.*

"Fun fact, when you get to be over two hundred years old it gets a lot harder to tell time." Rictor said, letting out a soft chuckle.

No one laughed, although their looks of curiosity deepened. Rictor guided Naomi over to an open space on the floor, and they both sat down.

"I think it is time you all understand a bit more about where I came from."

# CHAPTER THIRTY-EIGHT

"The first thing you should know about me is that I was not born, I was made," Rictor said, looking down at his hands. "I can't remember much until I was about fifteen or sixteen years old. I have been around for a while so the exact years are a bit of a blur to me. That time stands out so vividly because that is when they decided I was a viable candidate to have a series of specialized nanobots inserted into my body. There were five rounds of insertions with a two-month rest period between each round. During the two months, I was immobile as my body tried to decide whether it would accept the nanos. Any questions so far?"

No one said anything, so he continued.

"Obviously, I made it through the insertion process. After all the rounds were done I was put into a small furnished cabin where they monitored me. They measured how I developed, how I handled solitude, any physical or mental thing you can think of, they monitored. Those were the good years. I read a lot, learned a few languages, and got myself into top shape. No one bothered me."

He wiped his palms on his pants. *How long has it been since I have told anyone about the lab?*

"Next, they started giving me housemates. I woke up one morning to find another guy going through the fridge. I was paralyzed. I had no idea what to say or how to interact with him. He smiled at me and asked me what I wanted for breakfast. We developed a good friendship over the course of a few months. Then he left and was replaced by someone else. Not quite so friendly, but he was still better than being alone.

"They kept this routine up for a while, constantly changing who I was interacting with every few weeks or months. Then one day they put in a woman. She was beautiful. Before this moment, I had only seen the female scientists who observed me. It was a whole new experience meeting someone who just wanted to chat. I was naïve at the time and didn't expect anything. They left her in there for six months. We talked and laughed and grew quite close to one another. Or at least, I thought we were. Then she was gone. Something changed in me after that. Something inside me was broken and I was very aware of it."

"I stopped talking with anyone. No matter who it was, I just ignored them. Went back to my solitary routine. Then the real tests started. Before I continue, are there any questions?"

"How old were you at this point?" Kelley asked.

"I was about 23 or so."

"Did you ever try to escape?"

"That is why the real testing started," Rictor replied. "I decided I had had enough. I bolted out the door and just kept running. I had been running as fast as I could for about ten minutes or so, and then I hit a wall. An invisible wall of electricity that knocked me out completely. I woke up this time in a plain white room. I was lying on a cot and there was nothing else in there. I have no idea how long they kept me there, there was no way to tell time. I think I went crazy for a bit. Then one day a man opened a door that I hadn't even known was there and shot me with a drug of some sort, putting me to sleep. This time I woke up in a small apartment with a glass observation wall. I cried from joy that I wasn't in the white room anymore. This room was small, but there were some things to keep me busy.

"This particular instance was unique because I got to interact with the scientists through a small speaker in the wall. Every day they would ask me random questions. What color the sky was, what my name was, the date. It was dull, but at least I was interacting with people. I was petrified to disobey them again and they knew it. Eventually, they decided to start with interactions again, which was fine by me."

"Everything was fine. I was amicable and the guests were nice. Things were great. Then they introduced Mark into my life. When Mark was put in the room, they removed all the food. They sat both of us down and told us that in order for us to get any food at all, one of us would have to kill the other. Mark and I thought that was ridiculous. We told each other that we would never resort to killing someone for food. We weren't barbarians. Mark lasted forty-eight days before I woke up to him trying to choke me in my sleep. I fought him off and his head hit the coffee table. He died."

Naomi squeezed his hand, and he turned and briefly smiled at her before his face grew solemn again.

"It changed me, of course, knowing I had killed a man. Some might argue it was an accident or self-defense, but I struggled with it. Shortly after, a new scientist showed up. It was the woman from the cabin. She was much older than she had been, at least in her late-thirties, but she was just as easy to talk to. She opened up to me during our sessions. She would tell me about her relationships, her family, and her job. The talks helped me to get through my own emotions. Everything was finally starting to get back to normal when she began to change. I could tell that something was gnawing at her. I kept asking her about it, but she wouldn't say a word."

"Finally, I was able to break through. She visited me one night after our usual time and assured me that we weren't being monitored. She revealed that she was leaving the planet that night, that she was one of the Bound and would help me to escape if I wanted to come with her. I, of course, accepted. I would have gone anywhere to escape that cell. She unlocked a hidden door, and I was out. Finally, out."

"My happiness only lasted a few minutes. As we left the main facility, we met some...resistance. Many of the scientists who had tested me were there as well as armed guards. They shouted and threatened to shoot us if we didn't head back to the cell. I...lost it."

Images began assaulting him-blood stained lab coats, broken bodies, and the look--that terrified look she had given him. He focused on breathing until the memories faded. The room stayed silent.

"Something unhinged inside of me at the sight of them. I couldn't stop myself. I just attacked them until I knew they wouldn't be able to chase us. When I finally regained control, there she was, staring at me like I was some sort of monster; guess I was, then. She ran from me, and I let her go. I didn't see any point in chasing her. She had dropped her purse at some point, and I carried it with me for a time. There were files in it about what they had done to me. I journeyed across the world for a long time trying to find out where she had gone and to experience freedom for the first time.

"Over time I met with some more Bound and jumped on board hoping to find her. I have been with the Bound ever since."

Terran's eyes met Rictor's.

"So why stay on?" he asked.

"What?" Rictor was confused.

"Why stay on if you just joined to find a woman? It's been years since that happened. Do you really plan on finding her again?"

"No," Rictor shook his head, eyes downcast. She would be long dead by now.

"Then why are you staying?"

"Because..." Rictor paused.

*Because I'm too scared to do anything.*

"Because, I feel safe with the Bound and nowhere else."

A silence settled over the group. They stared at each other, waiting for someone to make a move. Finally, Laus stood. "So, what, you just lost track of time?"

Rictor scratched his chin considering his response. "Yeah, something like that."

"And you're sticking with that? How often does that happen?"

"It won't happen again. I'm back on the proverbial ball."

There was a long silence as Laus and Rictor stared at each other.

"I think Rictor has shared a lot with us, and we all need some time to process what he said. I suggest we all go to bed for now."

Nodding heads met Laus' suggestion, and the group split up to their respective corners to sleep. Rictor settled by the wall and tried to steady his breathing. He did feel safe with the Bound, but the real question would be if they felt safe with him, now that they knew the truth.

# CHAPTER THIRTY-NINE

Terran stood looking toward the inner ring of the third floor. The fact that Rictor had killed before should have shocked him. It should have made him angry or sad or something. Instead, his mind had been working in a different way. How could they use Rictor's abilities to reach Dagor? He had traveled to the shaft with Laus, and they hadn't been able to find a thing. Without a lot more information, the shafts were looking less promising. A finger tapped him on the shoulder and he turned to see Kelly smiling at him.

"Hello, Kelly," he smiled at his sister.

"What're you thinking about?"

"Everything," he said as he turned back to the inner circle. Farmers were picking through the crops to feed this level of the Pod. "You look like you're doing better."

"I am," she said, leaning against the guardrail beside him, "It's just been a couple of rough weeks. I didn't know how to handle it."

"And now?" he asked.

"Still don't, but it won't help being all sullen and mopey."

"Anything in particular help you out there?"

"Dad, actually." She looked at Terran, one eyebrow raised. "Have you talked with him much?"

"Just that first day," he admitted. "So much has happened it all seems so surreal. I have so many questions, but I don't have any idea where to even start, not to mention the anger that suddenly needs somewhere else to go. I thought if I ever saw him again, it would be different."

"Well, to be fair you thought he was still on Sisera instead of travelling through space. So there's that. And Dagor is pretty deserving on the whole 'angry for justice' department."

"True," Terran said as he studied the workers.

"How is Catherine?" Kelly asked.

Terran reached a hand down into his pocket and fingered the small box Glenn had given him. He hadn't opened it yet. *Why haven't I given it to Catherine?*

"She is still struggling. I have a notion of something that might help, but it will have to wait until I get back from the mission today."

"Do you think they suffered much?" Kelly asked.

"Not at all," he answered. "We will see Anna again."

"At the Capital?" Kelly asked raising an eyebrow.

"Yeah."

"Rictor has been on the ship for over two hundred years, and they haven't reached the Capital. What makes you think we will? Also, we are kind of stuck on a desert planet in an oversized underground bunker."

"I think there is more to the Capital than we know. Just because Rictor has been around for a while doesn't mean he knows everything. He has been struggling with his own demons."

They both fell silent as they thought about what Rictor had said the night before. It was odd to Terran that you could have such a picture of who someone was in your head only to be completely wrong.

"At least now we know how the androids are getting in." Terran shrugged. "Ish."

"Do you agree with the plan?"

"Assuming the calculations are right, very few people will get hurt, Kelly," Terran nodded, "So yes."

"I know, it's just I have this weird feeling that there is something going on." Kelly replied, "How well do we know Laus anyway?"

"He has done an awful lot for us," Terran grabbed her shoulders and gently turned her toward him. "Don't you think if he was bad he would have done something to us already or maybe just shot us when he had the chance?"

"I guess so," Kelly bit her lip, "I just have a bad feeling is all."

"Well, don't let it get you down. How about we go see if Peter's found anything out."

"Are you really not going to call him dad or father or anything?"

"Baby steps, Kelly, baby steps."

They found him a few minutes later at a small bench looking over a map. He was wearing a pair of tan coveralls covered in grease stains. He had started working on the top floor to see if any of the workers knew anything about the hidden level. So far, he hadn't gotten anything, but he was sure they were hiding something up there.

"Hello, Dad." Kelly said sitting down next to him.

"Hello, Kelly," he said as he hugged her.

"Peter," Terran said with a nod.

Peter nodded back.

"Find out anything?" Terran asked.

"Not yet," Peter replied with a sigh, "I got a few leads to talk. Apparently, there have been a few weird readings from equipment around the outside of the pod."

"Outside of the pod?" Terran asked.

"There are some maintenance stairwells around the outside of the Pod that servicemen use. On the ground out there, there have been some weird electrical readings."

"Is it something to look into?"

"Maybe in a bit. I would like to get some more information before we stumble around out there."

"Any word on the shafts?"

"Nothing," Peter said, "but, I think the other lead might pan out."

"So, you want to eat dinner tonight?" Kelly cut in.

"Sure, Kelly." Peter grinned.

"I have plans with Catherine tonight," Terran said.

"Next time then," Peter said with a small nod.

"Next time," Terran echoed.

Peter kissed Kelly on the forehead and checked his watch.

"I have to get going. You two don't get into too much trouble."

"Bye, Dad," Kelly said, giving a quick hug. "Can't wait to talk tonight."

"Me, too," he whispered with a smile. He got up from the bench and extended a hand to Terran, who shook it.

"See ya, Peter."

"See ya, son."

Terran and Kelley watched him get into the elevator and ascend the floors back to work.

"You should open up a bit toward him," Kelly said as she shoved him slightly.

"Maybe," Terran said pushing her back. "Anyway, I have to go check out a lead or two of my own. See you later, Kelly."

"Bye," she said, "Don't get too distracted staring into Catherine's big, beautiful eyes."

"Oh, shut up," he said as he gave her a quick hug.

Of course, he wouldn't have minded getting lost in Catherine's eyes; he just had different plans for the moment. He followed the walkway around the level until he reached a small side door leading toward the outer edge of the level. *So, there is something fishy going on outside.*

The door was locked, but Laus had given him a passcode that should be able to bypass most of the locks on the doors. Terran tried not to think too hard about why Laus had the code. He agreed with Kelly that something seemed off about him. It was almost too fortunate that they had met him. The passcode worked and the door opened revealing the staircases that extended far above and below Terran toward the other levels. The air was thicker and Terran undid a few buttons on his shirt to fight the heat. The door clicked behind him, and Terran noted that there was no entry panel on this side of the door. That was an interesting piece of information to not have been told about. He still had the small tablet that Laus had given them, so he wasn't too worried.

As he descended the stairs, Terran was surprised to find that the walls of the rocks around the levels were almost completely sheer. There were small ripples here and there, but in the grand scheme of how large the hole was, it amazed him how smooth it was. As he continued his descent, maintenance lights would come on as they sensed his movement, and reveal more stairs. As he descended deeper, light began to catch on the rock wall. Rugged, uncut gemstones were scattered all over the wall-agates, rubies, and sapphires all sparkled in the soft light provided by the maintenance lights.

On a whim, Terran took out a small pocket knife and tried to pry a ruby loose. Working around the edges, Terran was to retrieve a rock the slightly bigger than a marble. *I wonder if Catherine likes rubies.* He pried a few more gemstones from the wall, then continued down. They were rough, of course, but it was the thought that counted.

He continued down the stairs and tried to stay more alert. *I can't get distracted.* One of the more unnerving things about being outside the complex was the constant echo of his footfalls, which gave him the distinct feeling he was being followed. Every time he checked, however, he was greeted by nothing but the daunting sight of the Pod extending far above him.

He reached the bottom floor and was surprised to find that the stairway ended about halfway into the ground, as if it had settled over time. Terran spent some time trying to scrape away the dirt and was surprised to find that the stairway did seem to keep going. *That could be a good sign, stairs are meant to go somewhere.*

Terran dusted his hands on his pants and began walking along the outer edge of the complex. The lights lined up vertically along the pod, but only where the stairs were located, which meant that Terran would have to walk through long swathes of darkness with nothing but the light from his tablet to guide him. His footfalls were muffled on the dirt as he began his walk around the complex, but they still echoed enough to unsettle him.

As he made his way around the Pod, he kept his eyes on the outer wall and the ground beneath him. While most of the others had agreed with Rictor about how to get into the eleventh floor, Terran wasn't so sure. It seemed like a good idea, but chances were that those entrances would be closely monitored-- and what they needed was stealth.

He had gone past two more lighted stairwells before he tripped over a small lump in the dirt. As he fell, the tablet tumbled from his hands and hit the ground. There was a flash of light, then he was thrown into darkness. He hit the ground a second later and lay perfectly still. He took a moment to catch his breath and tried to listen for any unusual sounds. Silence. He got onto his hands and knees and reached for his tablet. He found it a few seconds later. His fingers told him the screen was cracked, and it refused to turn on. He turned around in a small circle brushing away the dirt around him. The lump he had tripped over appeared to be lever next to a small trapdoor on the ground leading down into the dirt. *I was right!* Smiling to himself, Terran reached down and patted the door. A shock erupted through his body that threw him away from the door into the wall of stone behind him. Everything went black.

# CHAPTER FORTY

Naomi watched Terran's unsteady breathing as he lay on the floor. Catherine and Kelly flanked either side of him, watching his face eagerly for any sign of consciousness. Laus' apartment was filled with the somber atmosphere of a funeral. *They don't expect him to live.* How could they? All they had seen was how he was now, not how he had been when Naomi had found him.

He had been face down in the dirt with a small trail of smoke curling from his body when they had found him. Naomi had run to him to check his vitals, and his heartbeat had been weak, not strong like it was now, and his breathing had come in small irregular gasps, not the strained long draws of breath he was forcing to come through his lungs. He was stronger than they thought. He had faced death once before and lived. He would do so again.

It was probably for the better that the girls hadn't seen him--both were fragile in their own way concerning Terran. A morbid chuckle escaped her as she thought about the boy. So much had changed when Terran had boarded the Lion's Roar, and it seemed that by attempting to kill him she had helped to shape him into what Dagor had feared. She didn't have a clue what it was about Terran that scared them, other than his seemingly enormous amount of luck at defying death.

Leaving the girls to their solemnity, Naomi went to visit Mirie. It had been a few days since she and Rictor had eaten dinner with her and Tessa. Naomi needed the pick-me-up that eating with the two of them always provided; not to mention they would have extras to bring to the girls who were practically mourning over Terran. She took the elevator to the third floor and stepped out heading toward Mirie's home. She was confronted with the sight of Tessa slumped against the wall, crying into her hands. The door to Mirie's apartment lay on the floor. It was twisted and torn with parts of the surrounding wall still attached to the frame. Long marks were dug into the wall on each side of the door frame where some beast had dugs its claws in to wrench the door free. Naomi ran over to Tessa and threw her arms around the poor girl.

"Tessa, are you OK?" Naomi whispered. "What happened?"

"The monsters..." the girl barely got the words out through the sobs, "they came...and took mommy away."

"Did they say anything, Tessa?"

"Something about a dagger and helping enemies: I couldn't hear much."

"Tessa, I want you to come with me. Is that okay?"

"Yeah."

Naomi grabbed the girl and ran to the elevator. The door shut behind them, and Naomi pressed the button to the level above Laus apartment.

"Tessa, did the monsters touch you at all?"

There was no response besides her sobs. *Poor girl.* Who knew how long she had been sitting there.

"Tessa, I need you to focus. Did they touch you anywhere?"

"I can't remember," Tessa choked out.

"I am going to make sure you're okay, so I am going to rub my hands over you, okay?"

"OK," she said

Naomi rubbed her hand over the girl's back, over her legs, then through her hair. She found two small chips clipped to her clothing--trackers, most likely.

The elevator stopped and they went to one of the side doors that led outside the Pod. Everything was silent except for Tessa's sobs. Naomi tossed both trackers down the hall, then punched in the code to open the door. She scrambled down the stairs to the next level. Reaching the landing of Laus' apartment, she pushed in the wall to the left of the door. It gave way and revealed an input. She punched in the next code and rushed inside. Both girls jumped up when she walked in, their faces filled with concern.

Naomi gently set her down on Laus's bed and began slowly working over her, taking more time to properly examine the girl. She found four more trackers, but no injuries. She took all four and put them in her pocket.

"Mirie was taken, and this little girl was bugged. I found the trackers and will take care of them. I won't be long."

She didn't wait for an answer as she headed out the door. She ran to the elevator and selected the fifth floor. She didn't have much time if she was going to keep everyone safe. Waiting for the elevator doors, she cursed herself for being careless with Mirie and Tessa. How did Dagor even know that Mirie was fraternizing with them? How could he know who they even were, since they were all wearing facial distortion masks?

She tapped her foot, waiting for the doors to open again.

As the doors slid open, Naomi walked out of the elevator into the crowd of people surging past. The sixth floor was always busy. Filled with workers, there was always a crowd headed from one end to the other. She weaved through several different groups, letting the trackers slide into the pockets of unsuspecting workers. Hopefully she had caught the trackers in time, but just to be safe they would have to move everyone to a different location.

She made her way back to the apartment, but hesitated at the door. What if she was too late? In her haste to get out, she had left behind her tablet. Taking a breath, she opened the door. Tessa was sitting on the bed with Kelly; Catherine was holding Terran's hand, who's condition hadn't seemed to change.

"Are we okay?" Kelley asked, gently stroking Tessa's arm.

"Maybe. We need to move though. This apartment may be compromised. We need to call Laus and find a new base."

"I'll do it," Catherine said, already reaching for her phone.

Leaving her to handle the logistics, Naomi made her way to Tessa and sat on the other side of the little girl.

"Hello, Tessa. How are you feeling?" she asked.

"I'm okay," Tessa said as tears began welling up around her eyes. "Is my mom dead?

"I don't know, Tessa," Naomi said, "but we will find her. The man who took her will pay for what he has done."

"I don't care about him," Tessa sobbed. "I just want my mom back."

Tears streamed down the little girl's cheeks as she buried her face in Kelly's lap. Naomi got up from the bed with as much decorum as she could muster and left the child to cry. Catherine stood and met her at the door.

"Laus is on his way. He is going to contact Rictor and Peter as well."

"That's fine, I just need to step outside for a moment."

"Naomi, I don't think it's wise for us to be seen outside at this moment," Catherine urged.

"If this apartment is compromised, it won't matter," Naomi said.

"But if it isn't you could draw Dagor straight to us."

Naomi looked back at Tessa.

"It's my fault, Catherine. Once again, it is my fault. I involved them, and that is their reward. A little girl lost her mother to a monster."

"Don't give yourself so much credit, Naomi."

Naomi looked back at Catherine, who's eyes were filled with rage.

"This was all caused by Dagor. He is the one who did this."

"Catherine," Naomi wasn't quite sure how to talk with her.

"Don't think everything is ok between us Naomi, because it's not, but if Dagor is alive, he is our main concern. We need to stay together, and we need to stay alert."

Naomi nodded.

"Then I'll take watch until everyone shows up."

# CHAPTER FORTY-ONE

The new apartment was larger than Laus's. It was also, somehow, more sparsely decorated than his. Except for a thin coat of dust that had settled over the floor, there was nothing in the apartment at all. Rictor didn't mind, of course. It was Terran and Tessa that he was worried about. Both were asleep on the floor in the center of the apartment under an overhead light.

Terran was doing remarkably better and would awaken in the next day or so.

Rictor was seated with the other surviving members of the Bound, and Laus was addressing them about how careless they had been. Well, really he was lecturing them, but trying to be polite about it.

"Do you understand what I am saying? No more fraternizing with anyone outside the group, besides Peter, who needs to." Laus finished.

"Sir, yes, sir," Rictor said mid yawn.

"This is serious, Rictor," Laus said, voice shaking.

"You want us all to stay in this apartment even though we already know how to get into the eleventh level-thanks to ol' Terran over there."

"We need a few days of caution. Terran is a prime example of being too hasty. Not to mention Naomi taking in a child covered in trackers to our apartment. Which now means that I am now in Dagor's radar."

"Terran," Rictor said matching Laus' gaze, "is a prime example of following a hunch and getting results. If we could study the door we could figure out how to short circuit it. We have your maps which means we know where we need to place the bombs. I don't understand why we are waiting. Except, maybe if you aren't exactly as keen to get rid of Dagor as you claim."

Laus didn't give in to the bait. "How are you planning on leaving the Pod? Much more importantly, how do you plan on leaving the planet? How do you proposed getting outside of the eleventh level after the charges are set? How do you plan to handle the androids that will undoubtedly be on guard at that entrance since they should have registered an electrical surge at that location"?

Rictor held his tongue at the rebuke. They were all valid questions. He hadn't really thought that far ahead. His plans had stopped right at the point that they killed Dagor.

"Fine," Rictor said as he sat back down. "But, the least you could do is get us those schematics so we could plan some more."

"We don't need them," Terran's voice called from behind them.

Everyone turned to see Terran sitting up.

"I have them all memorized." He tried to get up but fell softly back to the floor.

Catherine and Kelley both rushed to his side to help him up. He smiled gratefully at them and let them help him back to the small group of friends. Peter, Rictor noted, hadn't moved an inch. That man was strange to say the least.

"Well, the rest of us might want to know the floor plan as well Terran." Rictor said as Terran gratefully lowered himself to a seating position. "Sharing is caring after all; besides it will be harder to take someone in so delicate a state on a dangerous mission to blow up an entire floor of an underground civilization. Kind of high profile."

Terran barked out a short laugh, then covered his mouth and Rictor smiled to himself, realizing just how much the man had changed. Not too many months ago, Terran would have probably been offended at Rictor's joke. It was good to hear laughter, and the tension that had pervaded the group visibly lessened.

"Well, consider me keeping this information to myself as an insurance policy that I will get to go," Terran said. "I will be fine. The shock did some damage, but not as much as you might think. I just need a few more days. Plenty of time for us to come up with a plan. Peter does still need to go to work. He has access to many useful pieces of equipment that we will need to get past the latch. I will provide a list after this meeting."

"Sounds like a plan, son," Peter said.

"Now, Laus, is there any way we could send Naomi and Rictor to analyze the latch on the outer rim and see if they can find any others?"

"I don't know. It would be hard for them to go unnoticed," Laus said, shifting uncomfortably as Terran took control of the meeting.

"I could help with that," Peter interjected. "I have a small cloaking mechanism that I pulled from my rider. It only covers a small radius and only visuals, but it might be enough."

"Good," Terran cut in, sounding even more confident after Laus' hesitancy. "While they are gone, I will talk with Laus about the schematics. I might be able to draw out some usable plans."

"What about me and Kelly?" Catherine asked.

"Well, I was hoping you could stay by me," Terran said taking her hand. "I am not quite one-hundred percent, and you can help provide some different viewpoints and options for me to consider."

"Well, what about me?" Kelly asked.

Rictor noted an eagerness in her tone and looking around the group. To his surprise--and joy--he saw the same eagerness in everyone. They had needed a real leader. Laus was used to leading by rank, but Terran was the type who couldn't help but lead.

"You had the least amount of contact outside than anyone else. We will need you to get a feel for things--listen to conversations, get us food, that sort of thing."

"I get to be a spy?" She grinned with excitement.

"Yep. And a grocer. So, don't get too excited." Terran smiled at his sister, and she beamed back at him.

"When do we start?" Rictor asked. They needed to capitalize on the momentum they had just gained.

"Right now," Terran said.

"What was all that about?" Naomi asked as the pair stood outside the pods on the staircase leading down to the ground.

"What was what about?" Rictor asked.

"Terran," Naomi responded. "I like the kid, but he has really taken the reins on this one."

"Well, Naomi, he did a really good job." Rictor said with a chuckle.

"Why do you say that?" Naomi asked.

Rictor turned to her and pointed around them. "What are we doing?"

"Well, I only left because I was tired of listening to Laus. Between what Laus was telling us to do and what Terran suggested, I would rather have done what Terran said."

"But, you are doing it," Rictor said, "And that is the important part."

"You don't seem so upset about it," Naomi said continuing down the stairs.

"Well, I have never had the desire to lead from the front. Terran is someone who I could see furthering the cause of the Bound. He's a lot like Glenn, especially when Glenn first showed up. He has a presence about him, an air of confidence."

"So do you," Naomi chimed in.

"Not the same. Mine is more swagger."

They walked the rest of the way to the bottom in silence. Many people would have looked down at Terran because of his youth, but they didn't understand what Rictor did. Some people have a gift to lead. The best you could do for people like that was to guide them along, keep them focused on what was important. It had been what he'd tried to do for Glenn. Of course, they were all planning an assassination, so maybe he wasn't the best judge of character anymore.

They reached the bottom platform and paused to rest.

"I wonder when these were built," Naomi said.

"Probably shortly after the Terra-forming failed." Rictor leaned on the railing.

"You really do believe it all, don't you?" she asked resting besides him.

"I have been around too long not to." He shook his head. "It's hard for people who live such short lives to believe in anything bigger than themselves. A lot of people might say they do, but it takes faith built from life experience to really dig into belief."

"If we figure out how to leave, would you go?"

"You wouldn't?"

"Well, I don't quite have the faith built from life experience that you do," she said.

Rictor mulled over her words as he stared into the darkness.

"What if I asked really nicely?" he turned toward her.

"Ric, we don't have to pretend to be a couple," she returned his gaze.

"I never wanted to pretend anyway."

He kissed her under the dim light. They pulled apart briefly, then he drew her into an embrace.

"I want you to stay with me, Naomi," he whispered into her ear.

"I want to stay with you," she whispered back, "but, I don't believe in this Bound business anymore."

"Yes, you do, Naomi," Rictor said holding her tight. "You just struggle with the Emperor."

"What's the difference?"

"You know he is real, you just don't want anything to do with him."

"And that's better?"

"Pain heals with time, unbelief festers." He pulled her chin up to look at her again. "Will you stay with me until we finally reach the Capital?"

"At least until the next planet," she said laying her head on his chest.

They stood, holding onto each other in the dim light until Naomi pulled away again. Rictor didn't fight it.

"We should examine the door," she reminded him.

He followed her down the next flight of steps, a smile stuck on his face.

# CHAPTER FORTY-TWO

Terran watched Laus leave the apartment and ungracefully plopped down onto the floor. It was hard work keeping up his strength in front of the military man, but he knew he needed to appear strong. Catherine sat down next to him much more gracefully.

"That went well," he said to her.

"What?" she looked shocked. "I am pretty sure he hates you."

"Well, he is content to do what we need him to do for now. And, we won't need him much longer."

"Why do you say that?" Catherine asked. "Even if we take down Dagor, Laus will most likely lead the Pod and we will need him to help us find a way off this planet."

Terran smiled at her and didn't respond.

"I think Rictor has rubbed off on you a little too much," she said. "Just tell me what you have planned."

"Peter is hiding something," he said. "I think he has a way off."

"Why do you say that?"

"Just a feeling is all. There are just too many things that don't add up. I just feel like he was waiting for us here. And, if he was, then he was wanting to take us somewhere."

"He led us here," Catherine said. "If anything, the only suspicious thing about him is if he is really working for us or Dagor."

"Peter's a good guy. He is testing us right now. He is for us, but he wants to make sure we can be trusted. I think he is on the brink, but he hasn't left us yet, so that is good."

"You are either a genius or a conspiracy theorist."

"I was born the former, but I am becoming the latter. Probably better in the long run." He pulled her to him, and she scooted over by him. "Are you doing okay?"

"You were the one shocked by an electric latch and thrown into a rock wall. Shouldn't I ask you that?"

"Let me re-phrase my question, then. How are you handling the death of your father?"

Catherine stiffened and pulled away. "I am doing fine."

"Fine?" he asked. "I don't think you are. We haven't really talked about it at all, Catherine. You need to open up."

"Oh okay. Mr. Daddy-issues himself is lecturing me about how to handle the death of my father. You want the truth? If I had a gun, I would shoot Dagor where he stands. I can't grieve because Dagor is stopping me from it. Until he receives justice for what he did, I am not going to grieve. You lost a sister, aren't you angry?"

For the hundredth time Terran fingered the small box in his pocket. Would it just further enrage her? Would it calm her down? *Do I have any right to keep it from her?*

Terran let her get up and walk away from him. Why didn't he feel more anger about Anna? He should have been enraged that Dagor had stolen her away from him, but there was something stopping him. In fact, he didn't really feel anything at all. He forced his shaking legs to stand and made his way to the door.

"Where are you going?" Catherine asked.

"Just for a walk," Terran said. "I will be back soon."

He shut the door behind him, then turned to figure out which direction to walk. In front of him was a wide terrace overlooking a vast mountain range dusted with snow. He walked forward, his legs no longer shaking, and overlooked the mountains. Dark evergreens covered the majority of them, creating a sharp contrast to the glistening white snow that fought to shine through. A cold wind blew against his skin, and Terran was surprised to see his breath on the air. The sky was overcast and looked as if it were about to release a terrible storm.

"Hello, Terran," Ekundayo's voice came from behind him.

"Hello," Terran said, continuing to stare at the mountains.

"Do you like the view?" he asked.

"Yes, it speaks to me."

"I thought it would. Do you know why I brought you here?"

"It's about Dagor."

"Yes," Ekundayo said as he leaned ono the terrace next to him. He was wearing a heavy parka with thick gloves on his hands. Looking down at himself, Terran was only mildly surprised to find himself in similar garb.

"Well, what do you need to tell me?" Terran asked looking back to the mountains.

"Do you see that storm cloud?"

"Of course."

"There is a poison in the Bound on Torga. It has consumed some of your friends, but in you it is like this storm cloud. It is filled to the brim and ready to release itself, but if you prepare, you can withstand it and not let it destroy the beauty inside you."

Terran stood in silence thinking over everyone's reaction to Dagor and how at ease they were with the thought of killing him.

"Is Peter safe?" Terran asked.

Ekundayo laughed softly in his deep baritone for a few seconds.

"Peter is doing what I have asked him. The Bound aren't meant to be 'safe'. They are meant to do great things in the Emperor's name. That is all of humanity's calling."

"So, the whole destroy-everything plan is still going?"

"Terran, I understand it might seem like the collapsing of space is an ending, but it's not. It is the beginning of something so much better. It is just hard for you to see." He patted Terran on the arm.

"I have a surprise for you."

"Really? Is taking me to the top of a snow-capped mountain range not surprising enough?"

"I would hope I was a bit more exciting." Glenn's voice came from behind him.

Terran spun around and almost lost his balance at the sight of not-quite Glenn. It was a younger man without the scars. His stature was the same, and he still had his massive frame.

"I will let you two talk," Ekundayo said. He walked over to Glenn and whispered something that Terran couldn't hear. Glenn walked over next to Terran and gazed over the mountains.

"I am going to tell you a secret, Terran. I asked if I could, and I was given this moment to talk with you. "

"Ok..." Terran said as his stomach began twisting in knots.

"The Capital is not a physical place and physical things cannot interact with it."

"What?" Terran asked. "What did you just say?"

"You heard me," Glenn said, his now handsome features stared at Terran unwavering.

"Terran, you need to understand this. In the dark and deepest place of your soul, you must understand this. No one else does, but you need to help them to; otherwise, you will burn out and turn away. You understand?"

"I think so."

"Good. You need to go back now. Help the others to understand."

"Yes, sir."

Terran turned back to the mountains and immediately felt a force push him from behind. He fell over the terrace and headed toward the mountain range. As the ground started speeding toward him, he let out a scream that was torn from his mouth before it could form.

He hit the cool steel of the floor and turned around to see Catherine standing in the doorframe with a worried expression.

"Terran, what were you doing just now?" she rushed to his side.

His heart felt like it was about to break through his ribcage, and his breathing was shallow.

He could feel the cool sweat on his face and could have sworn he could still feel the ice-cold wind digging through his clothes.

"I had another vision." It was hard to get the words out from his chattering teeth.

Catherine helped him up and took him back inside. She laid him beside Tessa again under a small blanket.

"What did you see?"

"Secrets," he said and grabbed her hand. "Don't let the poison in."

"Poison? What poison."

Terran tried to tell her, but no words came out. Instead a great weight seemed to fall upon him and he had to close his eyes to fend off the light that seemed too harsh.

"Do I need to get Laus?" she asked.

Terran shook his head slowly and opened his eyes. "I just need a minute or two."

"I am going to call Rictor and Naomi, then."

Terran nodded and let her leave his side. He didn't know what Ekundayo wanted him to do with the information he was given, but if there was nothing else he could do he would make sure the poison that had infiltrated their group was pushed back.

# CHAPTER FORTY-THREE

The Bound stood in a circle in the center of the room under the dim light of the worn bulbs that laced the ceiling. Terran had just finished telling the group about his vision and what he interpreted it as. They had waited in patient silence as he had talked--no noise, no interruptions, just quiet contemplation.

Now that he had finished, Terran felt a well of nervousness begin to build within him, urging him to compromise his message. He ignored it and continued waiting. He would not be the first person to speak. He glanced at everyone around him in turn and settled on Peter. The man had shown a moment of surprise when Terran had described his vision.

"So, you don't think Dagor needs to be taken out?" Kelly asked.

"I don't believe we should murder him, no." Terran answered.

"You don't think he deserves it?" Catherine asked him. Her tone was accusatory.

"I do. I just don't think it is our job to kill him," Terran responded.

"So, what would we do? Put him in a cell so that his cronies could get him out?" Rictor cocked his head. "You can't imprison a man like that. He's too powerful. Prison would just be a vacation to him."

"Well, I don't quite know what we need to do, but I don't think murder is the answer."

"We have everything we need to do the plan. I say we go through with it," Naomi said.

It was true. Peter had finished bringing everything they had needed to complete the plan in with him piece by piece.

"We can still follow through with the plan. All I am saying is we need to capture Dagor, not kill him. One of us could watch over him while we figure out how to get off Torga."

"He murdered my father, your sister, and everyone I have ever cared about. This man does not need mercy." Catherine grabbed his hand as she spoke.

"I'm sorry, Catherine, I think he does. None of us deserved the opportunity to be one of the Bound. I almost missed getting the invitation at all. I think Dagor deserves the same opportunity."

"That is--"Rictor was cutoff as the door opened and Laus stumbled in, covered in blood. As he tripped and hit the floor, a flood of people came into the room. After they had filed in, Dagor walked in with an easy air. His face didn't distort in the light and Terran was almost positive that this was the real man before them.

"Hello, everyone," Dagor's voiced chilled the room as he walked forward. "I have been waiting to meet all of you since I found out that you had lived through a night on the surface. Of course, you seemed to have found a new friend. Peter, was it?"

"That is my name," Peter said.

Terran was surprised at the strength in his father's voice. He refused to speak, afraid his own voice would fail.

"It's a shame all of you will die today. I have quite enjoyed our little game of cat and mouse." He raised his finger to his ear and muttered a command.

The androids around him sprang into action and began running surging to the group. Amidst the roar of the crowd, Terran heard a distinct click, and a bright light erupted from where Rictor stood.

The first android was cut in half as Rictor swung a sword through it. With inhuman speed, he began to cut one android after another to pieces. The Bound huddled together behind their shining guardian as he struggled to fend off the horde. One of the androids slipped through and lunged toward the group with sharp claws extended.

A whine began next to him, then Naomi rushed past, meeting it head on. It swung at her, but as it's arm neared her it slowed, throwing the android off balance. Naomi rained blows on its head and torso until the machine fell to the ground. Even before it had finished its descent, another android slipped past Rictor and headed for the group. Naomi ran toward the thing and speared it to the ground. A few blows to the head left the body lifeless. Machine after machine fell as Naomi and Rictor worked in perfect union to fend off the horde.

Then Dagor was there at the front line with a gun leveled at Terran's chest. Rictor swung his blade too late as a blast left the end of the barrel. Terran felt a shove and fell to the ground. He heard a gasp and another body fell next to his. He heard Dagor scream in agony, but his mind was too numb from the sight of Catherine lying on the ground with blood pouring from her chest.

"Help!" Terran screamed looking around him for anything he could use to stop the bleeding.

He saw Dagor's hand still holding the gun that had shot Catherine on the floor, he saw a machine dig its claws into Rictor's back, and he saw another machine dig a claw into Naomi's leg.

This was it, Terran realized. This was the day he would die. They had failed. He shut his eyes and said a prayer of apology for failing. A warmth filled his body, and he opened his eyes to find the group sitting in the center of a circle on what looked like the bridge to a ship.

There were chairs in front of computers and from the front window he could see the black expanse of space. Peter walked from the circle and typed on a keyboard at one of the computers.

"We need to move quickly," he said walking back to the group. "Terran, grab Catherine. Kelly, help Naomi. I will take care of Rictor and Laus." He put Rictor across his shoulders and hefted Laus' body.

Shock overwhelming him, Terran acted without thought. He picked up Catherine and followed Peter. He heard Kelly and Naomi talking in hushed tones behind him, but didn't care. He didn't care about anything else but Catherine getting the help she needed. Peter turned a corner and went into a long room with several beds lined against the wall. Small curtains separated the beds and each had a large globe over the top.

Peter put Rictor face down on one of the beds, and Terran lowered Catherine as gently as he could on the one beside him. Kelly helped Naomi pull herself onto the bed to Rictor's other side. A whirring noise came from each globe that bathed everyone in a blue light for a few seconds. Each globe spouted arms from different angles and went to work on the wounded. Terran watched fascinated as the globe above Rictor began stitching the long gashes on his back. Rictor gave a small moan and another arm shot out from the globe and administered what Terran assumed was a painkiller. He glanced over toward Catherine, but the curtain was drawn tight.

He reached to pull it away to check on her, but Peter stopped him.

"They cut off her shirt to perform the surgery. She deserves some dignity, don't you think?"

Terran felt his cheeks burn and drew his arm back. The embarrassment turned into anger as the reality of where they were sank in.

"Why?" he turned to Peter his whole body shaking.

"Why, what?" Peter asked, keeping his voice low.

"Why did you wait to get us out of there? We could have died."

"We didn't."

"But, we could have." Terran clenched his fists. "Why did you wait?"

"It takes time for the teleporter to power up, I started the procedure as soon as Dagor burst in."

Terran wrestled against the urge to punch Peter. Instead he went over the wall and punched it as hard as he could. Pain shot up through his arm, and he could tell his wrist was at least sprained, but he kept walking back towards the bridge.

*I almost died. Again. Just because Peter wouldn't get us off that stupid planet. How could he do this to us?* His thoughts were interrupted by footsteps coming into the room. He turned to see Peter standing in the doorway.

"What?" Terran roared. "What have you come to screw up this time? All you have ever done is let us down and you have done it again. We could have died and all you have to say about it is that we didn't? What is wrong with you?"

"You selfish child." Peter strode across the room, closing the gap between them. "Do you think it was easy for me? Do you think I wanted to abandon my family to poverty? To see young men and women butchered in front of me? To see my son look at me with hate in his eyes? Do you have any idea how hard it was for me not to whisk you all way as far as possible from all this the moment I saw this? I did what I was told to. I don't answer to you Terran, I answer to someone much higher."

Terran snapped. He swung a right hook, catching Peter in the jaw. A loud crack erupted from his hand, almost assuring him that it had broken. Peter fell to the ground, but got back to his feet in a flash.

They stared at each other, both breathing heavy.

"Hit me again." Peter wiped blood from his mouth and smiled at Terran.

"What?"

"If you think hitting me is going to solve your problems, then go for it." Peter outstretched his arms. "A free hit, as hard as you can. Go for it."

Terran stared at Peter, fighting against his desire to follow through. Tears began to fill his eyes, and he collapsed to his knees.

"I'm not smart enough." Tears fell to the floor as he talked. "I couldn't save anyone. No matter how much I planned, Dagor was able to hurt everyone. I'm not special. I am just as worthless here as I was on Sisera. I--"

His voice broke off as Peter's arms wrapped around him.

"It's okay son. It's not your fault."

"Yes, it is," Terran tried weakly to push Peter away, but his hand crumpled under the pressure. *Why did I punch that stupid wall?*

"Terran, look at me."

Terran looked down.

"Look at me." Peter's strong hand lifted his head until they could look into each other's eyes. His lip was already puffy, and the blood was still flowing from his nose.

"You are not responsible for this, you are not alone, and you, most definitely, are not worthless."

"But... "

"No 'buts'," Peter pulled him in close. "We have been chosen by the creator of the universe to guide others to Him. How in the world would that make you think you are worthless?"

Terran's tears continued to fall as he pulled his father close. "I couldn't save Anna or Catherine."

"Don't worry about them. Anna is waiting for us and I don't think we should give up on Catherine just yet."

"I just, don't know what to do."

"Well, let's work together and figure that out."

Terran rested his head against Peter's chest.

"Thanks, Dad."

# CHAPTER FORTY-FOUR

Terran sat by Catherine's bed, the velvet box in his hands. The others were still asleep, but Terran hadn't been able to stay in his bunk for very long. A shower had helped after the episode with his father, and a tight cast had been wrapped around his broken hand. He had plenty of flexibility left, but he wasn't able to grasp things well, yet.

"I should have given this to you as soon as we landed." He placed the small box by her hand.

"Peter and I are going to do something drastic. I think it might work. The others don't know about it, but I think it's our best shot. When I get back, we need to talk about some things. If you are awake by then, I am really curious as to what's in that box."

He squeezed her hand, then kissed her on the forehead.

"I love you Catherine. Stay strong. I will be back soon."

He left her to the steady beep of the monitors that were helping to keep her stable, and went back to the bridge, where Peter was waiting for him.

They had talked for hours putting the plan together while everyone else was asleep.

"Do you think this'll work?"

"I think so." Peter finished typing coordinates into the computer and gave Terran a wink. "Maybe eighty-five percent."

"That's better than nothing." Terran said.

"I placed everything you will need by the teleporter. There is a watch with a cloaking mechanism built in, a phone with a direct line to the ship that will help to get you back here, and explosives."

Terran got up from the chair and made his way to the backpack. He put on the gear and flexed his hand, hopefully it would hold up.

"Stick to the plan and be safe, Terran."

"I'll try my best," Terran walked to the center of the teleporter and closed his eyes.

A gentle hum surrounded him, and he opened his eyes to find himself floating above the ground. He was back in the pod on the eleventh floor. The humming stopped and he fell the last few inches to the ground. *Time for payback.* He shouldered the backpack and ran to the first checkpoint, the elevator. The explosives were simple things-small bricks with a chip attached to them. Dagor would be in for quite the surprise. He pressed a button on his watch and a hologram of the pod shot out in front of him. He took mental note of the next checkpoint and started out. Terran passed a mirror and took a quick second to examine himself. His hair had grown out a bit since it had been shaved. His skin was still tan, his eyes still blue, but there was something different about him. He seemed, taller, maybe? *Wait, I can see myself.*

He scrambled to hit the button sequence on the watch and his image disappeared from the mirror. Maybe Dagor didn't have cameras on this level. Maybe everything was fine. *Just keep going.*

Pushing on, he passed doorways that lined the corridors until he found the second checkpoint--a pillar close to the main generator housing.

He pulled out the pod map again and took note of the third checkpoint. He closed the image and headed out, making a beeline for the next drop, but paused mid-stride before he had gone more than a hundred feet. There was a door where there shouldn't have been one. *It could be nothing, or it could something terrible.*

There wasn't anything special about the door; it was metal just like all the others with a simple handle. *Except it shouldn't be here.* Terran took hold of the handle and opened the door as slowly as he could manage. *Definitely something terrible.* The room appeared to be an observation deck looking over a hanger. Seated prominently in the middle of the hanger, sat the Gungir, or at least a ship that looked exactly like the Gungir. *Why would Dagor have a ship like that?* He snapped a quick photo with his phone and sent it to Peter. They could discuss it later.

He left the room and sprinted to the next checkpoint. A glance at his watch told him he was running out of time. The third checkpoint was a support beam near the inner wall of the level. Before he could set the charge down, thunderous footsteps erupted from all around him. Strong hands grabbed him before he could turn around, pinning his arms to his sides. The androids materialized around him as they marched down through the level. *Apparently, they have cloaking too.* The androids kept him marching until he stood before a door that did stick out compared to the others. The door was made of wood and was twice as wide as it needed to be. A giant "D" was etched into it.

One of the androids hit a few buttons on a keypad next to the door and it slid open, revealing a plush office. Granite pillars reflected the company of androids as they walked into the room, keeping their prisoner firmly in their grasp. Terran stared at his reflection in the floor as he was dragged forward and thrown in front of a wooden desk. Fingers were drumming an impatient staccato as he tried to find his breath.

"Well, of all the people I thought they would send to kill me, you were pretty low on the list." Terran shuddered as Dagor's voice seemed to crawl down his back. *I need to stand. I have to fight.*

"Maybe you aren't as important as you think." Terran stood to face Dagor, focusing on his breathing to stop the dizziness.

"Maybe so," Dagor flipped through some papers on his desk. After looking through a few stacks of the papers he pulled one out and smiled. "Now, Terran, do you understand what is actually going on here?"

"Besides you killing people?" Terran chanced a glance at his watch. A few minutes left before this would be over.

"Tsk, Terran. So naive." Dagor pushed his chair from the desk. Light glinted off metal, and Terran realized that Dagor had a metal prosthetic. Dagor drummed a quick staccato on the desk, leaving behind a series of holes where his fingers had hit. "Why are you fighting so hard for the Emperor? What has he done for you?"

"He got me off Sisera..."

Dagor barked out a laugh. "No, he didn't. Glenn got you off that planet. Well, technically Rictor and Naomi did, but ce'st la vie." He walked around the desk and sat on the front mere inches from Terran.

"I'm going to be frank with you. This plan was destined to fail, just like all your plans will. You are on the losing side, Terran. I can outthink any of you. I already took the chips out of the charges you set." There were three small thumps beside him as the charges landed next to his bag. "Don't think about trying to activate them either." Hands dug into his pockets and took out their contents, his watch was stripped from his arm; and an android kicked his knees out from under him, forcing him to kneel.

"I have a simple request for you, Terran. Join us, or die. We'll even spare the life of your sister..." He glanced at one of the papers on his desk. "Kelly is the one still alive I believe, or maybe you would like to keep Catherine alive? Assuming she isn't dead already."

Terran's shoulders shook as laughter escaped him. Dagor looked at him in disbelief as Terran began roaring with laughter. A backhand from a metal claw knocked him to the ground. Terran pushed himself back to a kneeling position.

"You have no idea what we are up to." He spit blood onto the tile. "You think you stopped us? You don't realize how predictable you are." *Just a little bit longer.* "You really think those bombs needed a detonator to go off?"

Dagor grew pale. "What?"

"Each of those charges is set to explode by an inner detonator. The chips on the outside were a distrac..."

"Rip the charges to pieces," Dagor yelled.

The androids sprang into action tearing apart the three charges on the floor. Terran got up from the ground as they turned to his backpack and began digging through it, looking for any more explosives.

"Now, what do you have to say for yourself?" Dagor turned just in time to see Terran tackling him onto the desk. They slid across the desk and onto the floor as a sticky warmth began covering Terran's body. He latched onto Dagor and held him close as robotic hands began tugging at him. A flash of light blinded him, followed by two gunshots. Terran's vision began to clear, and he saw Peter, standing with a smoking pistol in his hand. The androids lay on the floor, missing more than half of their torsos.

"What have you done?" Dagor screamed at him as he tried to plunge his claw into Terran's stomach. Terran grabbed the claw and pushed back against Dagor, but it wasn't enough. Dagor's now metallic fingers dung into his chest.

Then a blur tackled Dagor off him. Another gunshot sounded in the room and there was silence. Terran turned onto his side to see Dagor's face giving him a blank stare. *Is he dead?*

Dagor blinked, destroying the illusion, and Terran breathed a sigh of relief. He had too much information; they couldn't kill him.

"Well, now what?" Rictor stepped over him and looked toward Peter. His back was slick with blood.

"We throw him in a holding cell and figure out our next move."

# CHAPTER FORTY-FIVE

"How is he?" Catherine asked from her bed in the infirmary.

"He is." Peter was focused on the monitors by Terran's side. He pressed a few buttons then faced the group. The Bound were all awake and in for check-up.

"You know, I am almost positive that Terran is the luckiest man alive." Rictor's words were muffled by the large mouthful of protein he was eating. Naomi had barely been able to finish hers but Rictor had already eaten three of the bars since he had gotten out of bed.

"It's not luck." Catherine sat up slowly from her bed. "He is marked for something great. That's what my father said anyway."

"He's survived being injected with an illegal drug, a severe electrical shock, being beaten by your father, and a claw digging into his chest," Rictor finished the bar and reached for another. Naomi slapped his hand away. She needed to eat, as hard as it would be, and he was not getting her last bar.

"And apparently he is wanted by the Emperor's greatest enemy. He really won the lottery there." Peter let out a chuckle.

"Now what are we going to do?" Naomi asked as she opened the protein bar. She gagged at the smell, but took a bite. A sip of water seemed to help until the taste of the bar reached the back of her throat. She handed Rictor the rest of the bar and finished the glass of water. She would just eat later.

"We need to send Dagor out of the airlock," Rictor said between bites.

"I didn't think we were killing him," Kelly's voice shook.

"You don't have to participate, but I have a score to settle." Rictor said, finishing the bar.

"Now, Ric, we have been over this. Let's leave him be for a while." Naomi placed her hand on Rictor's shoulder and gave a gentle squeeze.

Terran stirred from the bed and his eyes fluttered open.

"How am I?" he asked.

"You're fine. Everything is healing nicely." Catherine smiled at him.

"Time for the elephant in the room. We need to get a Captain." Peter rose from his chair. "There are two people I need to talk to about taking the role of Captain aboard the ship. Catherine and Rictor, if you wouldn't mind, I would like to talk with you."

Terran watched her go and then walked over to the end of the infirmary where Laus lay silent, still recovering.

Naomi's heart began pounding in her chest. *What about staying behind? If Rictor becomes Captain, we will be trapped forever on this ship, waiting on an Emperor who never even bothered to help a widow.* She watched as they both followed Peter out of the room. Naomi scratched around the stiches in her thigh. With all the medical advances on the ship, she had assumed anti-itch cream would be readily available. She had been wrong.

Kelly made her way over to Naomi's bed and sat down where Rictor had been. "Do you mind if I sit here?"

"Go for it." Naomi sat on her hands. *Must not scratch.*

"I might be able to help with that." Kelly dug inside her bag and pulled out a small bottle. She squeezed a dime sized amount onto her hand and then applied it around Naomi's wound. The itching subsided instantly.

"You are a blessing." Naomi said, patting the child's arm.

"No sweat," Kelly smiled at her. "So, are you going to stay on with the ship?"

Naomi raised an eyebrow. *Either she is incredibly nosey, incredibly perceptive, or both.* "I don't know. It doesn't seem right to keep on with everyone else. I don't have my heart set on all of this just yet."

"We just took down an Envoy of Promioth who is trying to rule space, who had kidnapped your son to sabotage the good work that the Lion's Roar was doing in the name of the Emperor, and you find it hard to believe that it's all true?" There was a hint of a smile behind Kelly's serious expression.

"When you say it like that--"

"The truth," Kelly interjected.

"...it does seem a little ridiculous." Naomi continued. "My problem isn't with the facts, it's with who the Emperor is. I have watched my husband kill himself, I believed my son was beaten almost to death, I helped to kill an entire ship full of people, and I am supposed to believe that I was chosen to save people from the end of space and time. Doesn't that seem a little fantastical to you?"

Kelly was silent for a moment. Her lips were pursed and her brow was furrowed.

"But it's true," she said finally.

"What is?" Naomi asked.

"All of it," Kelly replied. "It doesn't matter what it sounds like. It's true. You are called to help other people."

"Yeah," Naomi began. "But, there's more to it than that."

"Not really. It's just the facts. You can choose whether to believe them or not, but it doesn't change the facts from being facts."

Naomi stared at Kelly, speechless. There wasn't anything to say. The child was right. Naomi grabbed her glass of water and took a sip. It was empty. She almost slammed it back on the table, but hesitated. *Why am I being so resistant to all of this?* She bit her lip, thinking through everything that had happened over the last few years. Something was holding her back.

"Can I ask you something, Naomi?" Kelly asked.

"Go for it."

"How did you fight those androids? They seemed to move in slow motion when they got near you."

Naomi smiled.

"Nothing like that. It was a simple magnetic shield on the belt I was wearing. It only had a small battery, so I knew it wouldn't last, but something had to be done to stop them from hurting us."

"For someone hesitant to stay on, you sure have done a lot to keep us safe." Kelly smiled at her again. Naomi tried to piece together a reply, but nothing came out.

Kelly, seeming to sense her need to be alone, walked back over to Terran's bed.

Silence settled over the room, interrupted only by the soft whirr of the monitors. Naomi twisted in the bed and swung her legs over the side. She slowly began to put her weight on her legs. They seemed stable. She took a step forward, and her injured leg buckled underneath the weight, throwing her to ground. She gritted her teeth through the pain and rolled onto her back. Kelly ran over and knelt beside her.

"What were you thinking?" She helped Naomi get her legs out from under her and began to check the stiches. "You're lucky you didn't tear these out."

"I thought I was strong enough to get out of bed."

"Well you aren't," Kelly placed on of Naomi's arms around her shoulders and helped her back onto the bed. "Do you want me to get your wheelchair?"

"No, thank you." Naomi turned away from Kelly and pulled the sheet over her.

*Chastised by a child for acting like a child.*

"Naomi," Kelly put a hand on her shoulder. "I would really like you to stay on the ship. I don't know how much that means to you, but I do."

"Why?" Naomi asked, keeping her back to Kelly.

"Well, because I like you. You remind me of my mom-before Dad left us and she got depressed."

*Her mother? That's all she needed. Some girl needing a mother figure.*

Naomi sat up in her bed.

"What's wrong?" Kelly asked, stepping back from the bed. "Do I need to get someone?"

"Get me the wheelchair." Kelly did as she was asked. "We need to head back down to Torga."

"Why?"

"Because we left Tessa behind."

Naomi sat in the wheelchair, staring at the teleporter. Kelly stood to her left, Catherine to her right.

"You need to get some rest." Kelly rested her hand on Naomi's shoulder.

Naomi shrugged it off. "Not until I see Tessa."

"I'm sure that Rictor will bring her here safely. Sitting here for *hours* on end won't help the matter."

Naomi glared at Catherine and flipped the lever that locked the wheelchair in place. "You both can leave. I will wait here for them. I won't believe that that child is working for Dagor. He might have gotten Mirie, but he couldn't have gotten her."

"Naomi," Catherine replied, "You need to prepare yourself. There is a very high chance that Tessa was used to track us too."

"If there is truly an Emperor in this universe, he would have spared a child."

Dagor is not the emperor.

"Why would he have replaced her? There is no reason to. Mirie had already given him everything he needed." Naomi took a deep breath. "I need her to be okay."

"We will have to scan her once she's on the ship. Just to make sure." Catherine stared at the teleporter, her brow knit together.

"Then that's what we will do. Stop telling me this isn't a good idea." Naomi looked back at the teleporter.

A soft hum filled the room and Rictor materialized in the circle, Tessa was in his arms.

He let her down and the child turned around. She stared in wonder at the consoles around her. When she caught sight of Naomi, she broke out into a smile and ran to her.

Tessa wrapped her arms around Naomi's neck and pulled her close. "I'm so sorry. I didn't mean to scream at you."

Naomi let her tears fall as she held Tessa. "It's okay sweetie. Everything is going to be okay from now on."

# CHAPTER FORTY-SIX

Much to Rictor's dismay, they had decided to wait a day to question Dagor. Terran knew he needed the rest at least, and it would help if all of them could actually be there when Dagor was interrogated.

Terran sat in his room, wrapping a new bandage around the stiches on his abdomen. Six long gashes marred his body. He took a deep breath and continued the process of wrapping the bandages. After the second pass around, someone knocked on the door.

"Come in."

Catherine stood in the doorway, holding a small velvet box. Terran smiled at her, but tried to keep wrapping the gauze.

"Let me help," Catherine said. She knelt beside him and took the gauze from him.

"Do you know what was in that box?" she asked.

"No. I didn't think it was my place to open it."

"It was a necklace my father gave my mother when they were married and a small vial of the perfume she used to wear."

Terran remained silent, unsure of how to respond.

"I wanted to let you know that I heard what you said, before you left."

Terran felt the heat rising to his cheeks and looked away from her.

"What did you want to talk to me about?" she finished the wrap and walked over to his closet. The room wasn't very big; there was little more that could have fit in the room besides the small bed and dresser. A small bathroom consisting of a shower, toilet, and sink was connected to the room, but there wasn't much space in there either.

"I wanted to talk to you about us." He reached for her hand. "We have been through a lot together and I just wanted to make sure everything was okay."

"Is there a reason we wouldn't be okay?"

"Well, no, but the last conversation we had was a little heated."

"Terran, I took a bullet for you, I think we are ok." She kissed him on the cheek. "Maybe that will help your mind along."

He smiled at her. *How could I have gotten so lucky?*

"Well, we need to get going. If we are going to try and figure out all this Dagor nonsense."

"I'm not sure if I should go." She looked away from him.

"What? Why not?"

"Well, I am still infuriated with him and I am almost certain I would at least attempt to hurt him."

"Okay then, get some rest. I will see you in a bit."

She smiled at him, then added quickly, "Oh, and Terran."

He paused in the doorway and looked back at her. "Yes?"

"I love you, too."

He smiled and left the room. It was a quick walk to the holding area where Dagor was being kept. Everyone else was waiting for him when he arrived.

"Ready to get some answers?" Peter asked.

They all nodded, and he opened the door. Dagor was seated in the middle of a bare room, bound to a chair. He metal prosthetic had been confiscated.

"Oh, look, it's the mindless drones of a bygone era." He grinned at them. "Do you really think keeping me locked up here will do anything? A bunch of fools think they can out think Promioth?"

Rictor walked over to him as he continued to talk.

"What do you think--?" Rictor slapped Dagor from behind.

"You are only going to speak when spoken to. Do you understand?"

"Yes," Dagor murmured. "Let's get this over with."

Kelly pushed Naomi forward, "Where is my son?"

"Don't know, don't care. Next quest--" Rictor slapped him again.

"Why!?" Dagor screamed.

"Because you deserved it. Give her a better answer."

Dagor looked at Naomi and spat.

"Everyone leave the room," Rictor said.

Dagor's eyes grew wide. "No, wait. I don't know where your son is. We took some photos of him and just acted like we had him. As far as I know, he never left the planet."

Naomi started to speak, but her voice caught and she waved to Terran.

Terran stepped forward, "How did you travel from Naomi's world to this one."

Dagor sneered at Terran, but caught sight of movement from Rictor and flinched. "I have a ship. Simple."

Peter laughed. "The interplanetary vessels won't work for you. They would shut off the minute you tried to use them.

Dagor rolled his eyes. "We don't use them, you idiot. We just use the rails and the jump ships' AI to navigate.

Peter glanced at Terran and they exchanged a worried glance. That was not good news.

"How many envoys are there?"

"We are as limitless as the stars and as...arrgh!" Dagor howled in pain as Rictor slapped him again.

"Okay, Okay. Look, I don't know. There is one for every inhabited planet. That much I know. How many of those there are, I have no idea."

"Where is Promioth?"

Dagor sneered. "Do you really think I would know that?" Rictor slapped him again.

"I don't know. I am not near as important as you make me out to be. "

"What were you doing on Torga?" Peter asked.

"I was running a test to see how long it would take to overthrow a planet. I was making good progress too."

Rictor pulled his hand back and Dagor ducked down. "Now you're learning."

"Why did you send Naomi to kill me?" Terran stepped closer to Dagor.

"Do you really not know? How backwards are you people?" Rictor raised his hand. "Look, you have visions, okay. Dangerous visions. Promioth sent out a mandate that everyone with the potential to have them was supposed to be taken out discreetly."

"What do you mean by dangerous?" Terran's heart began pounding.

"I don't know. I wasn't given that information."

The room sat in silence, broken only by Dagor's breathing.

"And Mirie?" Naomi's voice was weak.

Dagor began laughing. Rictor went to slap him, but Peter shook his head.

Dagor quieted down and sneered at them. "You fools. How in the world did you catch me? She was a plant. An android, working for me. You don't even understand how I found your hiding spots do you?"

The Bound stood awkwardly in silence.

Dagor barked out a laugh. "Now, should I tell you how it all worked out? I don't think so. Go ahead and slap me again. It won't matter." He stared at them, a smug smile stuck on his face.

"I think that's enough for today." Peter walked over to the door, and ushered them out. Naomi, did not stop with the group, instead she wheeled herself down the hallway back towards the infirmary.

"How much was true, do you think?" Terran asked.

"Probably most of it." Rictor replied. "I don't see why they wouldn't have envoys on every planet. Strategically speaking it makes sense."

Terran and Peter nodded.

"So, what are we going to do? Keep him locked up indefinitely?" Terran asked.

"I don't have any better ideas," Peter replied.

"I have one," Rictor looked at them. No trace of a smile could be seen on his face.

"Ric, I don't think that's wise. It's not our job to play executioner." Terran grabbed his shoulder. "Judgment belongs in the hands of the Emperor. Our job is to listen."

"And sometimes our job is to do the hard things," Rictor countered. "Just because something is tough, doesn't mean it shouldn't be done."

"He might still have information." It was the last defense Terran could think of.

"We can find out a different way." Rictor said.

"But imagine if we knew what to expect at the next planet, who we would be facing or what we would be facing. We could have a leg up on any defense anyone could throw at us."

"Well, not to burst your bubble, but I doubt he would ever really tell us the truth." Rictor began walking down the hallway.

"There is a seed of truth in every lie, Rictor." Peter finally spoke.

"Well you two ask the questions, I am going to check up with Naomi." He walked away.

"Think you can handle the questions? I need to go rest." Terran patted Peter on the back and headed to his room. Catherine was gone, but in her place was a little velvet box with a note attached to it.

"Open me," it read.

Terran did as the envelope demanded, and a small note fell out. Glenn had apparently left a note behind for either him or Catherine, he was just about to put it back when he saw his name scratched onto the paper.

He opened the letter to find it was a note from Catherine. It read:

Terran, keep a hold of this box of mine. If things ever settle down for us, maybe you can give this to me in a more romantic fashion.

With love,

Catherine.


Terran smiled and lay down on his bunk, drifting off to sleep.

# EPILOGUE

ix months after Torga

Rictor stood in front of the sink and patted his face dry. It had been a long time since he had been clean shaven, but it seemed appropriate. He wiped around the sink, taking care to dispose of any hairs that might have been left behind. He took a deep breath and walked over to the closet. Three uniforms hung in pristine condition. They were all the same, apparently someone had told Peter he might need extras. They were three piece uniforms consisting of a jacket, slacks, and undershirt. The jacket was a soft fabric that fit snug against his chest and shoulders. He paused, examining himself in the mirror, first zipping up the jacket, then unzipping it. Definitely zipped. The slacks were comfortable, a little loose, but nice. He put the belt on and looked back toward the mirror. Today was the beginning of something special. New responsibilities waited for him, and he was going to take them seriously. A knock on the door alerted him of the time.

"Come in."

Terran entered the doorway and stepped in. "I was..." He paused as Rictor turned around.

"Well, how do I look?"

"Different." Terran's eyes were still wide as he closed the door. "I brought your hat to you."

"I get a hat?"

"Apparently, it's tradition."

Rictor held onto the hat for a second, then tossed in on the bunk. "Unless Naomi requested it herself, I am not wearing a hat. I don't like them."

"It's your wedding," Terran chuckled.

Rictor smiled back at him. "That's right. Now, let's go to the bridge and get me hitched."

The front window of the ship was open, revealing a beautiful planet of blues and greens that took up most of the view. Peter stood in the center of the window facing them, with Kelly and Catherine standing to his right. Two hundred people from Torga sat in in the room facing the front. The room was filled with murmurs as Rictor and Terran walked down the only path in the room and stood to Peter's left. A tension filled the air as everyone looked toward the door leading to the bridge.

Rictor cracked his knuckles, then wiped his palms on his slacks again. Terran patted him on the shoulder. He looked at the girls, and Kelly winked at him. Catherine smiled. Both girls wore the black uniforms that they had adopted aboard the ship. Catherine wore slacks like his and Terran's, but Kelly had opted for a skirt.

A soft breath of air told him the door had opened. He looked toward the door. Tessa stood in the doorway, grinning. She walked slowly down the aisle, tossing flowers in front of her. She caught his stare, and he grinned at her. A melody started and Rictor glanced back to the doorway. Naomi stood motionless, waiting for Tessa to finish. Her dress was a beautiful cream color that shimmered in the starlight. She seemed to glow as she glided toward him. She stopped opposite him in front of Peter. At a loss of words, he tried to smile, but started to sob instead.

Peter cleared his throat. "Today is a tremendous day. Today we have come together to witness two lives become one. The road has not been easy. We have faced doubt, fear, and death to come to the point we are at now. We stand tall knowing that we have not been defeated, that joy has not been stolen from us. Instead, we celebrate the joy that so freely prevails among us. However, today is not about the rest of us. It is about these two. Naomi and Rictor, who have led this ship with patience, wisdom, and love. Today they stand before us and proclaim their love and dedications to the Emperor and each other. Naomi, do you swear before us all to look after Rictor, to lift him up when he is weak, to safeguard his heart from the lies of Promioth, and to stay by his side, till death do you part?"

"I do." She grabbed his hand.

"And you Rictor?" Peter continued. "Do pledge to love and care for Naomi? To lead her on the true path, to protect her, to provide for her, and to honor her in all that you say and do?"

"I do." He squeezed her hand.

"Then by the power vested in me by the Creator of the Universe, I pronounce you man and wife. You may kiss the bride."

Rictor pulled her close, "Always and forever."

She cupped his cheek, "Always and forever."

The room erupted in applause as they kissed. All too soon he pulled away and they made their way out of the room.

They walked back to his quarters and Naomi chuckled as she saw it. The room was sparse. There was a closet, bed, and a small side table, but that was it.

"You sure do live light," Naomi teased.

"I figured you had enough stuff for the both of us." He pulled her in for another kiss.

She pulled away slowly. "So, what's the plan? Do we actually get a honeymoon?"

Rictor flashed a grin. "Tomorrow, we head planet side."

"That's not the same thing."

"It is if the other groups are headed down next week."

She smiled at him and wrapped her arms around him.

"Are you ready for our next big adventure?" he asked.

"Always and forever."

# ABOUT THE AUTHOR

Michael Rogers is a speculative fiction writer, civil engineer, and tech enthusiast residing in the mountains of rural Virginia with his wife and two children. When he isn't tinkering with one of his seven 3D printers or solving water crises all over the state, he enjoys telling stories that mean something.

He has been deeply involved in missions in Mexico, Peru, and South Korea and believes that it is every Christian's calling to show God in everything they do with the gifts God has given them. Michael posts updates on his writing as well as funny and speculative content on Instagram as @mike.a.rogers.

You can keep track of all his books on his Writers Exchange author page: http://www.writers-exchange.com/Michael-Rogers/

**If you enjoyed this author's book, then please place a review up at the site of purchase, and any social media sites you frequent!**